A Man Apart
by Joan Hohl

಄ೱ

"Decadent," he pronounced. "Delicious."

Once again, Justin's low, ultrasensual tones sent an unfamiliar, unwanted and unappreciated chill down Hannah's already-quivering spine. At the same time, the spark of teasing devilment in his eyes caused a strange, melting heat deep inside her.

Hannah resented the sensation, but to her chagrin, she felt every bit as attracted to Justin as she was wary of him. All he had to do was look at her to make her, in a word, sizzle.

Dammit.

It had been a long time since Hannah had warmed to a man and she had certainly never *sizzled* for one. But innate honesty compelled her to admit to herself that she did indeed sizzle for Justin.

And she didn't like it at all.

Hot to the Touch
by Julie Hogan

ଚ ୨୮ ୧

Praise for the work of *USA TODAY* bestselling author Jennifer Greene

"A book by Jennifer Greene hums with an unbeatable combination of sexual chemistry and heart-warming emotion."
—*New York Times* bestselling author Susan Elizabeth Phillips

"A spellbinding storyteller of uncommon brilliance, the fabulous Jennifer Greene is one of the romance genre's greatest gifts to the world of popular fiction."
—*Romantic Times*

"Jennifer Greene's writing possesses a modern sensibility and frankness that is vivid, fresh, and often funny."
—*Publishers Weekly*

"Combining expertly crafted characters with lovely prose flavoured with sassy wit, Greene constructs a superb tale of love lost and found, dreams discarded and rediscovered, and the importance of family and friendship..."
—*Booklist* on *Where Is He Now?*

"Ms Greene lavishes her talents on every book she writes."
—*Rendezvous*

Available in June 2006 from Silhouette Desire

A Man Apart
by Joan Hohl
&
Hot to the Touch
by Jennifer Greene

ⓢ✧ⓔ

Rules of Attraction
by Susan Crosby
(Behind Closed Doors)
&
Scandalous Passion
by Emilie Rose

ⓢ✧ⓔ

The Rugged Loner
by Bronwyn Jameson
(Princes of the Outback)
&
At Your Service
by Amy Jo Cousins

A Man Apart
JOAN HOHL

Hot to the Touch
JENNIFER GREENE

*All the characters in this book have no existence outside the
imagination of the author, and have no relation whatsoever to anyone
bearing the same name or names. They are not even distantly inspired
by any individual known or unknown to the author, and all the
incidents are pure invention.*

*First published in Great Britain 2006
Silhouette Books, Eton House, 18-24 Paradise Road,
Richmond, Surrey TW9 1SR*

The publisher acknowledges the copyright holders of the
individual works as follows:

A Man Apart © Joan Hohl 2005
Hot to the Touch © Alison Hart 2005

ISBN 0 373 60315 0

51-0606

*Printed and bound in Spain
by Litografía Rosés S.A., Barcelona*

A MAN APART

by
Joan Hohl

JOAN HOHL

is the *New York Times* bestselling author of over
forty books. She has received numerous awards
for her work, including the Romance Writers of
America's Golden Medallion award. In addition
to contemporary romance, this prolific author also
writes historical and time-travel romances. Joan
lives in eastern Pennsylvania with her husband and
family.

Melissa & Tara
Gee, it's good to be back home again.

One

Justin Grainger was a man apart—and he liked it that way. He was content with his life. Possessing a nearly uncanny affinity for horses, he was satisfied with his work of running his isolated horse ranch in Montana.

But Justin was not a hermit or even a true loner. He enjoyed the easy camaraderie shared with his ranch hands and his foreman, Ben Daniels. And though Justin had never again wanted a woman on the property, since his failed marriage five years before, he had accepted the presence of Ben's new young wife, Karla. She had been the former personal assistant to Justin's brother, Mitch, who managed the family-owned gambling casino in Deadwood, South Dakota.

Justin had other family members he occasionally visited. His parents, retired now in Sedona, Arizona, were both still healthy and socially active. His sister, Beth, as yet unmarried, was off doing her fashion thing in San Francisco. And his eldest brother, Adam, headed up various family businesses from their corporate offices in Casper, Wyoming.

Adam was married to a lovely woman named Sunny, whom Justin had set out to tolerate in the name of family unity and had quickly come to admire, respect and love almost as much as his own sister. Adam and Sunny had a baby daughter, Becky, whom Justin quite simply adored.

On occasion Justin even spent recreational time with an accommodating woman—no strings attached. And that suited him fine. He claimed that horses were much easier to deal with, less contentious and argumentative, thus easier to talk to and get along with.

Although, these days, after a long, hot work-filled summer, a busy autumn, and winter just settling in, Justin was a bit restless and didn't grumble too much when he received an urgent and demanding phone call from Mitch the week before Christmas.

"I need you to come to Deadwood," Mitch said, in his usual straightforward way.

"Yeah? Why?" Justin replied, in his usual dry, less-than-impressed manner.

"I'm getting married, and I want you to be my best man," Mitch shot back. "That's why."

As an attention getter, his brother's explanation was a winner, Justin conceded…to himself. He never had conceded much of anything—except absolute loyalty and devotion—to any one of his siblings.

"When did you lose it, Mitch?" he asked in soft tones of commiseration.

"Lose what?" Mitch sounded slightly baffled.

Justin grinned. "Your mind, old son. You must have lost it if you're going to take the marital plunge."

"I haven't lost my mind…old son," Mitch retorted, a trace of amusement undermining his rough voice. "Trite as it might sound, it's my heart I've lost."

There was no way Justin could let his brother's remark pass without comment. "No 'might' about it," he drawled, enjoying himself. "That is trite. Sappy, too."

Mitch laughed. "I don't know what to tell you, bro," he said, suddenly dead serious. "I'm way deep in love with her."

Oh, yeah, Justin thought, hearing the heartfelt note in his brother's voice. Mitch was seriously serious. "It's Maggie Reynolds. Right?"

"Yes…of course."

Of course. Justin wasn't surprised, not really. A faint smile tugged at his lips. In fact, after all the rave reviews he'd heard from Mitch about Ms. Reynolds ever since she'd replaced Karla as his personal assistant, Justin should have been expecting the marriage announcement.

"Well?"

Mitch's impatient voice sliced across Justin's thoughts. "Well what?" he asked.

Mitch sighed loudly, and Justin managed to contain a burst of laughter.

"Will you be best man at my wedding?"

"Might as well," Justin drawled. "Why change the status quo now…as I always was the best man, anyway."

"In your dreams, maybe," Mitch said amiably going along with the old joke. "Because you're never gonna live long enough to see that day while you're awake."

"Ha! Don't bet the casino on it."

"As if…" Mitch made a snorting sound; he never gambled on anything, never mind the family owned casino. "You know damn well I never…"

"Yeah, yeah. I do know, so spare me the drill. When do you want me in Deadwood?"

"We've set the date for the first Saturday in the new year. But you could come for Christmas," Mitch suggested, cautiously hopeful.

"I don't think so." Justin slanted a wry look at the tall, glittery tree placed in front of the wide living room window. The tree—along with other assorted holiday decorations—was a concession to Ben's new bride. "You know I'm not—"

"Into Christmas," Mitch finished for him. "Yes, I know." He heaved a tired-sounding sigh. "This Christmas it'll be five years since Angie took off with that sales rep. Don't you think it's time to put it behind you, Justin, find a nice, decent woman and—"

"Back off, Mitch," he growled in warning, closing his mind to the memory of that bitter winter. "The only woman I'll be looking to find won't be either too nice or too decent, just ready and willing."

"Tsk, tsk," Mitch said, clicking his tongue in disapproval. "I do hope that if you're thinking of looking while you're here in Deadwood, you'll be discreet about it."

"Don't want me to shock the sensibilities of the future missus, hmm?" Justine taunted.

"My future missus and Ben's missus and Adam's missus," Mitch taunted right back. "Not to mention the sensibilities of our mother and sister."

"Ouch." Justin laughed. "Okay. I'll be extra discreet...even circumspect."

Mitch chuckled. "Whatever."

"By the way, is Karla going to be matron of honor?"

"Well...yes, but there'll be two of them."

"Two what?"

"Well, two attendants," Mitch said. "Maggie's best friend will be coming from Philadelphia via Nebraska to be Maggie's *maid* of honor."

"Philadelphia via Nebraska?"

"She lives in Philadelphia," Mitch explained. "That's where Maggie's from, you know."

"Yeah, I know, but...where does Nebraska come in?"

"Hannah's originally from Nebraska, and she'll be visiting her family before coming on to Deadwood."

"Hannah, huh?" Justin had an immediate image of an old-fashioned female to fit the old-fashioned name—prim, proper, virginal and probably plain.

"Yeah, Hannah Deturk."

Add *prudish* to the list.

"And you'd better be nice to her," Mitch warned.

"Of course I'll be nice to her. Why the hell wouldn't I be nice to her?" Justin said, genuinely hurt by his brother's warning, by the idea that Mitch felt it necessary to issue the warning.

"Well…" Mitch's tone was now conciliatory. "You've never made a secret about how you feel about women, and I just don't want anything to upset Maggie."

"You sound as smitten as Ben," he said. "You really do have it bad, don't you?"

"I love her, Justin, more than my own life," Mitch admitted in a quiet, but rock-solid tone.

"I hear you, and I promise I'll behave." He knew he'd never felt like that about a woman, not even his ex-wife, Angie, and was certain he never would.

Hell, he never wanted to experience that kind of intense emotion for any woman, Justin thought minutes later, frowning as he cradled the receiver. That path only led to pain.

First Ben and Karla, now Mitch and Maggie, he mused, staring into space, and all within one year.

Hmm. While Justin wasn't fanciful, he did wonder if there was some type of aphrodisiac in Deadwood's water, or maybe it was the atmosphere in the casino, some sort of love and marriage spell.

The day after Christmas, Justin set off for Deadwood, convinced he was impervious to anything like a spell or potion. He'd learned his lesson.

Hannah Deturk had not been exactly thrilled to be leaving Philadelphia at the end of the third week of December, of all times of the year, for the upper Midwest. South Dakota via Nebraska. To Hannah Deadwood, South Dakota was the back of beyond and, if possible, even more remote than the area of Nebraska where she had been born and raised.

After graduating college and relocating, first to Chicago, which was too windy, then to New York City, which was too big, and finally settling into

Philadelphia, Hannah had vowed that other than brief visits home to visit her folks, she would never go back to that desolate part of the country. She certainly wouldn't travel there in the winter months of November, December, January, February and March, and she even considered October, April and May pretty chancy.

Only a request by her parents or, as was the case, the marriage of her dearest friend, Maggie, could induce Hannah to take the three hard-earned vacation weeks she had allotted herself and spend them in Deadwood, South Dakota, of all places.

She didn't even gamble, for goodness sake, had never even visited the casinos in Atlantic City, a mere hour or so drive down the Atlantic City expressway from Philly.

And yet when Maggie had called her to tell her she was getting married in January and asked Hannah to be her maid of honor, Hannah hadn't so much as entertained a thought of refusing.

So, a few days into the new year, after spending Christmas with her family in Nebraska, Hannah found herself on the road, steering a leased four-wheel-drive vehicle through a blessedly light fall of snow, heading for Deadwood.

It was dark, and the snowfall heavier when

Hannah finally arrived in the town made legendary by its historical reputation of being wide-open and the larger-than-life characters of Wild Bill Hickok and Calamity Jane.

Those days were long-gone, as were the infamous pair. Other than having legal gambling casinos, Deadwood looked to Hannah much like any other small upper Midwest town.

She missed Philadelphia, where it would be evening rush hour and the traffic would be horrific. She even missed that.

Then again…perhaps not.

Smiling wryly, Hannah peered through the windshield to look for the turnoff Maggie had indicated in her directions. A few minutes later she brought the vehicle to a careful stop in front of a large Victorian house that had been converted into apartments.

No wonder Maggie had fallen in love with the house, Hannah thought, stepping out of the Jeep to stare through the swirling snow at the old mansion that had once been the Grainger family home. It was an imposing sight, and conjured images of a bygone era of grace and style.

"Hannah!"

Hannah blinked back into the present at the excited sound of Maggie's voice calling her name. Her coatless friend was dashing down the veranda steps toward her.

"Maggie!" Hannah flung out her arms to embrace her friend. "Are you nutty, or what?" she asked, laughing, as she stepped back to gaze into her friend's glowing face. "It's snowing and freezing out here."

"Yes, I'm nutty." Maggie laughed with her. "So nutty and crazy in love, I don't feel the cold."

"Got your love to keep you warm, do you?" Hannah dryly teased.

"Yes…yes." Despite her heartfelt assertion, Maggie shivered. "I can't wait for you to meet him."

"I'm looking forward to it," Hannah said, grasping Maggie's arm to lead her toward the house. "But meanwhile let's get inside, where I hope it's warm."

"Well, of course it's warm." Maggie flashed a grin. "Even up in my nest on the third floor."

Releasing her hold on Maggie's arm, Hannah turned back to the car. "You go on ahead, I'll just grab my bags and be with you in a minute."

"Did you bring your dress for the wedding?" Maggie called from the shelter of the veranda.

"Of course I did," Hannah yelled back over the

open trunk lid, shivering as the sting of wind-driven snow bit into her face. "Now go into the house."

A half hour later, her bags unpacked, the special dress she had frantically shopped for before leaving Philly hanging on a padded hanger to de-wrinkle, Hannah sat curled on the cushioned seat in the bay window alcove in Maggie's warm "nest," her hands cradling a steaming cup of marshmallow-topped hot chocolate.

She took a careful sip, and winced. "Mmm…delicious. But very hot. I scorched my tongue."

Maggie laughed. "It's supposed to be hot." Her eyes danced with amusement. "That's why it's called *hot* chocolate."

Hannah's pained expression smoothed into a gentle smile. It was so good to hear her friend laugh again, see the glow of happiness in Maggie's face that had replaced the bitter hurt of betrayal of the previous summer.

"You really are in love this time," Hannah said, taking another careful sip. "Aren't you?"

"Yes…though I wouldn't have believed it possible mere months ago…I really am in love." Maggie heaved a contented sigh. Her eyes took on a dreamy look. "Mitch is so wonderful, so, so…"

"Everything Todd was not?" Hannah interjected, her normally husky voice lightened by expectation.

"Todd who?" Maggie asked with assumed innocence.

Hannah grinned, finally convinced her friend was back on track at last. "Oh, you know, Todd what's-his-name, the jerk you were engaged to marry. The same jerk who eloped with his boss's daughter."

Maggie grimaced. "Oh, *that* jerk. Yes, Mitch is everything Todd was not." Her lips formed a soft smile. "And a whole heck of a lot more."

"Good." Allowing herself to fully relax, Hannah settled more comfortably into the corner of the alcove. Smiling, she studied her friend's radiant face. "You really are genuinely in love this time," she murmured in tones of wonder. "Aren't you?"

Maggie laughed. "Didn't I just answer that question moments ago? Yes, Hannah, I am deeply, genuinely, madly, desperately, deliriously…

"Okay, okay," Hannah broke in, holding up her hands and laughing. "I believe you."

"About time." Maggie laughed with her. "More hot chocolate? A cookie?"

"No, thank you." Hannah shook her head. "I still

have some chocolate—" she grimaced "—and I've already had too many cookies. They're delicious."

"Karla baked them."

Hannah frowned. "Karla?" Then, remembering, she said, "Oh, the woman whose job you took over, the one who's going to stand as matron of honor."

"Mmm." Maggie nodded. "She loves to cook, and baked these for Christmas. She brought some with her for us."

"That was thoughtful of her." Hannah smiled. "So, she's here already, too. I'm eager to meet her."

"Yes, she's here in Deadwood. Karla and her husband, Ben, and the baby." Maggie laughed. "Matter of fact, the whole gang's here."

"Gang?" Hannah lifted one perfectly arched brow.

"Yes, Mitch's family," Maggie explained. "They arrived in dribbles and drips over the past two days…"

"Dribbles and drips," Hannah interrupted, laughing. "Your Pennsylvania Dutch country origins are showing."

"Whatever." Maggie shrugged. "Anyway, they're here. Mitch's parents, two brothers, one alone, one with his family, and his sister. You'll meet them Friday evening at the rehearsal, and get to know them a little at dinner afterward."

"Dinner?" Hannah swept the room with a skeptical glance. "Where?"

"Mitch made arrangements for dinner at the Bullock Hotel."

"Oh." Naturally, Hannah hadn't a clue where the Bullock Hotel might be located, but it didn't matter. "And is that when I'll meet your Mitch?" Now, that did matter, a lot. She had witnessed the hurt and humiliation inflicted on Maggie by her former fiancé. Hannah had never been able to bring herself to trust or like the too-smooth Todd. Subsequently, to her dismay, her suspicions about him had proved correct.

"No." Maggie shook her head. "You'll meet Mitch tonight. He's going to stop by later. Though he's eager to meet you—I've told him so much about you—he wanted to give us some time alone together, to catch up." Her eyes softened. "He's so considerate."

Hmm, I'll be the judge of that, Hannah mused. But it sure sounded like Maggie did have it bad. "How does it really feel? Being in love, I mean?"

"All the things I mentioned before…and perhaps a little scary, too."

"Scary?" Hannah was at once alert, her protective instincts quivering. Was this Mitch Grainger a bully? She couldn't imagine her independent friend falling for a man who would intimidate her, but then again, Maggie had been about to marry that deceitful jerk Todd.

"Well, maybe not exactly scary," Maggie said, after giving it some thought. "It's all so new and sudden, and almost too exciting, too thrilling. You know how love is."

Whoa, Hannah thought, serious stuff here…. Too exciting? Too thrilling? Now she really couldn't wait to meet the man. "Actually, no," she admitted, wryly. "I don't know."

Maggie blinked in astonishment. "You're kidding."

"No, I'm not."

"You've never been in love? What about that guy you dated in college?"

"Oh, I thought I was in love," Hannah said. "Turned out it was a combination of chemistry and itchy hormones, commonly called lust." Her tone was dry, her smile self derisive.

"But…since then…?" Maggie persisted.

"Nope." Hannah swallowed the last of the chocolate; it had gone as cold as her love life…or lack of same. "There were a couple of infatuations, some sexual activity, but not much. There was one brief and I thought promising relationship I never told you about. But it really never got off square one, so to speak." She shrugged. "Nothing even remotely resembling what you've described."

"Oh, too bad. All this time we've known each other, and I never knew, never even guessed… you've always been so closemouthed about your personal life."

Hannah laughed. "That's because I didn't have one, at least nothing that warranted discussion."

"I never imagined…" Maggie sighed, then brightened. "Oh, I can't wait for you to fall in love someday, experience this excitingly scary champagne-bubbly feeling."

"I'm not sure I want to." Hannah slowly moved her head back and forth.

"Not want to?" Maggie exclaimed, surprised. "But…why not?"

"Because…" Hannah hesitated, carefully choosing her words so as not to offend her friend by voicing doubt. "I don't think I want to expose myself to that degree."

"Expose yourself?" Maggie frowned in confusion. "I don't get your point. Expose yourself to what?"

"That sort of emotional vulnerability," she said.

Maggie's amusement showed with her easy laughter. "You're wacko…you know that? Don't you realize that if I'm emotionally vulnerable, stands to reason Mitch is, too?"

"I suppose so," Hannah murmured. But is he? She kept the question and her doubts to herself. She had always considered herself a pretty good judge of character, and she had been right about Todd.

Wait and see, she told herself, lifting an eyebrow in question when Maggie, suddenly frowning, nibbled on her lower lip in consternation.

"Is something wrong?"

Maggie lifted her shoulders in an indecisive shrug. "Not really…it's just…"

"Just?" Hannah prompted.

Maggie sighed. "Well, I think maybe I should give you a heads-up on the best man, Mitch's brother, Justin."

"A heads-up?" Hannah grinned. "Why, is he some kind of ogre or monster?"

Maggie grinned back. "No, of course not. It's just…well…he's different, a little rough around the edges, not nearly as polished as Mitch or their oldest brother, Adam."

"Like, crude?" Hannah raised an eyebrow.

"No, no." Maggie shook her head. "Just a little

brusque. I understand he is something of a loner, thinks women are good for one thing only."

"I don't think I need ask what the one thing might be," Hannah drawled. A thought occurred that brought a glint of anger into her eyes. "Was this 'loner' brusque and perhaps a little rude to you?"

"Heavens no!" Maggie exclaimed on a laugh. "Actually, he was quite civil, really very nice."

"Then, how do you know that he—"

Maggie interrupted. "Because Mitch gave me a heads-up." She laughed. "He told me I should tell him at once if Justin said one word out of line." Her laugh turned to a giggle. "Mitch said if he did, he'd mop the casino floor with him. Which, after I met him, I thought was hilarious."

Thoroughly confused, Hannah was about to demand a fuller explanation when Maggie glanced at the clock, pushed her chair away from the table and stood.

"I think I'd better get dinner started," Maggie said. "I don't know about you, but I'm getting hungry. And I told Mitch we'd have coffee and dessert with him."

"Okay. I'll help," Hannah said, stretching as she stood.

"But…you're my guest," Maggie protested. "The first one I've had in this apartment."

"Guest, shmest," Hannah retorted. "I'm not a guest, I'm a friend…your best friend. Right?"

"Right." Maggie gave a vigorous nod, then qualified, "After Mitch, of course."

Oh, brother, Hannah thought. "Oh, of course," she agreed with a smile, skirting around the table. "What's on the menu?"

"Pasta."

Hannah rolled her eyes. "What else?" Being Maggie's second-best friend, she was well aware of her passion for past dishes. "What kind?"

"Penne with snow peas, baby carrots, walnuts and a light oil-balsamic-vinegar sauce."

"Yummy." Hannah's mouth watered. "And dessert?"

"A surprise." Maggie's eyes gleamed.

"Oh, come on," Hannah groused, grinning.

Maggie shook her head. "All I'll tell you is that Karla showed me how to make it." Her eyes now sparkled with a teasing light. "And it's a delight," she finished on a suspicious-sounding giggle.

After their fabulous meal, Hannah leaned back in her chair. "That was wonderful," she said, sighing with repletion.

"Thanks." Maggie arched an eyebrow as she rose to start clearing the table. "How's the career progressing?"

"Right on schedule. I figure by the time I'm eighty or ninety, I'll be the best damn consultant in the entire marketing industry," Hannah drawled, rising to help clean up.

Maggie shot a frown at her. "No, seriously, how is it going for you?"

"Very well, actually," Hannah answered, helping Maggie to fill the dishwasher. "I gave myself a raise by raising my fee in November. Not one of my clients objected. My end-of-year earnings have put me into a higher income tax bracket, and I don't even mind."

"That's great," Maggie exclaimed, rewarding her with a hug. "Congratulations."

"Thank you," Hannah said simply, going on to candidly admit, "At the risk of sounding arrogant, I'm rather pleased with myself at the moment."

"And why not?" Maggie demanded, her hands planted on her slender hips. "You should be pleased and delighted. You've worked your butt off getting yourself established. I know. I was there. Just as you've always been there for me. Remember?"

Hannah smiled, recalling the day the previous June when she had walked into Maggie's apartment to witness her friend slashing the exquisitely beautiful, extremely expensive wedding dress to shreds. "Remember? How could I forget all the pain—and fun—we've shared?"

"Well, while you're here, let's just remember the fun, and say to hell with the pain. Deal?"

Hannah laughed. "Deal."

They shared a hug and, sliding an arm around each other's waists, strolled to the other side of the room to settle back down on the window seat behind the table, chattering away while they waited for Mitch.

With each passing moment, Maggie's face took on a becoming glow, her eyes shining with anticipation. And with each of those moments, Hannah felt her own anticipation rise, as she wondered what kind of man this Mitch Grainger must be. Not to mention his enigmatic brother.

Two

Having listened to Maggie rave, through several long-distance phone calls, about how handsome, exciting, wonderful and flat-out sexy her employer and fiancé was, Hannah was prepared for the visual impact of Mitch Grainger.

So, when he arrived at the apartment a half hour later, she was neither surprised nor disappointed. Mitch appeared to be everything Maggie claimed him to be and then some. His manner was polite. He was gentle and tender with Maggie, and the perfect gentleman toward Hannah.

She couldn't help but notice that every time Mitch looked at Maggie, his eyes gleamed with near adoration, joy and male sexual hunger. Strangely, that gleam of light gave Hannah an odd little twist in her chest.

Surely not envy of Maggie and the emotions the mere sight of her so obviously induced in Mitch?

Envy? Of her very best friend? The very idea was both confusing and shaming. Hannah might have examined her unusual feeling more closely if there had been just the three of them around the small table.

But Mitch had not come to the apartment alone.

While Hannah had been prepared for Maggie's fiancé she hadn't at all been prepared for the impact of Mitch's older brother, Justin.

And what an impact he made. Hannah felt the reverberations in every molecule of her being—felt it and resented it. In looks, the brothers were quite similar, but altogether different in attire.

Mitch was dressed in a navy-blue business suit, ice-blue shirt, a striped, pale-blue and grey tie and a long gray obviously cashmere coat, the walking picture of the conservative businessman. Justin, on the other hand, had removed a brown, well-worn Stetson and shrugged out of a deep-collared suede jacket. Beneath his coat he wore a blue chambray shirt tucked into faded low-slung jeans plastered to his slim hips and long legs to cover the tops of smart-looking boots.

Justin Grainger towered over Hannah's five foot ten by seven and a half inches. His raw-boned frame was rangy but muscular, a tower of powerful masculinity.

At once, Hannah understood how Maggie had found it hysterical when Mitch threatened to mop the casino floor with his brother if he said one word out of line. While Mitch appeared quite capable of wiping the floor with most men, she knew his brother wasn't one of them.

Justin Grainger had dark hair, streaked with silver at the temples, and a little long at the nape. His eyes were gray, cold as the North Atlantic in January, sharp as a bitter wind, yet aloof and remote. And every time he turned his cold, calculating, but somehow tinglingly sexy sharp-eyed gaze on Hannah, she felt a chilling thrill from the tingling top of her head to the curling tips of her toes.

Hannah's immediate assessment of the two brothers was that Mitch was forceful and dynamic, whereas Justin was a silent but simmering volcano of leashed sexuality, with the potential to erupt without warning all over any innocent, unsuspecting female to cross his path.

Fortunately, having survived that one unsuccessful and unsettling relationship two years before—a relationship in which she had been burned so badly she hadn't even confided in Maggie about the affair or aftereffects—Hannah was neither innocent nor unsuspecting. To be sure, she was suspicious as all get-out.

On Maggie's introduction, Hannah accepted Mitch's proffered hand first. It was warm, his grip polite. But she barely registered his greeting, since all she could hear was the sound of static electricity as she took Justin's extended hand. She not only heard it, she felt it zigzag from her palm to every particle of her body.

Hannah slid a quick glance toward Maggie and Mitch only to find that they had moved across the room to the hallway closet to put away the men's coats.

"Miss Deturk."

That's all he said. Her name. Not even her first name. His voice was low, disturbingly intimate. Hannah's hand felt seared. She hadn't realized his fingers were still firmly wrapped around hers. She turned her gaze back to his, her mouth going dry at the sight of tiny flames flickering in the depths of his cold gray eyes.

Feeling slightly disoriented, and resenting the sensation, she slid her hand free, murmuring, "Mr. Grainger."

"Justin."

"If you wish." She inclined her head, feeling like an awkward teenager, not having a clue she gave the impression of a haughty queen condescending to acknowledge one of her lowest subjects.

A smile shadowed his masculine, tempting lips. "May I call you Hannah?"

Oh, hell, she thought. His voice was even lower, more intimate, and too damn beguiling. Certain her brain had been rendered into nothing more than a small blob, Hannah could manage only to parrot herself.

"If you wish."

"Well, ready for dessert?" Maggie's bright voice dissolved the strange misty atmosphere seemingly surrounding her and Justin Grainger.

Thank heavens for small mercies, Hannah thought, turning away from him.

"Do you have coffee?" Mitch asked.

"Of course." Maggie crossed to the small kitchen area.

Grateful for a moment's respite from Justin's nearness, Hannah hurried after Maggie to help. She served the coffee, careful not to look directly at him. She thought she had herself under control when she again seated herself next to him at the table.

The moment she was settled, she knew she was wrong.

Beneath Justin Grainger's keen gaze, Hannah's enthusiasm waned for the coffee and the surprise dessert promised by Maggie.

"What is it?" Mitch asked, eyeing the dessert dish Maggie set before him, which appeared to contain a mixed-up blob of ingredients.

Maggie grinned. "Karla calls it Heavenly Hawaiian Surprise. It's got pineapple and cherries and pecans and marshmallow and sour cream, and trust me, it is heavenly."

"We shall see, or better yet taste," Mitch said, his teasing eyes alight with affection.

His brother beat him to it. Scooping up a spoonful of the mixture, he popped it in his mouth.

"Decadent," he pronounced. "Delicious."

Once again Justin's low, ultrasensual tones sent an unfamiliar, unwanted and unappreciated chill down Hannah's already quivering spine. At the same time, the spark in his eyes caused a strange melting heat deep inside her.

Hannah resented the sensation but, to her chagrin, she felt every bit as attracted to Justin as she was wary of him. All he had to do was look at her to make her, in a word, sizzle.

Dammit.

It had been some time since Hannah had warmed to a man and she had certainly never sizzled for one. But innate honesty compelled her to admit to herself that she did indeed sizzle for Justin.

And she didn't like it at all.

The conversation around the small table was general; for Hannah, desultory. Appearing for all the world comfortable and relaxed, inside she felt stiff, frozen solid.

Later that night, after the brothers had finally left, Hannah lay awake in the surprisingly comfortable roll-away bed Maggie had prepared for her. She examined the conflicting emotions Justin Grainger had so casually and seemingly effortlessly aroused inside her mind and body.

She felt empty, needy. It was almost frightening. How could it have happened? Hannah asked herself. She was hardly the type to become all squishy and nervy from the mere expression in a man's eyes and the low, sensual sound of his voice.

Certainly, Justin had not said or done anything out of line. He had been every bit as polite and respectful as had his brother Mitch.

Except for his eyes. Dear heavens, Justin Grainger's sharp and compelling eyes.

A shiver trickled through Hannah, and she drew the down comforter more closely around her. She knew it wasn't the coldness of the air but an inner, deeper chill that wouldn't be banished by burrowing under three down comforters.

Hannah decided that getting through the next days—the rehearsal, the dinner, the wedding and reception ought to prove more than a little interesting. In fact, she was afraid it would be an endurance test.

Was she up to the sort of sensual challenge those glinting, gray eyes promised?

Hannah believed she was. She was her own woman, which was why she had struck out on her own, preferring to work her tail off to establish herself rather than work for somebody else.

There was just one tiny flaw in all this—while Hannah *believed* she could handle the situation, return home unscathed by Justin Grainger, she wasn't absolutely certain.

And *that* was frightening.

* * *

"So what did you think of her?" Mitch asked as he and Justin settled into his car after leaving the large house.

Her? Justin hesitated. "Who?"

Mitch glanced over to give Justin an are-you-kidding? look. "Maggie, who else. You remember—the woman I'm going to be marrying in just a few days."

"Well, of course I remember," Justin retorted, feeling like an idiot and not liking the feeling. 'But if you'll recall, there were two women in the apartment," he said in his own defense. "Although I did notice you had eyes only for Maggie."

Tossing him a grin, Mitch flicked on the motor. "I do recall that there were two, smart-ass," he chided. "I also recall that you seemed to stare at Hannah a lot."

Justin shrugged in what he hoped was a carefree way. "Hey, she's an attractive woman."

"Yes, she is," Mitch agreed. "But, that doesn't answer my question. What did you think of Maggie, your future sister-in-law?"

"She is both beautiful and nice, as you well know," Justin answered, relieved to have the topic back on Maggie and off Hannah. "And she is most obviously head-over-heels in love with you. Although I can't imagine why."

"Because I'm sexy as hell?"

Justin gave him a droll look. "Since when?"

"Since I was fifteen," Mitch shot back, as he shot out of the parking lot at the rear of the house. "Of course," he qualified, "I was following your bad example."

"Hmm. Bad example, huh?" he drawled. "Personally, I never considered it bad to be sexy."

After returning to the hotel, Justin closed his room door behind him and leaned back against it. He inhaled deeply and released the breath on a soft "Whew."

Old fashioned? Prim? Proper? Virginal? And probably plain? Had he really held such a preconceived opinion of who Hannah would turn out to be?

"Hah." Shaking his head as though he had just taken a blow to the temple and was still groggy in the mind, Justin pushed away from the door muttering to himself.

"Hannah Deturk is the most cool, composed, beautiful, long-legged woman this ol' son's weary eyes ever landed on."

He chuckled. "And you, Justin Grainger are talking to yourself."

Well, at least he wasn't cursing, Justin consoled himself, releasing a half groan. He was surprised at his unexpected emotional, and physical, reaction to the blond goddess.

Sure, it had been a while since he'd been with a woman, but not nearly long enough to explain the immediate surge of lust he'd experienced at first glance. He'd felt like a teenager in the throes of a testosterone rush.

In that instant Justin decided he had to have Hannah Deturk, in every way possible. Either that or he just might expire from the mind-blowing need.

The tricky part was; how and when? Well, he knew exactly how, Justin mused, a smile twitching the corners of his mouth. But the trick was when. Time was limited.

There were only a few days to go until the wedding. As Maggie and Hannah hadn't seen each other for six months, they'd likely be spending most of those days—and nights—together, chattering away.

Poor Mitch was going to be sleeping alone from now until his wedding night. He'd probably be a bear until then, working overtime to conceal his feelings.

Then Justin realized something—Mitch wouldn't be the only man working to control strong urges.

Damnation.

He mulled over the problem of private time and place with Hannah as he sat on the edge of the bed and pulled off his best pair of boots. Standing to shuck out of his clothes, he folded them neatly before sliding them into the plastic laundry bag provided by the hotel. His mother had been a real stickler about neatness.

Naked as a newborn, he stretched his length between the chilled sheets, doused the bedside light and started up at the ceiling. Of course, he really couldn't see the ceiling, as the closed drapes shut out even the tiniest glimmer of moonlight and the room was as dark as pure nothingness.

It didn't matter to Justin, because he could still see a shimmering image of Hannah Deturk.

"Oh, hell," he muttered, his breathing growing shallow as his body grew hard. "Think, man. When are you going to have the chance to approach her?"

The days leading up to the big event were out. There was the rehearsal late in the afternoon the day before the wedding, to be followed by the re-hearsal dinner. That night was out, as well. Justin knew full well his family would make a lengthy celebration of the dinner.

Naturally, the actual day of the wedding was out.

The day—or night—after the wedding? Justin mulled over the problem, allowing his body to cool down a few degrees. He was in no hurry to get back to the ranch, he could spare a few days for fun and games.

Not in a hotel room. Justin gave a sharp shake of his head against the pillow. Not with Hannah. He didn't want to delve into why it mattered. It never bothered him before where he spent time romping with a woman—a hotel room, motel room, her apartment, it made no difference to him. This time, if there were to be a time with Hannah, it did matter.

So then, if not the hotel, where?

He could probably have the use of Mitch's apartment, seeing as how he and Maggie were off the day after the wedding to one of those island re-sorts exclusively for couples.

No, that wouldn't do. Mitch's apartment was on the top floor of the casino, and there was no way

Justin would escort Hannah either through the front entrance of the casino or up the back stairs.

Without knowing how he knew, Justin felt Hannah was definitely not a back stairs kind of woman. Scratch Mitch's place. The same for Maggie's attic hide-away. He felt positive that Hannah would not for a second even consider her friend's home for what he had in mind.

Suddenly he was struck by a memory. There was an apartment two floors below Maggie's place. Karla had lived there before marrying Ben. It hadn't been rented since then. So they would have privacy for their baby, Ben and Karla were staying in it now. They were planning to leave the morning after the wedding, as well.

Perfect. All he had to do was inform his brother of his intention to stay in the apartment for a couple of days after the wedding. It would be empty. Besides, the house belonged to the family, and he was a member, wasn't he?

The best part was he had already laid the groundwork by telling Mitch he would be looking for female company while he was in town.

Suddenly Justin laughed aloud. Damned if he wasn't planning a seduction. Hell, he had never in his life made plans to actually seduce a woman.

He had simply homed in on a female who appealed to him, made his move and, if the woman was willing, let it all happen.

His laughter faded as fast as it had erupted. Of course, everything depended on when Hannah was planning to return to Philadelphia and, more important, if she would be willing to spend some mutually entertaining time with him.

Of course, Hannah hadn't appeared overwhelmed by his masculine appeal. Come to think of it, she had barely spoken or looked at him during dinner. But he had a feeling something shimmered between them from the moment he touched her hand. And damned if he wasn't going to give it his best shot.

"So, I understand our family's going to go off in separate directions right after the big day," said Justin who was seated at a small table in Mitch's office the following morning. He'd called his brother and invited himself for breakfast. They had finished their meal, and Justin sat back in his chair, sipping at a mug of steaming coffee.

"Far as I know, everybody's taking off about the

same time," Mitch replied from opposite Justin, his hands cradling a matching mug. "Aren't they?"

"I'm not." Justin took another sip. "Ben can take care of things at the ranch, so I think I'll lug my gear over to the apartment Ben and Karla are presently occupying and camp there for a couple days."

"Why?" Mitch raised his eyebrows.

Justin gave him a slow, suggestive grin. "I do recall telling you I'd be on the lookout for some female companionship, didn't I?"

Mitch grinned back. "You're incorrigible."

"Not at all," Justin denied. "I'm just hot to trot, is all. You don't mind if I use the place for a while?"

"Why should I mind?" Mitch shrugged. "The house belongs as much to you as it does to me." He gave Justin a wry look. "As long as you wait until everybody has left to track down a playmate."

"Everybody?" Before Mitch could respond, he went on, digging for information. "Just the family, or does that include other guests?"

"Other guests?" Mitch frowned. "What other guests? Since Maggie's parents decided not to fly in from Hawaii after we informed them we'd stop by on the way to our honeymoon, the only other guests are employees and a few local residents."

"And Hannah." Justin kept his voice free of inflection, other than a slight hint of disinterest.

"Oh, yeah, Hannah." Mitch pursed his lips. "Hmm…you know, I don't have a clue as to her plans. Maggie hasn't said a word. I'll have to ask her."

"Is it important?" Justin had to focus to retain his near-bored tone. "I mean, does Hannah come under your no-shock edict?"

Mitch pondered the question for a few seconds, then said, "I haven't given it a thought. Does it matter?"

"Only if it's going to cramp my style. Such as it is."

Mitch shook his head. "I wasn't aware that you had a style. I thought you just jumped the first woman that appealed to you."

"Only if she's willing."

Mitch raised his eyes, as if seeking help from above. "You are not to be believed." His lips twitched. "My very own brother, a philanderer, of all things."

"Hey," Justin objected. "I am not a philanderer. I'm a normal male, with a healthy sexual appetite. And do you have any idea how long it's been since I've appeased it?"

Mitch let rip a deep, rich laugh. "I don't think I want to know anything about your sex life, thank you."

"Sex life? Who the hell has a sex life?" Justin chuckled. "I talk to horses most of the time, and most of the time I don't mind. But, every now and again, a man needs a woman. And in my case, buddy, it's been months."

"Okay. Okay." Mitch held his hand up in surrender. "I give up. Have your R and R, but try not to lose the ranch at the tables downstairs."

Justin didn't bother to respond. Mitch knew damn well he wasn't stupid; he would set a limit, a fairly low one, and stick to it. He hid an inner smile. "If things break my way, I'll be too busy with more important—and a helluva lot more interesting—things than gambling."

Three

Friday arrived much too soon to suit Hannah. Although they talked almost nonstop, there hadn't been nearly enough time for her and Maggie to catch up with each other's lives. Not once had either one of them run out of things to say.

The rehearsal was scheduled for five in the small church just a few blocks from the big Victorian house. Dinner would be at the Bullock Hotel immediately following the rehearsal.

By four o'clock Maggie was a nervous wreck. "All this over a rehearsal?" Hannah said, trying hard to contain a laugh. "I can't wait until tomorrow. You'll probably be a basket case. Instead of walking in front of you, Karla and I might have to walk behind, in case you collapse on the way down the aisle."

"Not at all," Maggie said, giving a dainty but superior sniff. "Don't forget, I'll have Mitch's brother Adam to walk me down the aisle." She no sooner had the words out, when she burst out laughing. "And believe me, friend, Adam's big enough to handle delicate little ol' me."

"Shall we be off?" Hannah asked.

"I suppose we'd better," Maggie agreed.

Giggling like two teenagers, they clattered down the stairs and out of the building to Hannah's rented SUV.

The streets had been cleared of snow and the short jaunt to the church took only minutes. That parking lot, also cleared, already contained several vehicles.

"It looks like we're the last to arrive," Maggie said, her voice quavery with tension.

"Yes, it does," Hannah agreed, tossing her friend an exasperated look. "And will you calm down, for pity's sake? It is only the rehearsal."

"I know…but…"

"No buts." She pushed open the door. "Let's go and get this show on the road, so we can get to dinner." She grinned at Maggie, hoping to ease her nerves. "I'm starving."

The rehearsal went off without a hitch…for everyone except Hannah. She was fine at the beginning. Maggie introduced her to more of Mitch's family including his brother Adam. Hannah had immediately liked him.

Adam was just as tall and handsome as his brothers, a little older, but pleasant and charming. His eyes, unlike Justin's, were warm, friendly. So she was feeling good, relaxed, until she began leading the procession. The sight of Justin, standing beside Mitch at the end of the aisle, had the strangest effect on her.

In direct contrast to Mitch, who was wearing a dark suit, white shirt and striped tie, Justin was dressed in a soft brown pullover sweater, tan casual pants and the same black boots he'd worn at Maggie's that first night.

Hannah couldn't help but wonder if he were planning to wear the boots for the wedding. The errant thought flittered through her mind that at least the boots were shined.

But his footwear or clothes weren't the cause

of her weird reaction. It was his eyes, his laser-sharp eyes. After slowly raking the length of her body, they seemed to bore right through her, to her every thought, every emotion. And Hannah's range of emotions were running wild, shaking up every particle of her being.

She suddenly felt nervy, excited and vaguely frightened, chilled and hot all over, as if in anticipation of something earth-shattering about to happen.

Weird hardly described it.

It seemed to take forever for her to traverse the relatively short aisle, and yet she reached the end way too soon. And there he was, his piercing gray gaze glittering with a sometime-soon promise of that anticipated, dreaded, earth-shattering event. The heat causing the glitter left little doubt in her mind what he intended that event to be.

Hannah's breathing was labored, uneven. Relief rushed through her when she stepped to the side, out of his direct line of vision. Hannah rigidly avoided his eyes through the rest of the proceedings.

After that, everything went off without a hitch…until they arrived at the hotel.

Dinner itself was fine. The food served was ex-

cellent, Mitch's family friendly, easy to talk to…
that is, except Justin. He had waited until Hannah
was seated, then, deliberately, she felt certain,
seated himself directly opposite her. At once he
proceeded to renew sending his silent, visual messages to her. Hard as she tried—and she gave it her
best shot—Hannah couldn't misinterpret his intent.

She was not without experience in the nuances
of eye conduct and body language. He had plans,
for her and him together, those silent messages
promised. And, as she had suspected in the church,
every one of those plans were sexual in nature.

While Justin's hot-eyed gaze revealed his car-
nal thoughts to Hannah, his occasional and brief
comments were bland, almost banal.

Hannah didn't know whether to be amused or
run for her life.

She attempted to assure herself her feelings
were caused by revulsion, but she knew she was
lying. The truth, which she would fiercely deny if
questioned, was that her feelings stemmed from
excitement.

Hannah was fearful her feelings, the heat
steadily building inside, were clearly revealed on
her face, in her eyes. She hoped the picture she

presented to the company, even the most keen of observers, was that of cool, controlled composure.

Especially to Justin.

Justin could read Hannah like an open book. Far from being repelled by his stare of unconcealed desire, Hannah was receptive, her own needs and desires revealed in the depths of her so-cool eyes.

He couldn't wait to get her alone, feel her mouth yielding to his kiss, her naked body sliding against his, her long legs curling around his waist.

Stop it, Justin ordered his wayward thoughts. Damned if he wasn't getting hard, right there under the table. He drew a mental image of himself, trudging across the frozen tundra, chilled to the bone.

Moments later he was surprised by the strains of music from a group positioned in front of a small dance floor at the end of the private dining room. Leave it to Mitch to have arranged for dancing after dinner.

In a flash, Justin was on his feet, circling the table to Hannah. "I suppose we're expected to rehearse the wedding party reception dance, too," he said, holding out his hand in invitation.

"Ahh…" she responded, her voice laced with uncertainty and a strong hint of reluctance.

"That's right," Maggie said, laughing—bless her heart. "We want everything perfect."

Hannah sighed, but complied, placing her hand in his as she rose from her chair.

Justin's own heart was starting to speed up as he led Hannah to the dance floor. While he wouldn't be able to feel her satiny skin sliding against him, or her tempting mouth pressed to his, or the embrace of her slender legs, he was determined to feel the thrill of her supple body held close to his in the dance.

Not exactly the dance Justin would have preferred, but it would have to do…for now.

Fortunately, the group was playing his kind of music, a ballad, allowing for only slow dancing. At the edge of the dance floor, Justin drew Hannah to him, circling her waist with his arms, leaving her little choice but to circle his neck with her own. The sensation created by the feel of her tall body held closely against his was thrilling beyond anything he had ever felt while fully clothed.

Scratch that last thought, he corrected himself, drawing in a quick breath at the sensations sent skittering through him at the touch of her hand sliding from the back of his neck to the center of his chest. Though he knew her movement was intended to keep some distance between them, Justin was forced to suppress an involuntary shiver at the scorching feel of her palm against him, right through his shirt.

"What are you afraid of?" he asked, his voice pitched low for her ears only. "You don't like dancing?"

Hannah lifted her head to gaze at him, a wry curve on her maddeningly tempting lips. "Not particularly," she drawled. "And I don't need my suit pressed, thank you."

He laughed, refraining himself from telling her he intended to press a lot more than her clothes. He held himself in check for one reason; he had heard the slight breathy catch in her voice underlying her dry tones.

Deciding to play it cool, he made a half step back, feeling a chill, even from that tiny span between them.

"I'm glad you find me so amusing," she said, keeping her hand solidly pressed to his chest.

"Oh, I find you a lot more than amusing," he said, fighting an urge to be explicit, and a bigger urge to show her, right there on the dance floor.

But no, the room was full of people, most of whom were family members. If he gave in to the urge, Mitch and Adam would be all over him like a bad rash in no time. He'd hate like hell to have to deck the two of them in front of the family. The thought made him smile.

Hannah felt…bedazzled. Where the heck had that almost boyish, impish smile come from? she wondered, feeling an unfamiliar warmth around her heart. What in the world was Justin thinking about to cause that smile?

"You look pensive," he murmured, trying to move her closer to him, relenting when she resisted.

Having lowered his head, his breath tickled her ear, all the way to the base of her spinal cord. Two conflicting thoughts tangled together in her bemused mind—wanting this dance to end soon and hoping it would go on forever.

Throwing caution aside, she decided to be candid. "I was just wondering where that smile came from…and who it was for."

He laughed. Damn, Hannah wished he wouldn't do that. His laughter had an even more intense effect than his smile. It was low, infectious, relaxed, and scattered the warmth in her chest, setting off minisparklers throughout her body.

Now he grinned. She swallowed a groan.

"Actually, I was thinking about having to take down both of my brothers in front of everybody here."

Startled by his reply, Hannah stared at him. "But…why would you think of such a thing?"

His eyes gleamed with devilment. "In self-defense, of course. Why else?"

The music stopped. She made a move. He didn't. His hold was unbreakable. She swept a quick look around to see if anyone was watching them. There were three other couples on the floor: his parents, Mitch and Maggie, and Ben and Karla. The three couples were too absorbed in one another to pay any attention to her and Justin. Still, Hannah had just opened her mouth to protest, when the music started again. He moved, taking her with him, and they continued dancing.

Hannah sighed, heavily so he couldn't possibly miss it, but she had to ask, "Why on earth would you need to defend yourself from your brothers?"

"Because they'd jump me for sure," Justin responded patiently, as if the answer should be obvious.

Hannah didn't know whether to hit him or scream at him. She did neither. She sighed again and narrowed her eyes. "Okay, if you want to play games. Why would they jump you?"

"Because I want to play games," he explained, the gleam in the depth of his so cool eyes literally dancing.

"Justin…" Her voice held a gravelly, distinct note of warning.

"Okay. But don't say you didn't ask." He shrugged. "I figured if I acted on impulse, pulling you tightly against me and ravishing your mouth with mine, Mitch and Adam might think it was their duty to rescue you from the clutches of their womanizing brother." Laughter skirted on the edges of his serious tone. "And in that case, of course, I'd have little recourse but to sweep out this barn with them."

Sweep out this barn? Barn? Hannah sent a quick glance around the well-appointed dining room. But she didn't question his remark. Her attention had focused on one word. "Womanizing?"

Justin nodded solemnly, immediately ruining the effect of his somber expression with another one of those breath-stealing smiles.

She stopped moving so suddenly his big body crashed hard into hers, knocking the breath out of her. Reflexively he tightened his arms around her, steadying her while keeping them both upright, her body crushed to his.

"Nice," he murmured, his breath ruffling the tiny hairs at her temple…and her senses.

"You're a womanizer?" she blurted without thinking, her voice betraying her shock.

"No, sweetheart," he denied, his tone adamant, thrilling her with the casually stated endearment, his lips setting off a thrill as they skimmed a trial from her ear to the corner of her mouth.

"But, you said…" she began, stirring—not struggling—to put some small distance between them. Her puny efforts proved unsuccessful.

"I know what I said." His arms tightened even more. "Stay still. You feel so good." His mouth took a slow, erotic journey over her surprised, parted lips. "You taste so good. I could make a feast of you."

Because she suddenly craved a deeper taste of him, she felt a faint curl of panic. Afraid of the strange sensations churning inside her, Hannah turned and pulled her head back, away from his tantalizing mouth.

"You've got the wrong woman," she said, somehow managing to infuse a thread of strength into her breathy voice.

"No." Justin shook his head, but loosened his hold, allowing her to move back a half step. "I've got the right woman." His smile and eyes were soft, almost tender. "Hannah, I am not a womanizer."

She frowned. "Then why did you say you were?"

"Because my brothers tease me about my lifestyle every time we're together." He grinned. "Matter of fact, Mitch called me a philanderer just the other day." He heaved a deep sigh. "It was unkind of him. I was crushed."

"Right," Hannah drawled, raising an eyebrow in disbelief. "I know it's none of my business, but…" she hesitated. It most certainly was her business: Justin Grainger had definite and obvious designs on her.

"But?" he prompted, a dark brow mirroring hers.

"What is your lifestyle…exactly."

"Pretty damn boring," he said, releasing her when the music stopped. "I ranch, and I don't go to town, any town or city, too often."

"Have you ever been married?" she asked.

"I was. I've been divorced now for almost five year," he said, his voice hard and flat. "And no,

I don't want to talk about it. I want to forget about it."

Feeling rebuffed, Hannah's spine stiffened. "I don't recall asking you to talk about it…or to dance in the first place as far as that goes. Now, if you'll excuse me?" She didn't wait for an answer but strode away, head held high.

A little while later—though it seemed like hours to Hannah—the party began to break up. At last, she thought, rising and scooping up her handbag. After not having exchanged one word with Justin since returning to the table, she not only didn't say good-night, she avoided eye contact with him.

Feeling a need to escape the room, and Justin, she found Maggie, who was lingering over saying her farewells to the others, and murmured her intention of getting the car.

Hannah saw the snow flurries a moment before she reached the hotel exit. Fortunately, only a fine coating of white covered the parking lot. She didn't notice the thin layer of black ice beneath the snow as she stepped outside.

She took only three steps before she felt the heel of her right boot begin to slip. Hannah tried to regain her balance, but knew for certain she was going down.

"Son of a…" she began, her arms flailing.

"Whoa," Justin said from right behind her, his strong hands grasping her upper arms to catch her, ease her upright. "Is that any way for a lady to talk?" His hands moved, swinging her around to face him.

"I wasn't feeling much like a lady at that moment," Hannah said, still catching her breath from the near tumble, and not the nearness of the man, she assured herself.

"I can understand your reaction. That was a close one." Though it would seem impossible, his voice contained both concern and amusement. "Good thing I was only a few steps behind you."

"Thank you," Hannah said, a bit shakily, forcing herself to look directly into his eyes.

"You're welcome." His smile was a tormenting tease, his eyes held that gleam again.

He was close, too close. She could smell the clean, spicy, masculine scent of him, feel the warmth of him through her winter coat. "Were you following me?" She attempted a step back; he drew her closer.

"Yes." His lips brushed her ear, his warm breath tickling the interior.

A thrill shimmered the length of her spine; Hannah told herself it was the chill in the air, the feel of the cold fluffy snowflakes kissing her cheeks. "Why were you following me? What do you want from me?" Stupid question, as if she didn't already know the answer. Nevertheless, when it came, so blunt, so determined, she was shocked…and a lot more than thrilled. She felt allover warm and excited.

"Long, hot nights on smooth, cool sheets."

Four

At last the wedding day arrived. The candlelight ceremony was scheduled for six, with the reception following immediately at the hotel.

To Hannah's amazement, after the nervous fits Maggie had suffered the day before, her friend had been calm and remained so throughout the day.

Although she revealed not the slightest hint of it, Hannah felt like the basket case she had expected Maggie to be. Of course, her inner jitters had nothing whatever to do with her encounter with Justin in the parking lot, she kept telling herself.

Yeah. Right.

So stunned had she been by Justin's blatant suggestion—suggestion, heck, it was an outright declaration of intent—Hannah retained only a vague memory of him, chuckling softly as he walked her to her car. And, darn it, how had he been so surefooted, when he'd been wearing heeled boots, too?

"Time to dress," Maggie happily announced, ending Hannah's brooding introspection.

At last. At last. Hannah smiled, nodding her agreement. She was of two minds about the coming hours; relieved at finally getting it over with, and filled with conflicting amounts of trepidation and anticipation, more of the latter than the former.

Calling herself all kinds of a ditz didn't do a thing to calm down her seesawing emotions.

One thing was for certain. Hannah was determined there would be no slipping on black ice. At her advice, both she and Maggie wore low-heeled winter boots and carried their fancy wedding shoes in shoe bags. At least they didn't have any concerns about holding up their dresses out of the slushy mess, as both garments were cocktail length. Maggie's dress was a simple and elegant, long-sleeved white velvet, with a nipped-in waist and full skirt. She looked both innocent and gorgeous.

Hannah's dress was as simple and elegant—a sheath with three-quarter-length sleeves and a modest neckline.

They arrived at the church with five minutes to spare until show time. Apparently everyone else, including the groom, was already in place. Karla and Adam were waiting in the small foyer. Adam took their coats, and Karla handed them their bouquets. Maggie's was made of white orchids. Hannah's bouquet was the same as Karla's, a mix of dark-red rosebuds with lacy ferns and delicate white baby's breath.

Now Hannah knew why Maggie had insisted she hunt down a dress in forest green. Hers was only a shade darker than Karla's.

Music from the organ filled the church.

Flashing Maggie an encouraging smile, Karla stepped out, heading down the aisle. Offering her own smile to the bride, while drawing a calming breath for herself, Hannah followed two steps behind Karla.

And there he was, standing beside Mitch, looking devastating in a white shirt, somber tie and dark suit that was fitted perfectly to his wide-shouldered, narrow-waisted, long-legged body.

As she drew nearer, Hannah lowered her gaze, fully expecting to find black slant-heeled boots. Surprise, surprise. Justin was actually shod in classic black men's dress shoes.

When she raised her eyes, her gaze collided with his smoldering stare.

Good grief! The man was a menace. Hannah felt hot. She felt cold. She felt exhilarated. She felt exhausted. In short, she felt like a woman fiercely physically attracted to a man. A man who didn't so much as attempt to hide his intention from her.

Unaware of the ceremony going on about her, she automatically received Maggie's bouquet.

Her heart pounding, her pulse racing, finding it increasingly difficult to think straight, Hannah almost completely missed the exchange of vows.

"With this ring, I thee wed."

The firm, clear sound of Mitch's voice broke through Hannah's mental fog. She blinked, and just caught the movement of Justin handing Mitch a plain gold ring.

Her cue. Releasing a soft sigh of relief for coming to her senses in time, Hannah slipped a larger matching gold band from her thumb, just as Maggie repeated the vow.

Moments later Mitch kissed Maggie, to the applause of the guests, and it was over. They were married.

Hopefully, till death did them part, Hannah thought, frowning as she saw Justin take Adam's place in line, leaving his older brother to escort Karla.

What was the devil up to now? Steeling herself, she took Justin's arm to follow the newlyweds down the aisle to the church foyer.

"Your place or mine?" Justin murmured, his eyes glittering with a positively wicked gleam of amusement.

He knew. Damn the man, he knew exactly how she was feeling, *what* she was feeling, as if the word *ready* had magically appeared branded on her forehead in capital letters.

"I don't have a place here," Hannah muttered, riveting her gaze on the back of Maggie's head. "My place is hundreds of miles from here, in Pennsylvania."

He chuckled.

Hannah cringed, covering it with a tight smile as she hugged first Maggie, then Mitch, wishing them good luck before turning to stand beside Mitch to form the greeting line. Not daring to so much as glance into Justin's eyes again, she stood stiff, staring directly ahead. It didn't do her a bit of good, as he continued to torment her in that low, deep, nerve-rattling sexy voice.

"My permanent place is not as far away. In Montana," he murmured, his head so close to hers she felt his warm breath caress her ear. "But I have a temporary place here, as I know you do. Conveniently, both places are at the very same location, that beautiful old Victorian house."

Hannah was genuinely shocked. "Maggie's apartment? I…I couldn't, wouldn't dream of it!" she softly protested, suddenly realizing she had not said no to *him,* but rather to meeting him at Maggie's adorable little flat on the third floor.

"Of course not," he agreed, drawing her startled gaze just as he smiled at Karla who settled in line next to him. His eyes still gleamed with a sinful light. "But I haven't the least hesitation in using the roomier apartment on the first floor for some fun and games."

Fun and games. The overused expression, following the tired line of your place or mine, didn't sound as worn-out and dated coming from Justin's sensuous mouth. Truth be told, the soft invitation sounded much too tempting.

At a loss for a coherent retort, Hannah felt a wave of relief as she turned her head to find the first of the guests, Justin's parents, who were laughing and crying and hugging Maggie and Mitch in turn.

Justin merely lowered his head closer to her, his whispered words tickling her inner ear and every nerve ending in her body. "I'll be moving in for a couple of days tomorrow, right after Karla and Ben vacate."

Hannah had to suppress a visible tremor as his tongue swiftly speared into her ear.

"Feel free to visit at anytime…day or night," he murmured, increasing the tremor a hundredfold. "Come early…and often—" he chuckled at her quick, indrawn breath, "—and stay late…like a couple of days."

Thank goodness, at that moment Justin's father swept her into a celebratory embrace, as she found it difficult to pull a comeback from her mush of gray matter. The man was nearly as tall as his three sons, but not as strong as them, and not nearly as ruggedly handsome as Justin—darn his too-attractive hide.

His mother, a lovely woman, and almost as tall as Hannah took her hands and leaned forward to kiss her cheek. "You look beautiful in that dress, Hannah," she said, delicately dabbing at her eyes with a tissue. "Both of you do, you and Karla."

"Why, thank you," Hannah responded, lowering her head to kiss the older woman's still smooth cheek. She had liked Mrs. Grainger from their first meeting. "Maggie picked the color. She insisted I search until I found the perfect dress."

"And you did. It's a perfect color for so soon after the holidays," the older woman said, smiling as she stepped into Justin's waiting arms. "It's lovely on you."

Wrong on both counts, Mom, Justin thought as he swept his mother into a hug and planted a kiss on her cheek. That dark green was great against Hannah's blond hair and creamy complexion any time of year. And she didn't look merely lovely, she looked ravishing. And as for it being lovely on her, he'd rather see it off her. And he intended to…soon.

Naturally, Justin didn't say any of that to his mother. She just might have decided to step in and protect the lovely Hannah from her "bad boy" son.

He complimented her instead. "As always, you not only look wonderful, Mother, you smell terrific, kinda sexy. I'll bet Dad loves that scent."

"Justin Grainger!" His mother sounded shocked, but she couldn't quite control the amusement twitching the corners of her lips. "Behave yourself."

"He doesn't have a clue how to do that," his father drawled, the glimmer in his eyes similar to the light dancing in his son's. "But, you know what?" he said, drawing his wife from Justin's loose hold. "He's exactly right. I do think that perfume's sexy. It turns me on."

His mother gasped and proceeded to scold her grinning husband. Justin thrilled to the soft sound of laughter from the woman by his side. He smiled at Hannah.

"They're a trip, aren't they?"

"I think they're perfect together." Her returned smile caused sudden heat and potentially embarrassing sensations in all parts of his body.

"I think we'll be perfect together, too."

"To quote a wise woman I recently met, 'Behave yourself, Justin,' before you embarrass me," she said sternly, giving him a brief, pointed look at one particular part of his anatomy, "As well as yourself."

He laughed aloud, he couldn't help it. This gorgeous woman thoroughly delighted him.

Hannah simply shook her head in despair of him and turned her attention to the line of waiting guests. Then she ignored him until the last couple of guests had finally departed.

Thinking her advice prudent, at least until he got her on the dance floor at the reception, Justin conducted himself like the perfect gentleman throughout the boring ordeal of being prodded and pushed into position by the fussy photographer during the snapping of the wedding pictures.

While he drew impatient with his self-imposed restraint, and at the seemingly endless procedures, he still was distracted and amused by the quick, suspicious glances Hannah winged his way every so often.

Although he felt at the point of busting loose, Justin maintained his circumspect demeanor during the time-honored rituals of the start of the reception. He didn't even suggest that Adam again change partners with him as the wedding party made their entrance.

Toasts were raised, seemingly never-ending toasts. As best man, Justin gave the first one, and even managed to deliver it without firing one risqué shot at Mitch. Adam stood up after him, and followed his lead of propriety. It was their father, the unrepentant, rugged seventy-five-year-old zing-tosser that scored with a couple of sly innuendoes.

Braving their mother's startled and annoyed expression, Justin joined his brothers and the guests in laughter. He was happy to notice that Maggie, Karla, his sisters and even the tempting Hannah were laughing.

Within seconds, at a teasing, endearing smile from his father, his mother gave in to laughter, too.

It set the mood for the celebratory party. Growing impatient to hold Hannah in his arms, Justin remained stoic throughout the rest of the preliminaries.

There was dinner. A buffet fairly groaning with the weight of the food. Servers stood behind the long table, slicing roast beef, baked ham and roasted turkey. Then there was an array of all kinds of hot vegetables, salads and fruits.

Would this never end? Justin wondered, filling his plate then only picking at the food. Not anytime soon, he concluded, hearing the announcement for the bride and groom's first dance.

The first dance ended and the frontman for the small band called for the attendants to take the floor. Schooling himself, Justin swept Hannah into his arms and onto the floor, keeping a respectful distance between them.

She gave him a wary look, as if recalling the way he had held her the night before.

Justin offered her a polite smile. "Did you enjoy your dinner?" he asked, his tone every bit as polite as his smile. "I noticed you didn't take very much to eat."

Hannah still looked wary. "I really wasn't hungry."

"I suppose you didn't notice, but I wasn't, either." He smiled at Adam and Karla as they danced past. "At least, I wasn't hungry for food."

"Justin." Her voice was soft, stern. Her gaze narrowed on his. "Are you going to start up again?"

"Oh, honey, I've barely begun." He grinned. "May I see you back to the house?"

Her eyes glittering defiance, she raised her chin. He was tempted to take a tasty bite of it.

"No. Thank you." She gave him a superior, mocking smile. "I have my own car."

Releasing her hand, Justin took a half step back,

feigning shock. "You mean, my brother didn't send a limo for his prospective bride and her attendant?"

"Of course not. Why should he? I rented a large SUV. And he did have the limo to bring them here from the church."

"Even so, I'd have sent a limo for my intended." His eyes refuted his self-righteous tone. Reclaiming her hand, he whirled her around.

"And do you have an intended hidden away somewhere?" She was slightly breathless from his sudden quick movement. A becoming color bloomed in her cheeks.

Justin was intrigued, wondering if his swirling action had caused her pink breathlessness, or if it had sprung from her question. "No." He gave a fast and sharp shake of his head. "No intendeds for me." He lifted a dark, chiding eyebrow. "If there were, I wouldn't be here, now, wanting to make love with you."

She made a sound that to him was part gasp, part sigh. He waited for a response from her, feeling breathless himself.

At that moment the music ended, and she slipped out of his arms and damned near ran to the bridal party table.

* * *

For someone who was usually calm and collected, Hannah was feeling more than a little rattled. Rattled, excited and annoyed.

No intendeds for me.

What was he trying to tell her with his emphatic statement, the quick negative shake of his head? He had no use for women? Hannah gave a silent but definite "Ha!" Justin obviously had one use for women.

Just then, Maggie found her. "Hannah, I want you to come with me." Her friend grasped her arm, tugging to get her moving.

Trailing along, thoroughly confused by the urgency in Maggie's voice, Hannah asked, "Where are we going…and why such a hurry?"

"We're going up to the suite Mitch reserved for us for tonight," Maggie explained—kind of—continuing to tug on Hannah's arm.

"I don't understand." Now she was more than confused.

"Of course you don't." Maggie exhaled as the doors to the elevator slid together after they stepped inside. "I want you to help me out of my dress."

"Me?" Hannah could only stare at her in disbelief. "Maggie, isn't that Mitch's job?"

"Yes, yes, I know all that." Maggie waved the question aside. "But Mitch is the one who asked me to give you another heads-up." The doors swished open, and Maggie swished into the corridor. "Besides," she added over her shoulder, "I would like you to take my dress back to the house for me."

"I'd be happy to take it with me." Tired of trailing in her friend's wake, Hannah strode forward to walk with her to the suite. "Heads-up about what?" she asked, with wide-eyed innocence, as if she didn't know damn well it would concern Justin somehow.

"Justin." Maggie unlocked then flung open the door and ushered her inside.

Who would ever have guessed? Hannah thought, resigned to hearing more negative tidbits about Justin's character, or lack of same. She sighed, might as well get it over with. "What about Justin?"

"Well…" Now, after having given Hannah the bum's rush from the reception room, Maggie hesitated.

"He's a wanted felon?" Hannah asked, facetiously.

"No, of course not." Maggie tossed an impatient look at her. "Apparently, he's something of a…uh…philanderer. You know, the no-strings, love-'em-and-leave-'em type."

Big shocker. Hannah had figured that one out for herself. If she hadn't, she wouldn't have been about to bid good-night to Maggie and Mitch, wish them happiness, give them both a congratulatory hug and head for the nearest exit.

"I suspected as much," Hannah said, with self-imposed equanimity, walking around Maggie to unhook and pull the waist-length zipper on her dress.

"You did?" Maggie swung around to face her. "How?"

Hannah actually contrived a reasonable-sounding chuckle. "Dearest friend, Justin has been making…shall I say…explicit suggestions to me since the rehearsal supper last night."

"Aha," Maggie crowed. "Mitch was right. He said he thought Justin was hitting on you. That's why he asked me to clue you in."

"I appreciate the concern." In point of fact, even though she had figured Justin wasn't looking for a real relationship, Hannah wasn't at all sure she did appreciate the concern, or the information. She gave a frowning Maggie a serene smile. "Where is your bridegroom, by the way?"

"Oh my gosh," Maggie yelped. "He'll be here any minute. If you don't mind," she said, stepping out of the dress, "I'm going to toss this into the bag and toss you out of here so I can get ready for him."

Laughing with genuine amusement, Hannah retrieved the long, heavy plastic dress bag and held it open while Maggie slipped it onto a padded hanger and beneath the garment bag.

"Okay, I'm outta here."

"Wait," Maggie ordered, stopping Hannah as she turned toward the door. Bending to a low table, she scooped up her bouquet and shoved it into Hannah's free hand.

"What are you doing?" Hannah demanded. "You're supposed to toss that to the single women downstairs." She tried to hand it back to Maggie, who refused to take it.

"What single woman?" Maggie backed away. "As far as I'm concerned, *you* are the only single woman here…which means, you'll be the next bride."

"But, Maggie, you know there is no—"

"I know, I know, but who knows what's in the future? Mr. Right might be just around the corner." Laughing at Hannah's skeptical expression, Maggie backed up another step. "Will you just take it and get out of here?"

Hannah heaved an exaggerated sigh. "Okay, you win. But only because I don't want to be here to cramp his style when Mitch arrives."

"Thanks, love," Maggie fervently said, rushing to Hannah to give her a hug. "For everything, especially being my friend. I'll call you after Mitch and I get back."

"I'll be waiting," Hannah said, holding the bag up from the floor as she moved to the door. "Be happy." She smiled, opened the door, then turned back to murmur, "Love you."

Maggie's return smile was misty. "Back at you."

Five

Avoiding Justin as she made her escape, Hannah didn't breathe fully until she locked the door behind her in Maggie's cozy attic flat.

Nervous, edgy, both afraid—and secretly hopeful—that she'd hear Justin rap at the door any second, she carefully hung Maggie's dress away before removing her own dress. After a quick shower, Hannah slipped into her nightshirt and robe, then proceeded to collect her stuff. She was leaving, going back to Philly, first thing in the morning.

She was *not* running from Justin, Hannah kept telling herself, knowing all the while she was lying. She knew, without a shred of doubt, Justin would not force any issues or hurt her in any way. Why she was convinced he would honor her decision, whatever that might be, she didn't know, but she felt certain she was right.

So, if she was not running from fear of Justin, what was she running from? She was attracted to Justin, fiercely attracted. She had never, ever wanted a man, his touch, his kiss, his possession as much as she wanted Justin Grainger.

It scared the hell out of her.

He scared the hell out of her.

Not physically. Emotionally.

As sure as Hannah was that Justin would never physically harm her, she was equally sure he could devastate her emotionally.

She had been warned. Justin himself had told her he was the family "bad boy," and to protect her, Mitch had instructed Maggie to inform her of his brother's love-'em-and-leave-'em reputation with women.

Perhaps, Mitch had had a heart-to-heart with his wayward brother because, by 2 a.m. he had neither rapped on the door nor rung Maggie's phone.

Hannah knew the exact time, because by 2 a.m., she had not slept, had not so much as closed her eyes. Her restless, wakeful state had nothing to do with not having heard from him, she assured herself. She absolutely did not feel let down, disappointed…damn near bereft.

Sigh. She had done a lot of sighing.

Somewhere around 4 a.m., well, actually, 4:14 to be exact, Hannah faced the cold hard fact that Justin had been amusing himself by teasing her, stringing her along. For all she knew, he simply might have been deliberately coming on to her to rile his brother Mitch.

If that had been Justin's aim, he had scored a direct hit. Problem for Hannah was his barb had scored a direct hit on her, as well.

Her own fault. She had walked fully conscious into the cross-hairs. Served her right if she was feeling the sting of his arrow. She deserved the piercing stab in her chest. She had known full well that his make on her was all about sex, anyway.

So, the hell with Justin Grainger. She'd forget him in no time once she was back in Philly, back to her real life of work and friends.

But first she had to get some rest. She had a lot

of driving in the morning to get to the airport in time for her flight. Sleep, stupid, Hannah scathingly told herself. Clenching her body against the aching emptiness inside, she shut her eyes tight, denying the sting burning her eyelids, and concentrated on the word sleep.

Her alarm went off at seven, approximately one hour and twenty minutes after she had finally drifted off.

Groaning, Hannah levered herself off the cot and stumbled into the bathroom. Even though she had showered last night, to get an early start this morning, she pulled off her nightshirt and stepped under a spray of tepid, wake-up water.

It helped, but not a helluva lot. Heaving a deep sigh, followed by a wide yawn, she brushed her teeth, applied a layer of concealer on the dark half-moons beneath her eyes, and finished with a light application of tinted moisturizer and blush to each cheek.

Frowning at her image in the mirror above the sink, Hannah left the bathroom, made up the cot. Deciding to grab something to eat in the terminal concourse, she skipped breakfast for a fast get-away. Quickly dressing, she stomped into foul-weather boots, pulled on her coat, gathered her baggage and sent a final glance around the cozy flat, checking that everything was in order.

Swallowing another sigh, which she adamantly refused to admit was of regret, Hannah left the apartment and clattered down the stairs to the second-floor doorway. Yanking open the door, she stepped into the hallway and practically into the arms of Justin Grainger.

"What kept you?" he said, a lopsided smile on his smooth, clean-shaved face.

Startled, rattled, Hannah stared at him. "Wh–what?"

"I thought you'd never get it together this morning." His warm gaze caressed her face, settled on her mouth. "I heard your alarm go off all the way down two flights of stairs—what the hell have you got, anyway, a miniature Big Ben?" Before she could open her suddenly tingling lips to reply, he caught her by one arm to lead her along the hall to the other stairs. "I hope you didn't waste time eating. I've been holding breakfast for you."

"But...but..." Hannah stammered. Dammit, she never stammered. "Why?" she demanded, allowing him to relieve her of her suitcase and carry-on with the other hand as he urged her down the stairs and to the open door of the apartment where Karla and Ben were staying.

"Why not?" he asked, ushering her inside and firmly closing the door behind them.

More unsettled than she would have believed a man, any man could make her, Hannah ignored his question to ask one of her own. "Where are Karla, Ben and the baby?"

"They left before daylight. I helped them load the SUV. They're going to visit her folks in Rapid City before heading back to the ranch," he explained.

"So, why were you holding breakfast for me?" But before he could respond, she went on, "And how did you know I'd agree to have breakfast with you?"

Justin held up one finger. "I thought you might be hungry." He grinned—too darned sexily—and held up another finger. "I didn't know. I hoped. Will you?"

He had done it again. Thrown her off track. "Will I..." she blurted, before she collected her senses. Never in her adult life had a man held the power to so fluster her.

"Share a meal with me." His grin turned into a sensual smile; his lowered voice was sheer temptation. "Among other even more satisfying pleasures."

"I, uh…" Damned if she wasn't stammering again. Grabbing a quick breath, she stammered, "I…really…I don't…uh…think that…would be wise," she finished, all in a breathless gush.

"Maybe so," he drawled, in that same low, tempting tone. "But it would be fulfilling …for all our hungers."

"I know." Hannah blurted out without thinking, amazed at herself for doing so. "But that's beside the—"

"No, that *is* the point," he interrupted, setting her bags aside to cradle her face in his warm palms. "I want to be with you so bad I ache all over," he murmured, lowering his mouth to within a breath of hers. "And I feel, no, I know you want to be with me every bit as badly."

"How…" Hannah swallowed. Her voice was barely there, because suddenly her throat was tight, dry. "How do you know I want what you want?"

"Ahhh, sweet Hannah," he whispered, his breath slipping between her slightly parted lips and into her mouth. "Your eyes give you away." His mouth skimmed across hers, setting off a sensation that sparkled throughout her entire being. "Admit it…" His voice gathered a wicked, teasing thread. "So we can get on with other things, beginning with breakfast, which I can smell is ready."

It wasn't until he mentioned it that Hannah caught the mouthwatering aroma of freshly brewed coffee, meat sizzling and something she couldn't quite identify, but which tantalized her taste buds.

"Okay," she said, giving in, not to him, she told herself, but the rumble of emptiness in her stomach. "I'll have breakfast with you." Chastising her weakness, she hurried on, "But then I must get moving or I'll miss my plane."

"There'll be other planes." Very softly, very gently, he touched his mouth to hers.

Hannah couldn't answer. She couldn't breathe. His half kiss had turned the sparkle inside her to tongues of flame.

She stood mute while Justin lifted the strap of her handbag from her shoulder and slid her coat from her arms. She didn't protest when he stashed her coat, handbag and two cases into a small closet. Turning back to her, he smiled, melting what felt like her fire-charred insides, and held out a long-fingered hand.

"Come…let's have breakfast."

* * *

Hannah was well and truly stuffed, pleasantly so. Cradling her second mug of coffee in her hands, she sat back in her chair, replete, one hunger satisfied.

"More?" Justin raised one dark brow, smiling at her over the rim of his coffee mug, reigniting another, even more basic hunger inside her.

"Good heavens, no." She returned his smile, if a bit shakily. "Thank you. Everything was wonderful."

"You're welcome." He lowered the mug; his lips were moist from the beverage and much too appealing. "And thank you, I'm glad you enjoyed it."

"I certainly did. Do you cook a lot?"

"Not often, I admit, but I can cook."

"A man of many talents?"

"Oh, honey, you'd be amazed."

Always before, Hannah had resented a man calling her honey, yet, somehow, coming from Justin, it didn't bother her. The fact was, she rather liked it.

"Refill?" he asked, raising his mug.

"I don't think so." She shook her head before swallowing the last of the coffee and setting her mug on the table. Hannah stood, telling herself to get moving before she gave in to the desire to stay and indulge herself. "I've got to go home."

"Why?" he asked with a grin. "I was tempted to say—Home is where the heart is—but," he shook his head. "I decided that was a bit too obvious."

Though she really tried, Hannah couldn't contain a smile. "And practically everything you've said to me, every suggestion you've made, wasn't obvious?"

He pulled a long face—an attractive long face. "And here all the time I thought I was being subtle."

She burst out laughing. "Subtle? Justin Grainger, you are about as subtle as a jackhammer."

"You deeply wound me." His words were belied by the devilish light in his eyes. He set his cup aside and started toward her. "Is that any way to being an affair?"

"Affair?" Hannah felt a thrilling jolt. "We, uh… we're not beginning an affair." She took a step back. He took two steps forward. "We hardly know each other." She held up one hand…as if she actually believed that would stop him.

Of course it didn't. Justin kept moving, slowly backing her up until her spine made contact with the kitchen wall. He raised his hands to cup her face. His palms were warm, gentle. His long fingers stroked her cheekbones.

"Justin." Hannah would have drawn a deep breath, if she could have found anything other than the most shallow wisp of air. "Don't." Her breathless voice was a mere half-hearted whisper, hardly a deterrent.

Still, Justin paused, his mouth within inches of hers. He sighed, as if held motionless by that one word don't. "Oh, sweet Hannah, don't tell me no," he murmured. "If I don't kiss you soon, I'll explode."

Hannah raised her hand to his shoulders to move him back. She felt the muscles grow taut beneath her suddenly gripping fingers. And then, amazing herself with her boldness, she slid her hands to the back of his neck, grasped his hair, and pulled his head to hers to devour his mouth.

Justin did a fantastic job of devouring in return. Holding her head still with gentle fingers, he angled his mouth over hers. His tongue outlined her lips, teased the sensitive inner skin, before exploring deeper, engaging her tongue in an erotic dance.

Hannah could barely breathe, and she didn't

care. His mouth was heaven, his tongue a seeking, probing, ravenous instrument of sensual torment.

His hands deserted her head to glide down her spine, cup her bottom, draw her to the fullness of his body. All rational thought dissolved, swept away by a torrent of sensation, part agony, part pleasure, all terribly exciting and arousing.

He could have this effect on her with one kiss? Hannah marveled, in an obscure corner of her disintegrating mind. What would making love with him do to her?

On the spot, without having to give it a moment's thought—which was good, since she couldn't think anyway—Hannah knew she had to find out, possess him while she experienced his possession of her.

"Hannah, sweet Hannah," Justin groaned into her mouth, lifting his head to stare into her pleasure-clouded eyes. "You can't kiss me like that then tell me you must leave, that we're not beginning an affair."

"I know," she admitted in a raw whisper.

Justin drew back another inch to study her expression. "You want me, don't you, sweet Hannah?"

She didn't answer at once, but stood staring

back at him. Able to breathe a little, and almost think, Hannah was struck by the realization of having lost count of the times he had called her "sweet Hannah." She had been called many things in her life, from "squirt" by her older brother, to "the cool one" by her friends, to "beautiful," even "stunning" by hopeful lovers but never "sweet." If anybody had said she was sweet, she'd have bristled, been annoyed. Babies were sweet, not mature, adult women.

So, then, why did she melt at the endearment murmured through Justin's so-tempting lips?

"Hannah?" The thin, sharp edge on his voice yanked her from her muddled reverie.

She blinked. "What?" Then she remembered his question. "Oh…yes," she answered with complete honesty. "I do want you, Justin," she confessed, spearing her fingers into his thick dark hair.

His soft laughter had a joyous ring. Releasing her bottom, Justin flung his arms out to his sides. "Then take me, sweet Hannah. I'm all yours."

Hannah accepted his invitation by pressing her mouth to his.

Without breaking contact, Justin moved Hannah away from the wall, through the small dining room and in the direction of the bedroom.

Drowning in multiple sensations, Hannah was only vaguely aware of his arms curling around her waist, holding her entire body tightly to his. But she was fully aware of heat rising inside her at the feel of his hard muscles against her softer flesh.

Entering the bedroom, Justin shut the door with a backward tap of his bare foot. Still without breaking the kiss, he carried her to the side of the bed. Setting her on her feet, he released her, stepped back and brought his hands to the hem of her sweater.

Trembling with need, Hannah raised her hands and the sweater swished over her head, landing who knew, or cared, where. She was fumbling with the buttons on his shirt when an errant but important realization stilled her fingers.

"You need to know that I'm not on any kind of birth control. I haven't used anything for over two years now."

He frowned at her statement. "That's pretty risky, isn't it?"

"Not at all." She shook her head, a bittersweet smile shadowing her lips. "I…haven't…er…indulged—" She broke off to shake her head once more. "You know."

"You haven't had sex in two years?" His voice, his startled expression, hovered somewhere between amazement and disbelief. "Are you serious?"

"Yes." She sighed.

His expression turned pained. "You don't like sex?"

She had to smile. "Well, I don't dislike it." She sighed again. "It's just that," she lifted her shoulders in a hapless shrug when his frown deepened to a near scowl. "I haven't felt attracted…that way…to a man, any man, since I ended a relationship a little more than two years ago."

"Why did you end the relationship?" he asked, in a tone that said he wasn't sure he really wanted to know.

"It was mutual," she answered. "It simply wasn't working for either of us."

"What wasn't working?" His gaze probed intently into hers. "The sex?"

"Well…yes," Hannah confessed, lowering her eyes to the allure of his half-naked chest, suddenly aware of her own near nakedness. "I owe it to you to admit that I fear I may be, uh…unresponsive." She drew a deep breath before rushing on, "I've never had an orgasm."

"You're kidding."

Tired of feeling like a feminine failure, Hannah lifted her head and boldly stared straight into his shocked eyes. "No, I am not kidding. Dammit, do you think any sane woman would kid about something so serious?"

"No, I suppose not," he agreed. Then he asked, "You said you wanted me. Did you mean it, or were you just experimenting with me?"

"I meant it." Hannah's tone was filled with conviction. "I do want you."

"Good," Justin purred, the flame of desire flaring again in his eyes. Lowering his head, he brushed a taunting kiss over her mouth. "Then let's get on with it, see if we can't give you that orgasm."

The mere brush of his mouth robbed her of breath, sent her senses whirling.

"What about...um," she said between quick breaths, "protection?"

Justin smiled. "Luckily for us," he said, shoving his hand in a jeans pocket and retrieving a foil-wrapped package, "I *do* practice safe sex."

Six

Hannah lay where Justin had placed her, right in the center of the queen-size bed and watched as he stretched his long length next to her.

"Hannah, Hannah," he murmured. "What am I gonna do with you?"

She gasped and opened her eyes in wide innocence. "You need instructions?"

Justin laughed gently. "That does it, sweetheart. Now you are really gonna get it."

"Really, really?" Hannah curled her arms around his neck to bring his mouth back to hers.

She was thoroughly enjoying herself, never before had she teased and laughed while making love. "Will I like it?"

"Let's find out," he whispered, taking command of her mouth with his.

Deepening his kiss, he slid a hand over her shoulder, down her chest to the rounded slope of her breast. Gasping, Hannah arched her back, seeking more of his exciting touch. Growling into her mouth, he cupped her breast, found the hardening peak with his fingers.

Heat flowed like molten lava from the rigid peak to the core of her femininity. Hannah was on fire. She couldn't breathe but she didn't care. She wanted more and more.

Squirming to get closer to him, she lowered her arms and pulled him tightly against her straining body. Her hands made a tactile exploration of his broad back, his narrow waist, his slim hips, his long well-muscled thighs.

She needed something…something.

"Slowly, sweetheart," he softly said, his lips following the trail laid out by his hand. "We have all day." His tongue darted out, electrifying her as it flicked that aching peak. "There's plenty of time."

That was easy for him to say, Hannah mused,

moaning deep in her throat at the exquisite sensations his tongue sent quaking through her. She was on fire, every inch of her burning for…that elusive something.

Grasping his hips, she urged him to her, arching in an attempt to align their bodies. Resisting, holding himself back a few inches from her he slid his hand down the center of her quivering body.

"Justin." Hannah cried out as his stroking hand found, delved through her mat of tight blond curls and into the very core of her.

"Justin!" she cried out again, her voice now a near sob, as he parted the delicate folds to explore the moist heat within. "I…I…please!"

"Please what, sweet Hannah?" He delved deeper as he raised his head to her mouth, spearing his tongue between her parted lips, capturing her gasping breaths.

She arched her hips into his tormenting hand, and slid her mouth from his. "I need…need…" she paused to pull some air into her lungs.

"Me?" he whispered enticingly, slipping the tip of his tongue into her ear.

"Yes, I need you, your body…now!"

"At your service, sweet Hannah." Continuing to tease her by gliding his tongue to the corners of her mouth, Justin settled himself between her thighs.

Hannah immediately embraced him with her legs, urging him closer, closer. She gave a hoarse cry when he thrust his body deeply inside her. He set a quick, hard rhythm. Holding on to him for all she was worth, she arched back her head and strove to match his deep strokes. It was a very short ride.

The fire inside her blazed out of control. Hannah felt the unbearable tension quiver, then snap.

"Justin!" Her voice was raw, strangled as her body convulsed around him. In reaction to the sheer pleasure pouring over her, and without conscious direction, her nails scored his buttocks, thrilling once more when he attained his release, growling her name, over and over.

Pure ecstasy. Hannah wanted to tell him, thank him, but at first she couldn't find the breath. Then, when her breathing evened enough to speak, before she could put the thought into words, she succumbed to the sleep that had eluded her during the long night.

"Hannah?" Getting control of his own breathing process, Justin lifted her sweat-slick head from her equally moist breast to look at her. Her eyes were closed, and she looked serene, disheveled but serene. She was breathing at a normal sleeping rate. "Knocked you clear out, did I?"

Smiling, he disengaged, lifted his depleted body from hers. Stretching out beside her, he drew her soft, pliant body to his, pillowing her cheek on his chest.

"Ahhh, Hannah, sweet Hannah," he murmured, not wanting to wake her. Well, with the swift response of his body to the satiny feel of hers, he actually did want to wake her, but he held himself in check, letting her rest.

She'll need it, he thought, rubbing his cheek against the silken, tangled mass of her hair, his body growing harder at the memory of her long blond tresses spread wildly on the pillow in the throes of passion.

And Hannah was passionate. Justin could still hear the echo of her voice pleading with him, her nails raking his skin, crying out to him in the intensity of her orgasm.

Her response had triggered the strongest, most shattering orgasm he had ever achieved, he thought, aching to repeat the experience.

Good grief, were Hannah's former lovers complete idiots? How could they not be as fired up—

roasted, in fact—as he had been to her quick, passionate sensuality?

A shot of sheer male satisfaction flashed through Justin as he realized he was the first man to bring Hannah to ultimate completion.

And ultimate was the only way to describe it. She lay thoroughly satiated and relaxed in the protective cradle of his arms, one of which was growing numb. Justin didn't care. Ignoring the sensation and the discomfort of his hard body, he closed his eyes.

"Sweet, beautiful, Hannah," he whispered, kissing the top of her head as he drifted into a light doze.

The afternoon sun rays were slanting into the room when Hannah woke. She felt good. No, she mused, yawning. She felt wonderful…but hungry. No, that wasn't quite right, either. She felt famished, in another part of her body as well as her stomach.

She made a tentative move in the confines of Justin's caging embrace, sliding her body against his.

Justin. A thrill skipped up her spine at the memory of what they'd shared. With his mouth, his hands, that strong hard body, he had given her a gift beyond her wildest imagination. Not only in her delicious release, but by freeing her fears of being frigid.

"I was beginning to think you had died."

His breath tickled her scalp, his low, intimate tone tickled her libido. "For a moment there, I think I did." Tilting back her head, she smiled up at him and nearly melted at the tender expression on his handsome face. "Isn't that what the French call it. The little death?"

"Yeah." His mouth curved invitingly, a flame springing to life in the depths of his eyes. "Wanna do it again?"

"Yes, please," she said, sliding her free hand up his chest to toy with one flat male nipple. His response was so swift it was breathtaking.

Grunting like a caveman, he heaved himself up and over her, settling her flat on her back. Precisely where she wanted to be at that moment. She opened her legs for him.

"Not so fast, sweet Hannah," he said, laughing down at her as he lowered his head to hers. "You had your way with me the last time. This time it's my turn."

She pouted at him. Still chuckling, he crushed her pouting lips with his hungry mouth.

This time the little death was even more intense; the release, mind and body shattering. Never had Hannah expected to feel as if she were soaring above the clouds. Talk about a natural high! Justin's slow, fantastic loving had brought her to the point where she had actually screamed in response to the sensations of joyous bliss.

Hannah might have been embarrassed by her uncontrollable outcry, if Justin's shout hadn't almost immediately followed her own. Still buried deeply inside her, he lay, spent and relaxed, his head pillowed on her breast. Moving beneath him, she rubbed her leg over his buttock and down the long length of his muscular thigh.

He murmured something against her breast, letting her know he was alive, if not altogether awake.

"I'm hungry," she said, sliding her fingers into his hair, combing through the sweat-dampened, long, tangled strands.

"Are you trying to kill me, woman?" he muttered, raising his head to stare at her in feigned astonishment. "I'm in my thirties, you know, not my late teens."

Hannah giggled. "I thought I felt something stir awake inside me," she lied, laughing into his teasing eyes.

"You thought wrong. It's out for the count." He grinned, rather leeringly. "It'll take a while before I'm ready to spring into action again. Do you think you can bear the wait?"

"I guess so." She sighed, then grinned back at him. "But I don't know how much longer I can bear your weight."

Justin groaned and rolled his eyes. "Give me strength. The woman's tossing puns at me now," he groused, lifting his body to roll over, sprawling next to her.

Hannah gave an exaggerated sigh of relief. "That's better." Arching her back, she stretched the stiffness out of her arms and legs. "I'm hungry."

"You said that." He grinned and looked down at the front of his body. "And I explained that—"

"For food, *man,*" she taunted, getting back at him for twice calling her woman. She wrinkled her nose in distaste. "So drag your so depleted carcass off this bed and help me get something together to eat."

"Slave driver," he complained, laughing as he practically leaped from the bed. "I'm not doing another damn thing, bossy *woman* until I shower and shave." Circling the bed, he scooped her body up into his arms and headed for the door. "And you, sweet Hannah, are going into the shower with me."

Smothering yet another giggle, Hannah curled her arms around his neck and rubbed her face against his shoulder. "I've never showered with a man before," she softly confessed.

Justin stared down into her eyes. He shook his head, his expression compassionate. "You've never done a lot of fun things with a man, have you?"

"No."

"Did you enjoy your, er, first thing?" He arched his brows, then wiggled them.

Hannah laughed, feeling her cheeks grow warm. "Immensely," she admitted. Darn it. What was it about this man, anyway? She hadn't blushed since…hell, she couldn't recall ever having blushed.

"Then, trust me, sweetheart, you're going to enjoy this, too," he promised.

He was dead right. Hannah thoroughly enjoyed

every minute of the playful splashing, lathering, caressing, kissing beneath the spray of warm water. Who knew how long they would have remained there, if not for the audible grumbling sound of hunger from her stomach.

It was almost as much fun drying each other off.

Clean, but still naked as a newborn, Hannah dove back under the covers while Justin shaved. When he walked boldly naked into the bedroom, she unabashedly watched, admiring his lean, muscular and magnificent body as he stepped into briefs, jeans and pulled a cable-knit sweater over his head.

"See anything you like?" he asked, arching a dark brow over laughing gray eyes.

"Actually, I like the whole package," she readily admitted. "You're a very attractive and nice man."

"Boy, that last compliment is a relief." He heaved a deep sigh. "For a minute there, I thought you wanted me only for the pleasure of my body."

"Well," Hannah said teasingly. "There's that, too."

"Thanks. Hey, aren't you ever coming out from hiding? I thought you were hungry."

"I am. But I have no clean clothes here." She

made a face at their clothing scattered around the bed. "I'm waiting for you to be a gentleman and fetch my suitcases."

"I knew you were a slave driver," he muttered.

Justin was back in moments. He set the bags next to the bed, then stood watching her.

"Out," she ordered, flicking a hand at the door.

"But I wanna watch," Justin said, in tones similar to a petulant little boy.

"Are you some kind of voyeur?" Hannah asked, grabbing a pillow and throwing it at his head.

He ducked. The pillow missed him by inches. "No." He grinned. "But you watched me. Hell, I could feel you watching me. It was like a touch. And now I want the privilege of watching you."

"You don't have time to watch me," she countered, enjoying the banter. "I told you, I'm hungry."

"Then I suggest you get your tush in gear and get dressed." He moved back to prop himself indolently against the door frame. "Because I'm not budging."

Giving him a narrow-eyed glare that only brought a wolfish grin to his lips, Hannah flung back the covers and stood. "All right, then, dammit. Watch your fill."

Laughing softly all the while, Justin did watch, his appraising look missing nothing as she dug through the largest of the cases. Secretly thrilling to his caressing gaze, Hannah took her sweet time stepping into almost-there panties, fastened the front closure of her bra, wriggled into hip-hugging jeans and shrugged into a turtleneck sweater.

"You are one absolutely stunning woman from head to toe, sweet Hannah," he said in near reverence.

"Thank you," she whispered. Feeling her face grow warm again, this time with pleasure, she turned away, opening the other bag to search out footwear. Like him, she didn't bother with shoes, slipping into satin ballerina slippers.

In the meantime, Justin moved to open a dresser drawer, making do with a pair of heavy-duty socks to keep his big, narrow feet warm.

He held out his hand to clasp hers. "Now, let's go rustle something up for lunch—" he shot a look at the dark beyond the window "—or supper." He laughed. "Hell, for all we know, it may be a midnight snack."

"Not quite," Hannah said, letting him lead her from the room. "I looked at the clock. It's only nine-fifteen."

"Only, she says." He groaned, and fumbled for the light switch as they entered the kitchen. "We haven't eaten since early this morning. We're both ravenous…and the woman says it's *only* nine-fifteen."

Hannah laughed, at him and at herself. She must be losing her mind, she decided happily, because she not only didn't mind him calling her woman, she was beginning to like it. No doubt about it, her mind was starting to disintegrate. She masked her laughter with an exaggerated groan at the sight of the table still cluttered from their breakfast.

"Yeah," Justin agreed, propping his hands on his hips. "It's a mess. Tell you what, sweet Hannah. I'll make a deal with you."

She gave him a skeptical look. "What kind of deal?"

He frowned and shook his head in sad despair of her. "You have a suspicious mind, Ms. Deturk."

"Damned straight, Mr. Grainger," she retorted. "What deal?"

"Here's the deal. I'll get dinner, if you'll clean up the breakfast debris."

"Deal," Hannah accepted at once, fully aware

she was getting the better end of the arrangement. Crossing to the table, she went to work, while Justin went to the fridge.

"That was delicious," Hannah commended Justin, raising her wineglass in a salute. "You're a very good cook."

"Either that," Justin said, inclining his head and raising his own nearly empty glass in acknowledgement of her compliment, "or you actually were famished."

"I was," she admitted. "But that doesn't mean I'd have praised anything you set in front of me." She grinned. "I'd have eaten the meal, but I wouldn't have praised it, or your culinary skill."

"I wouldn't go so far as to call it a skill. I simply can manage to prepare a reasonably palatable meal. Now, my mother, she's a skilled cook."

"I like your mother, by the way," Hannah said. "She is a lovely woman. I admire the way she handles her husband and her overgrown sons…all three of whom I also like."

"Three?" He appeared crushed. "Just my father, Adam and Mitch? What about me? Don't you like me?"

Hannah's expression and tone went hard and serious. "If I didn't like you, Justin, do you really believe for one minute I would be here with you now?"

"No." He gave a quick shake of his head, his voice as serious as hers had been. "No, Hannah. I don't, for even a second, believe you would be here now, if you hadn't found something about me to like." The seriousness fled, and the gleam sprang back into his eyes. "What is it that appeals to you? My body? My…"

"Is fantastic," Hannah interjected, holding back a laugh. "And you use it to advantage."

Justin arched a brow but continued with what he had started to say, "My personality?"

She mirrored his dark arch with her lighter eyebrow. "I didn't know you had one."

He laughed.

Her pulse leaped and her senses freaked. How was it possible for one man's laughter to cause such exciting sensations inside her, Hannah mused, loving the feelings, yet scared of them at the same time.

"I like you," Justin offered the unsolicited opinion. "I like your gorgeous body, too."

"I kind of figured you did," she responded wryly.

"But I'd like to do a further exploration of the terrain." He grinned...more like leered. "Just to be sure."

"Uh-huh." She eyed him warily. "But that will have to wait. My plane left hours ago. I've got to phone the airline, see if I can book another flight."

"You've already missed your flight," Justin pointed out, his voice soft, persuasive. "Why can't you wait till morning to call and reschedule?"

"I, er..." She faltered at the brazen look of renewed passion in his eyes. At her hesitation, he shoved back his chair and stood.

"Come on, let's get the supper things cleared away," he said, collecting his plate and cutlery.

Rising, Hannah began to follow his example. "And after the supper things are cleared away, we'll go to the bedroom...."

"Good," he flashed a self-satisfied grin at her.

"To pick up the clothing we discarded and scattered all over the bedroom floor."

"Yeah, yeah," he muttered, not meaning one yeah.

Ten minutes later Justin found himself hanging the damp towels on the mounted wall racks in the bathroom. "You know, this could have waited till morning, as well," he called to Hannah, who was busy neatly folding their clothing.

"Yeah, yeah," she mimicked his agreement. "But you'll be thanking me tomorrow."

In truth, Justin did thank Hannah in the morning, but not for remaining resolute about picking up their stuff. He thanked her with words and caresses and deep, searing kisses for what he swore was the most fantastic night of his life.

Seven

"What about Beth?" The gleam in his eyes grew brighter. "Didn't you like her?"

It took a few minutes for Hannah to make the connection. She and Justin were in the middle of breakfast. This time he had cooked oatmeal, served with brown sugar. He was watching her, waiting for the dawn of comprehension to break over her sleep- and sex-fogged mind.

"Oh, your sister, Beth." Hannah felt like a dull wit. At least she hadn't said, "huh?" "I like her, very much. She stopped by Maggie's apartment a few days ago. We had a nice chat. Besides being warm and friendly, she's a gorgeous woman, a striking combination of your mother and father."

"Yeah, she is," Justin agreed, popping another spoonful of cereal into his mouth. After swallowing the oatmeal, he downed half the orange in his glass. "Adam's wife, Sunny, is no slouch either."

Nodding, Hannah took a ladylike sip of her juice. "She's lovely, and their daughter, Becky, is absolutely adorable. I immediately fell in love with her."

He chuckled around the last of his cereal. "She has that effect on everybody." He arched a quizzical dark eyebrow. "You like kids?"

"Very much." Finished eating, she dabbed her mouth with the paper napkin she had spread over her lap, and gave him a teasing smile. "Some of my best friends have kids."

"So," he said, getting up to fetch the coffee carafe to fill their cups. "What about you?"

Frowning, Hannah gave him a blank look. "What about me?"

"Don't dodge, sweet Hannah," he chided. "I've told you about myself. Now it's your turn."

Her mind may have been a little slow that morning—apparently a wild night of unbelievably fantastic sex had that effect on her—but it hadn't come to a complete stop. "You did no such thing," she retorted. "You quizzed me about my opinion of your family."

"Well, I sure couldn't give you my opinion of your family, since I haven't met them."

"Now who's dodging, Mr. Thinks-He's-So-Clever Grainger?" She grinned as she mimicked his one eyebrow lift.

He took a careful sip of his steaming coffee and grinned back at her. "Okay, what do you want to know...all my deep, dark secrets?"

"Do you have any?"

"No."

Hannah laughed, she couldn't help it. She just loved... Whoa, hold it. Loved? Don't go there, Hannah, she cautioned herself. Avoid that word like the plague.

"Are you really the bad boy your mother called you?" she asked. Not that she believed he'd confess to her all about his philandering ways.

"Of course not. I'm worse."

"Indeed. In what way?"

"You know," he drawled, "I don't know what you do for a living, but you should be in police interrogation."

"I'm in marketing," she said wryly. "And don't try changing the subject. It won't work. I want to hear all the lascivious details."

"Lascivious?" Justin tilted back his head and laughed. "You are really something, woman."

Woman. Again? Time to drag the knuckle-dragger into the twenty-first century. "Yes, actually, I am something. And don't call me woman. My name is Hannah."

He looked astounded. "You're not a woman? Damn, you could have fooled me. Yesterday morning and last night. Mostly last night. And I'll call you woman whenever I want to."

"Okay." Hannah pushed back her chair and stood. "I'm out of here." Turning away, she walked to the phone mounted on the kitchen wall.

"Wait a minute." His hand covered hers on the telephone receiver, holding it still.

She hadn't even heard him move.

"Hannah, sweetheart," he crooned into her ear. "I was only kidding. What are you doing?"

"Precisely what I said I was going to do today," she said. "I'm going to phone the airline to book another flight, hopefully for tonight or tomorrow morning."

"Hannah," he murmured, his voice a low, coaxing siren song. Releasing her hand to cup her shoulder, he turned her into his arms. "Don't go."

She raised her eyes and dropped her guard. His gaze was shadowed, compelling. Oh, heavens, she had to get out of there, away from him, because if she stayed with him…she could wind up being hurt. Hannah knew her thinking was right and yet. And yet…

"Hannah." Justin slowly lowered his head, to brush her mouth with his. "Don't go. Stay here, with me, for a week, or at least a few more days."

His tongue outlined her lips, and Hannah was a goner. Against her better judgment. Against everything she had believed about the folly of a rushed relationship, she knew it was too late to stop, too soon to bolt.

She wanted more of him. It was as simple and frightening as that. Surrendering more to her own needs and desires than to Justin's plea, Hannah raised her arms, curling them around his strong neck to draw his lips to her hungry mouth.

"You said you had been married."

"Hmm," said Justin.

Hannah couldn't see his face, since she lay tightly against him, her cheek resting on his chest.

Justin's angled body was curled almost protectively around her. The fingers of his one hand played with a strand of her long hair. The protective position of his long body sparked a memory of the night of the wedding reception.

After leaving Maggie in the bridal suite, Hannah had returned to the hotel lobby and gone straight to the coat-check counter. Draping the garment bag containing Maggie's gown over the counter, she exchanged her high heels for the boots she had worn earlier. Shrugging into her coat and toting the garment bag and the shoe bag, she considered slipping away, before Justin began looking for her.

She started for the lobby doors, but with a sigh, changed direction to go to the banquet hall where the reception was being held. Hannah had been brought up the old-fashioned way. Good manners dictated she say goodbye to Justin's family, thank his parents—whom she had learned had footed the bill for both the rehearsal dinner and the reception—for a lovely time at both events.

Peeking inside the hall, Hannah's determination faltered. Justin was standing next to the table, talking and laughing with his father and Adam, and looking far too tempting.

She was on the point of turning to leave when little Becky had come up to tug at his pant leg. Gazing down at her, his laughter changed to a tender smile, and instead of kneeling to talk to her, he bent down, his body curved protectively over her. With her pretty little face turned up to her uncle, Hannah saw her mouth move, saw Justin's move in reply before, with a laugh, he swept her up into his arms and headed for the edge of the crowded dance floor.

Hovering in the doorway, Hannah had watched, expecting Justin to whirl Becky around the floor. He hadn't. Setting her on her feet, he'd bowed like a proper gentleman, taken her tiny hands in his and danced her onto the floor.

For some ridiculous reason the sight of Justin, so careful and caring of his niece, had brought a lump to Hannah's throat and a hot sting to her eyes.

With a firm shake of her head, a stiffening of her spine—and her resolve—Hannah had used those few precious seconds while the music played to pay her respects to the Grainger family, then steal away from the hotel, and Justin.

Hannah was brought back to the present when a thought struck her. "Justin, do you have children of your own?"

Heaving a sigh, he rolled onto his back, spreading his arms wide in surrender. "No, Hannah." He opened his eyes to look at her, his expression somber. "Angie...my ex-wife, said she wanted to wait a little while before starting a family." His lips twisted, as if from a sour taste in his mouth. "Before the 'little while' was up, she put on her running shoes and sprinted away with another man." He made a rude, snorting noise. "Would you believe, a traveling computer-software sales rep? Pitiful, huh?"

"I'm sorry," she said in a subdued tone. "I shouldn't have pried."

"No." Justin moved his head back and forth on the mattress; the pillow had somehow wound up on the floor. The icy look in his eyes had thawed...somewhat. "It's okay, Hannah, you may ask anything that comes to mind."

"Did you—" Hannah hesitated, before taking a chance of making him angry, bringing back the frost. "Did you love her very much?"

He managed a slight smile. "We didn't know each other very well at the beginning. You could say it was a whirlwind thing. But yes, at the time, I loved her."

Despite his omitting the words *very much,* Hannah had to fight to control herself from betraying the sharp twinge of pain in her chest. "Are you still in love with her?" It would explain his love-'em-and-leave-'em attitude toward women.

"No." He stared directly into her eyes, his voice firm. "You want the truth?" he said, not waiting for a reply before continuing, "I realized I wasn't really in love with her a month after we got married."

She frowned. "But then…" She broke off in confusion.

Justin moved his shoulders in a shrug. "She was hot, and I was horny."

Hannah didn't know quite how to respond to his frank admission, so she circumvented that particular subject. "Have you ever truly been in love?"

"No," he answered with blunt candor. "Have you?"

Hannah smiled. Turnabout was fair play, she supposed. "No," she said, equally frank and candid. "But, like you, I thought I was for a time." Her smile turned into a small grin. "But unlike you, instead of a measly month, I believed that I was in love for almost a full year."

"So, what happened? That no-orgasm thing?"

Hannah felt her neck and face grow warm. This blushing was getting pretty damned annoying. Her expression must have revealed her feelings, because he grinned in a manner of sheer male hubris. She really couldn't challenge him on it, for he certainly had cured that *thing*. Many times.

"Partly," she admitted, on a sigh. "But that wasn't the major issue."

"What!" Justin exploded, jackknifing up to sit facing her. "Was he an idiot...or were you?" As before, often before, he didn't allow her time to answer. "Not the major issue? If you believed you were in love, I would think it would be the most important issue."

"Yes, I believe you would," Hannah said, her tone patient, her silent sigh sad. "Justin, there are more things to a relationship than sex, at least if there's any hope of the relationship lasting."

"Yeah, yeah," he brushed off her scold. "Compatibility, similar likes and all the rest of that jazz. But good sex is a very large component, and great sex even more so."

Yes, indeedy, Hannah thought, without a trace of humor but with a large amount of disappointment. Justin Grainger definitely was sexually motivated.

She sighed again. "Turned out, we weren't very compatible," she explained. "He was altogether career oriented. He ate, drank and slept his career, and it got worse with every move he made up the corporate ladder. There was no time for fun, friends, long, deep conversations."

"Or even the fun of longer, deeper, lovemaking," Justin interjected.

Hannah chose to ignore his opinion, then doggedly continued. "Understand, I was recently out of college and devoted to the marketing business I was getting off the ground. But I was often able to leave my business concerns in the office when I locked up for the night."

"And he couldn't do that?"

"No." She shook her head, at the same time wondering why she was bothering to explain all this to him when they obviously weren't going to be seeing each other again after she returned to Philly and he went back to breed horses in Montana. But she soldiered on, "I didn't simply quit, you know. I tried to make it work. I even learned to cook, a chore he knew I wasn't exactly crazy about."

He laughed.

She bristled. "Well, I never could understand why anyone would put so much time and effort into preparing an elaborate meal for someone to consume in fifteen minutes, leaving the cook to clean up afterward."

Justin laughed harder. "I'm sorry. I'm not ridiculing you."

Hannah glared at him. "Then what's so damn funny?"

"The fact that you've put my own feelings about the culinary art so elegantly into words." He had brought the laughter to a more acceptable grin. "If I want an elaborately concocted meal, complete with fine wine and candles on the table, I'll go to a fine restaurant and let an expert prepare it."

"My sentiments exactly," Hannah concurred, grinning back at him, not for a minute realizing that they were in the midst of the kind of deep conversation she had just complained about being missing from her previous relationship. Maybe that was because she never considered she and Justin ever would be in any kind of relationship…other than the physical one they were briefly conducting.

"So, what do you say we consign whoever-he-was to the dull life he deserves and get on with our own pursuits?" His grin slid into an invitingly sexy smile.

"Which are?" she asked, suddenly aware of

them sitting there, naked to the waist, and the thrill of expectation dancing along her exposed spine.

"The dreaded kitchen duty first." The sexy smile reverted back to a grin. "Then a shower." He hesitated. "And I think it's time I stripped the bed and tossed these sheets into the washer."

"Okay." Though she readily agreed, Hannah was disappointed. Drat the man and his sensually teasing ways. "I'll remake the bed."

"You're on." Springing from the bed, he scooped up his crumpled jeans and put them on before reaching for the same sweater he'd worn the day before.

Quickly sliding from the bed, Hannah picked up the robe he had earlier flung aside, and slipped into it, belting it securely, while admiring the back he turned away to gather his clothes.

Justin Grainger was a magnificent specimen, his broad muscular back, his slender waist, the tightness of his butt, the long muscles of his thighs and calves. She sighed. Hell, she even thought he had handsome feet!

Pathetic, she chastised herself. Who the devil ever thought of a male's feet as handsome?

She did, that's who, and the realization was pretty damn scary. Hurrying out of the room, Hannah kept telling herself what she was feeling was simply a strong physical attraction, a very strong physical attraction. Nothing more.

Working smoothly together as they had the day before, Hannah and Justin had the kitchen clean in less than twenty minutes.

"Know what?" Justin said to her as she was rinsing out the dish cloth. "I'm hungry."

Dropping the cloth into the sink, Hannah turned to him and pointed out the obvious. "We just finished clearing away the breakfast things."

"Yeah, I know," he agreed, favoring her with that blasted devil smile. "But have you looked at the clock?"

Naturally, Hannah shot a glance at the wall. The clock read 1:44. Unbelievable. She and Justin had finished breakfast somewhere around nine. For some weird reason, knowing the time made her aware of the hollow feeling inside her. She shifted her gaze back to him.

"You know what?" She pulled his trick of forging ahead without waiting for a response. "I'm hungry, too."

He flashed his most sexy smile. "Good. Let's grab some lunch."

Within ten minutes, again working easily together, they sat down to a meal.

Where before they had cleaned up the kitchen in compatible silence, this time they chatted away about this and that, nothing earth-shattering, simply kitchen talk.

From the kitchen they returned to the bedroom to gather the dirty laundry. They had no sooner set foot inside the room when Justin placed a hand on her arm, stopping her in the process of bending to start collecting clothes.

"You know what?" he asked again, and once more going on without pause, "I think it would be a waste of that invitingly rumpled bed." He raised that brow and flashed that wicked smile. "Don't you?"

Hannah wanted to say no. She really did. But her vocal chords and tongue wouldn't cooperate, and what came out was a hushed and breathless "Yes."

Later, lying replete and boneless beside him, Hannah silently marveled at the sexual prowess of the man holding her firmly against him. She loved the feel of his warm skin against hers, his breath ruffling her hair, his hands smoothing, soothing her back with long strokes of his hand. She gave a soft, contented sigh. Could she possibly love…

Don't go there. Hannah repeated the order she had given herself once before. This was merely fun and games. A few days out of the ordinary.

Allow yourself a few more days of physical indulgence, then run for home as though your very emotional stability depended on it...for it just might.

Spurred by her introspection, Hannah rolled out of Justin's arms, off the bed and grabbed up her robe. "I'm taking a shower," she announced, making a bee-line for the bathroom.

"Hey, wait," Justin barked, coming after her.

He was too late. She flipped the lock jut as he reached for the doorknob.

"Hannah," he pleaded with a soft laugh. "Let me in."

"You've been in," Hannah dared to playfully remind him. "A lot. And I loved every minute of it," she conceded, smiling at his exaggerated groan. "Now I want to have a long shower and shampoo my hair. I'll see you in about a half hour...if you're lucky."

"A half hour?" Justin shouted. "What the hell am I going to do for a half hour?"

"I'm sure you'll figure something out." She turned the water on full force to drown out any reply he might make.

Hannah felt wonderfully clean as she stepped from the shower. She also was rather proud of herself, as she had finished five or so minutes faster than she had promised Justin.

Holding her robe around her, she entered the bedroom. The room was empty, not a half-naked, too-attractive man in sight. To her surprise, not only was the floor clear of their clothes, the bed had been stripped and remade.

The man in question continued to amaze her. Whoever thought Mr. Philanderer would turn out to be so domesticated?

Taking advantage of the moment or privacy, Hannah dug in her suitcase for a clean set of clothes. When she was dressed, she stepped into her slippers.

Feeling warmer, and relatively protected by the clothing, Hannah plugged in her blow dryer and went to work on her hair with a round brush. She was making progress, the long strands no longer dripping, when Justin breezed into the room.

"The sheets are in the washer. It'll shut off in about fifteen minutes." He went to a dresser to remove fresh clothing. "As you'll note, I remade the bed."

"And now you want applause?"

He grinned. "No, a kiss will do for a reward."

"I don't think so." She shook her head.

Up went the eyebrow. "You don't trust me?"

"Not for a heartbeat." Trying not to laugh at his sorrowful expression, she grabbed her brush. "You get your shower, while I finish drying my hair."

He heaved a deep, noisy sigh. "You're one tough lady, sweet Hannah. You know that?" Grumbling loudly, Justin strode to the bathroom.

Never in a million years would Hannah have believed she could have so much fun with a man. She had hardly even laughed with—Well forget that one. He had been much too serious and full of himself, among other things.

Giggling Hannah decided on the spot that she would stay on, perhaps until the end of the week with Justin. She felt relaxed and happy. Why not enjoy his company, the fun and laughter, if only for a few more days?

After all, once the few days were over, she'd be flying back to her real life in Philadelphia. Justin would be heading back to his ranch in Montana.

They'd probably never see each other again.

The thought was oddly depressing.

Eight

Hannah was home in her apartment in Philadelphia. It was Sunday. She had flown into the airport late the previous Friday and had been home for a week and one day.

She had yet to hear a word from Justin.

Well, what had she expected? Hannah asked herself, making a half-hearted attempt to dust the living room. They had spent five days together. Five wonderful days that had left her so relaxed, her assistant had noted it the moment she had walked into the small suite of offices Monday morning.

"You look positively glowing," Jocelyn had exclaimed. "Were you in South Dakota, or did you hide away somewhere in some exclusive spa?"

Hannah had to laugh. Actually, she felt terrific. "No spa, I promise I was in South Dakota the whole time."

Jocelyn leveled a measuring look at her. "Well, something put that sparkle in your eyes. A man?"

Hannah knew her soft sigh and satisfied smile gave her away. The warmth spreading up her throat and over her cheeks was answer enough. Damn her new propensity to blush.

"Aha!" Jocelyn crowed. "Was he handsome? Was it romantic? Was he great in bed?"

"Jocelyn, *really.*" Now Hannah's cheeks were burning. "You know I'm never going to answer such personal questions."

"Sure." Jocelyn grinned. "But I don't need a blow-by-blow—" she giggled "—pardon the pun. Your expression says it all."

Hannah blinked, startled. "It's that obvious?"

"Yes, boss. I'm sorry, but it is. You needed a break."

That was Monday. This was Sunday. Hannah was no longer amused, or glowing. She was hurting inside, and she feared the tiny lines of tension were about to make another appearance.

But then, she had known all along that their moment out of time couldn't last. What had she been secretly hoping for, that Justin would be on the very next flight east, following her back?

No, she hadn't hoped for that, even secretly.

But one phone call just to find out if she had arrived safely would have been nice, not to mention thoughtful. Had she really believed Justin was thoughtful? Hannah chided herself. Just because he helped her prepare meals, pick up their clothes that were forever flung without care to the floor, smooth the bedding that was inevitably rumpled? Because the last time they had made love there had been a sense of desperation? And because his goodbye kiss had been deep, lingering, as if he couldn't bear to stop?

Hannah knew better. At any rate she should have. They had played house, she and Justin, like little kids. Okay, not exactly like kids.

Hannah shivered at the memory. It had been fun, playing house together. It had been more than fun, it had been wonderful, an awakening of her senses and sensuality.

Tears misted her eyes. Why the hell had she

gone and done something as stupid as fall in love with him? For she *had* fallen in love with Justin, no strings for me, Justin, philanderer extraordinaire.

Not fair, Hannah, she told herself, swiping her eyes with her fingertips. He had never made any promises. He had been up-front with her, had offered her nothing more than fun and games. She had gone into the affair with her eyes open. She had no one to blame but herself for the empty feelings of pain and longing she was experiencing now.

Life does go on, Hannah assured herself, and so would she. There was no other choice. She had friends, a career, a business to run…a living room to dust.

Justin was on the prowl, roaming the house, unsettled and cranky. Karla would attest to it; she had been witness to his moodiness. She was beginning to eye him warily, as if uncertain what he might do.

It was the weather, he told himself, staring out the window at the nearly foot of snow on the ground that was growing higher in the driving blizzard. He felt trapped, that's what was bugging him, he thought, turning away from the scene.

Justin knew damn well his restlessness had nothing at all to do with the inclement weather. He had been raised in Wyoming, and had lived in Montana for almost ten years, had taken over the running of the ranch soon after he had graduated college. Snow, ice, winter and spring rains hadn't bothered him, except in regard to worrying about the horses.

But Justin knew full well that the animals were in their stable stalls; warm, fed and watered by Ben and the rest of his ranch hands.

"Can I get you something, Justin?" Karla asked, as he stalked into the kitchen.

Wondering what in hell he was doing there, Justin said the first thought that jumped to mind. "Is there any coffee in the pot?" It was a dumb question, and he knew it. There was always coffee in the pot. It wasn't always freshly made, but he had never demanded fresh, although he preferred it that way.

"Yes." Karla smiled at him as she opened a cabinet and took down a mug. "I just made it." She shook her head when he reached for the mug. "Sit down, I'll get it for you."

Not about to argue with the woman who prepared some of the best meals he had ever tasted,

Justin moved to the table, collecting a carton of milk as he went by the fridge.

The coffee was exactly as he liked it, strong, hot and freshly brewed.

"Would you like something to go with that?" she asked, carrying her own mug to the table. "Cookies, a slice of pie or coffee cake?"

Ever since Ben had brought Karla to the ranch as his bride, there were always cookies in the pantry and pie in the fridge. He liked her coffee cake best…although her apple pie was also delicious.

Justin glanced at the wall clock. It was several hours to go until suppertime. "Couple of cookies sound good. Do you have any of those oatmeal, raisin, walnut cookies?"

Karla laughed and headed for the pantry. "As those are both Ben's and your favorite, I always keep a supply on hand. I baked a double batch yesterday."

While Karla was inside the large storage room, Ben strolled into the kitchen from the ranch office, where he had been checking stock on the computer. In effect, Ben had virtually taken over the running of the ranch, leaving Justin feeling superfluous and adrift. He didn't resent Ben…how could he resent a man for doing a great job, especially when the man was next thing to a member of the family?

No, Justin didn't resent Ben. He simply felt useless.

"Where's my bride?" Ben asked, going straight to the cabinet to pour a cup of coffee for himself.

"Ran off with the milk man," Justin drawled, sipping carefully at the hot brew in his mug.

"Neat trick." Ben grinned as he strolled to the table. "As we don't even have a milk man."

Justin waved a hand in dismissal. "Minor point."

"You rang, Your Lordship?" Karla emerged from the pantry to favor her husband with a smile. "Was there something you wanted from me?"

Ben flashed a wicked grin. "Yeah, but this isn't the time or place. The boss is watching." He jerked his head at the plate she was carrying. "I'll settle for some of those cookies you've got there."

Their affectionate banter created a hollow sensation in Justin's midsection. Telling himself it had nothing to do with one Hannah Deturk and the bantering, laughter and tender moments they had shared, he attempted to fill the hollow place with cookies. His ploy didn't work.

Through the long, seemingly endless days that

followed, nothing worked. Including Justin. Leaving the majority of the ranch responsibilities to Ben, Justin brooded and prowled the house like a hungry mountain lion.

Hungry was the key word, and it had nothing to do with his stomach. How often had he reached for the phone, to place a long-distance call to Philadelphia? Justin couldn't remember, but he knew damn well why he had never actually lifted the telephone receiver.

What could he say to Hannah? I miss you, and I'm hard as hell? Yeah, he derided himself. That ought to turn any woman's mind and will to molten lava. And Hannah wasn't just any woman. Oh, no. Sweet Hannah was her own woman, a fact she had made abundantly clear to him from the beginning.

Sure, she had agreed to spend a few days of mutual pleasure with him, Justin conceded. And the pleasure had been mutual, of that he had no doubt. For a man who had not so much as stayed a full night with a woman since his marriage ended, the pleasure had been intense, teeth-clenching ecstasy. As for Hannah, well Justin felt certain that not even the most skilled of actresses could have faked the depth of her response.

Still, their shared desire, and compatibility out of bed, had not kept her from leaving when she said she would.

Without saying it aloud, she had made it abundantly clear that she had a life back east and she wasn't about to change it. Her determination to leave was unshakable. Despite his murmured plea for her to stay a while longer and the implied enticement of his last kiss, she had whispered a farewell, slid behind the wheel of her rental vehicle and driven away without looking back.

Unaware of heaving a heavy sigh, Justin stared out the window. The blizzard had long since blown itself out, but the temperature had not risen above the twenties since then. The snow remained, the unrelenting wind driving it into five-foot and higher snowbanks.

Damn, other than the inconvenience of getting back and forth from the house to the stables, Justin had never minded the snow before. What in hell was wrong with him?

"Why don't you take a vacation?" Ben's voice broke through Justin's thoughts. "Someplace where the sun's shining and the temp's in the eighties. Find yourself a woman. You're workin' on my nerves, and you're starting to worry Karla."

"I'm working on your nerves and making Karla edgy?" Justin said in a soft, tightly controlled voice to keep from snarling at the man. "Maybe you and Karla are the ones needing a sun-filled vacation."

"Not us," Ben denied. "Karla and I are happy here, sunshine or not."

Justin lifted an eyebrow. "And you think I'm not?"

"Oh, gimme a break, Justin. I've known you a long time, remember?" Ben shook his head. "In all that time I have never seen you like this, stalking about the house, staring out the window, sighing every couple minutes, not even when Angie took off with that smooth creep."

"I sigh every couple of minutes?" Justin drawled in feigned amusement, feeling a twinge of alarm and ignoring the reference to his ex, because *that* wasn't important. The strange sensation was. "I'll think about it," he said, ending the conversation by turning back to the window.

"Okay, I can take a hint," Ben said with a short laugh of resignation. "I'll mind my own business."

"I appreciate it."

Justin only vaguely heard Ben's chuckle as he left the room. Staring out, he didn't see the barren scene of winter white on the other side of the window. An image had formed in his mind, an image Hannah had drawn for him with her description of Pennsylvania. The verbal picture she had given him was of a different landscape, a vision of rolling countryside, lush and green, bathed in sparkling spring sunlight.

Blinking, he frowned, then turned and strode to his bedroom. Going to his desk he opened his personal laptop, and went onto the Net. He had some research to do.

Several hours later Justin shut down the computer and picked up the phone to call the company pilot in charge of the ranch's helicopter. After asking the pilot to pick him up at the pad a short distance from the house, he pulled a bag from the closet and dumped enough clothes into it to last him a couple of days.

Following the near ennui he had been experiencing since he had returned from Deadwood, the rush of anticipation he was feeling was invigorating.

Justin placed another call before striding briskly from his room. He had what he figured was an interesting and potentially very profitable idea he needed to discuss with his brother, Adam.

His battery recharged, Justin gave a brief explanation to Ben as he drove him to the landing pad. The chopper was already there, blades slicing through the frigid air.

"Not to worry," Ben assured him. "I'll take good care of the horses."

"I know you will." With a wave goodbye, Justin headed for the helicopter.

"By the way," Ben yelled over the roar of the spinning blades. "You look and sound like your old self again."

Near the end of the second week of February, Hannah faced up to the suspicions she had been mentally dodging for close to a week, suspicions induced by the vague feeling of queasiness she had in the morning, the slight tenderness in her breasts. Needing more proof than just symptoms, she stopped by a pharmacy on her way home from work.

The strip from the particular home pregnancy kit she had purchased turned the positive color. Not an altogether complete confirmation, Hannah knew. There had been cases where the strip results had proved wrong, but…it definitely required a visit to her doctor.

How could it have happened? Not even in their most heated, impromptu and wild love play, had Justin forgotten to use protection.

Of course, no one ever claimed the protective sheaths were infallible, Hannah mused as she studied the inside of her freezer, trying to decide what to have for dinner.

Having heated in the microwave the frozen meal she'd chosen Hannah sat in front of it, considering the options available to her should her doctor's examination prove conclusive.

Sliding the plate aside, Hannah laid her fork on the place mat and picked up the cup of green tea she had brewed for her dinner beverage, instead of her usual coffee.

Coffee. She sighed. She loved coffee, especially in the morning, all morning…several cups of coffee, regular, not decaf.

Hannah knew she would have to forgo her favorite drink if she decided to—

Oh, hell. Hannah took another sip of the tea. It wasn't bad tasting. It wasn't coffee, but actually was rather good as far as substitutes went.

That is, unless she chose an alternative. The thought set a wave of nausea roiling in her stomach. She gulped the tea in hopes of quelling the sensation.

She couldn't do it. Though she supported a woman's right to choose any of the options, Hannah knew that she really had only one option. Should the doctor confirm her pregnancy, Hannah was going to have a baby.

A baby. Visions of soft blankets and tiny booties danced through Hannah's mind. A fierce rush of protectiveness shot through her, and she slid a hand down over her flat belly.

Her child.

Justin's child.

The sudden realization was both thrilling and somewhat frightening. How to tell him?

Justin had been up-front with her from the beginning. He had wanted nothing from her except a brief physical affair. Their affair had been the most wonderful experience Hannah had ever known. Of course, she hadn't considered the possibility of falling in love with him.

Over the days they had been together, Hannah had learned a lot about Justin. Yet at times she felt she hardly knew him at all.

As a lover, she couldn't imagine anyone his equal. There were moments when his voice was so tender, his touch so gentle it brought tears to her eyes while at the same time setting her body on fire. And there were other times when his voice was raw and ragged, his touch urgent, his love-making fierce and demanding.

And Hannah had reveled in every minute of both approaches.

Then there were the periods when all they did was talk, sometimes teasingly, other times seriously.

Hannah had learned that Justin was honest to a fault. When he shared something of himself with her he was blunt and to the point. Not a bad quality to possess. She knew a woman had betrayed his trust and that he had no intention of walking that route again.

She also knew Justin liked kids. He had confessed to Hannah that he adored his niece, Becky. But Justin had never mentioned a desire for children of his own, other than to say his ex had wanted to wait a while before starting a family.

If the doctor confirmed her pregnancy, Hannah didn't know whether or not to inform Justin. After all, she reasoned, if Justin had any interest in a child of his own, he wouldn't have been so scrupulous about protection.

For all the good it had done them.

Still, he had a right to know he had fathered a

child. It was her duty, as an honest person, to let him know.

She just didn't know how to tell him.

Nine

Valentine's Day. The day for lovers. Hannah not only didn't leave work early, she worked over an hour later than usual. She even skipped lunch. Tired, only vaguely hungry, and not so much as considering a restaurant, especially on this special day for sweethearts, she went straight home.

Her heart skipped many beats as she stepped from the condo's elevator to find Justin propped languidly against her door. A bag was on the floor next to his crossed ankles.

The bag, along with the very sight of him filled

her with a flash of hope that he had come to Philadelphia because he realized that they belonged together.

Gathering her senses, and applying her common sense almost at once, Hannah told herself to play it cool until she heard from his lips the words she desperately longed to hear. How easy it would be for her to then tell him of her pregnancy suspicions.

Heaven help her, he looked…wonderful, like the horseman he was. With his Stetson, heavy wool jacket, jeans and slant-heeled boots, he looked exactly as he had the first time she'd seen him.

"Hi."

The low, intimate timbre of his voice nearly stopped her breathing completely. Damn his gorgeous hide. She had to repeat to herself her cautioning advice to play it cool.

"Hi." Hannah was amazed by the steadiness of her own voice, her ability to speak at all, as her throat was suddenly dry. "What are you doing here?" Door key at the ready, she aimed it at the key hole. No minor feat, considering the tremor shaking her fingers.

"I came to see you. Are you going to invite me in?"

"Yes, of course, come on in." Hannah walked inside with as much decorum as she could muster. "I didn't mean what were you doing here, at my apartment," she said, not sure if she was making conversation, or babbling on in response to the sudden attack of nervousness coursing through her. "I meant what are you doing here, in Philadelphia?"

"Well," he said, grinning as he shrugged out of his jacket, removed his hat, "I wanted to see you. Though that isn't the only reason I'm here, in the northeast."

Hannah's spirits soared at first, then took a nosedive, her hopes going down in flames. Still, she maintained her composure and took his jacket and hat and hung them away in the coat closet. The flight bag she set behind the nearby chair.

"I see." She tried to match his casual tone and didn't quite make it. "Well, I'm glad you stopped by," she said, dredging up a shaky smile to hide the sting of pain burning inside. "So," she held on to her smile for dear life. "Why else have you come east?"

"I'll tell you after dinner…" Justin hesitated, frowning. "You haven't had dinner, have you?"

"No," Hannah shook her head. "I worked late and didn't feel up to the crowds in the restaurants tonight."

"Oh." He nodded, then raised a dark brow. "You eat out often?"

Hannah wanted to scream at him. Didn't the man know that it was Valentine's Day? And what difference did it make to him whether or not she ate out often? This was only an afterthought visit, anyway.

"Occasionally," she answered, smothering the curse and a sigh. She gestured for him to sit down. "Would you like something to drink?" she asked, too politely, certain that if he said coffee she'd throw up.

"No, thanks." He sat down on the plush lounge chair. "I'll wait for dinner."

Did he actually expect her to cook for him? He'd wait until the cows came home, she fumed, using one of her father's favorite expressions. Hannah gave him a level stare and mirrored his eyebrow action. "I hope you realize that there will probably be long lines at all the better restaurants tonight," she said, making it perfectly clear she had no intention of providing a meal for him.

"I don't need a restaurant." His smile was knowing, making her aware he understood her unsubtle hint. "I've ordered dinner to be delivered here."

The audacity of the man. Why didn't it surprise

her? Everything inside him radiated audacity and…and…sheer male sensuality.

Stop that train of thought immediately, you dimwit, Hannah ordered herself. Stick to the subject at hand. "How did you know I'd be in town?"

"I didn't." Justin shrugged, then laughed that deep, thrilling, damnably exciting laugh that set her pulses racing. "But I figured I'd take a chance. I'll tell you all about why I'm here while we eat."

"But…" Hannah began to ask him how he had gotten past the security guard in the lobby, only to be interrupted by the buzz on the intercom from that very same man.

"There's our dinner," Justin said, moving to the intercom beside the door. "I'll take care of this. You go set the table."

You go set the table, Hannah grumbled to herself, whirling around to do as he ordered. As he ordered. Who the devil did he think he was?

Hannah had finished setting the table except for the water glasses she had retrieved from the cabinet. But she didn't know whether he wanted water with whatever it was he had ordered for dinner or if he'd prefer wine, which of course, she couldn't have. She set one glass on the table and was filling the other glass for herself from the refrigerator's water dispenser when she heard him open the door and speak to a delivery man. The distinct aroma of pizza wafted through the apartment.

To her amazement, instead of bringing on a wave of queasiness, the smell made her mouth water and her stomach rumble with hunger.

Carrying a large pizza box with one hand and a white paper bag in the other, Justin walked jauntily into the kitchen, his smile more appetizing than the smell of the food.

"Dinner is served, madam," he said, carefully sliding the box onto the table. "This," he added, holding the bag aloft, "is our dessert."

Someday, maybe, hopefully, you'll get your just dessert for being such a rogue, Hannah thought, but simply asked aloud, "What do you want to drink to go with it?"

"Beer?" he asked.

"Yes." She turned to the fridge.

"Beer with the pizza, and coffee with dessert."

Her stomach twitched in protest. Wishing he hadn't mentioned her previously favorite beverage, Hannah took a can of beer from the fridge and moved to the table to reach for the glass at his place.

"I don't need a glass," Justin said with a dismissive wave of his hand, popping the top while seating himself in the chair opposite hers. "Sit down and serve the pizza."

Starting to seriously resent his assumed right to order her around, Hannah fixed him with a fuming look. "You know, you could have served it while I was getting your beer."

"No, I couldn't," he said with a smile, indicating the box with a nod of his head. "The opening's in front of you. And in case you haven't noticed, the lid's taped shut."

Hannah couldn't decide if she wanted to laugh at his obvious teasing, or toss her glass of water at him. She did neither. Drawing the box closer, she broke the paper tape and lifted the lid.

The delicious aroma hit her first, making her almost groan with hunger. Then two other factors struck her, making her gasp in surprise. The large crust had been worked into a heart shape, and the words, Sweet Hannah, had been formed with small slices of pepperoni.

She laughed with delight. It was the strangest, most wonderful Valentine's gift she had ever received. "Wherever did you get this?" she asked.

"The pizzeria a couple of blocks down. I told the counter man what I had in mind. Turns out, he owns the place and he smacked his hand against his forehead and said, and I quote, 'Why didn't I think of that? I coulda made a bundle.' I told him to keep it in mind for next year." He grinned. "Are you ever going to serve it?"

Hannah pulled a sad face. "Must I?"

"Only if you want to eat…and don't want me to starve to death at your kitchen table."

"Well, in that case, I suppose I'd better." Laughing, if rather weakly, Hannah scooped up a slice and slid it onto his plate. "May I ask what gave you the idea in the first place?" she said, serving herself a slice.

"Hmm." Nodding, Justin murmured around the big bite he'd taken into his mouth. "I came up with the idea when I decided I wasn't in the mood to stand on line at a restaurant, at a candy store or a florist," he said after swallowing. "Hey, this is pretty good." He followed that with a swig of beer. "And I wasn't in the mood because I was tired after driving around since early this morning." He took another big bite.

Ready to bite into the slice she had served herself, Hannah paused, unable to resist asking, "Why have you been driving since early this morning…and where?"

* * *

Before responding to her questions, Justin polished off his slice and held his plate out for another. His hesitation wasn't because he was that hungry, although he was, but because he was carefully choosing the words of his explanation.

"Actually, I've been driving around for two days. I flew into Baltimore the day before yesterday." Justin couldn't miss the tightness that stiffened Hannah's spine, so he rushed on. "I picked up my rental car, checked into a hotel, then went to keep an appointment with a real estate agent."

She frowned. "Here? In Baltimore?"

"Yes. You see, I'm doing some scouting for Adam. We're thinking of investing in a horse farm here in the East, to breed Thoroughbreds. The agent found farms available in several states and set up appointments for me."

"What states? And why here in the East?" she asked, frowning.

"Maggie told me there were a lot of horse farms out here." He answered her second question first.

"Well, Maggie should know," Hannah said. "She was born in Berks County."

Justin nodded. "So she said. She suggested Virginia, Maryland and Pennsylvania." He polished off a third slice of pizza, grinning as he again held out his plate to her.

Hannah shook her head as if in disbelief of his capacity for food, but slid another slice onto his plate.

He plowed on. "I started in Virginia, where there were two possibilities. From there I drove into Maryland, where there were three. I stayed in a motel in Pennsylvania last night and got an early start this morning. I toured one in Lancaster County, another two in Bucks County, and the last one in Berks, in the Oley Valley."

"Oh, I've been there," Hannah said, patting her lips with a paper napkin. "My assistant is a dedicated antique-shop crawler. I go with her every so often, and one time she drove through the valley, to Oley Village, I guess that's what they call it. It's not very big, but charming."

"I didn't get to see the village or town, or whatever it's called. But the valley is beautiful, even in winter. And the property I looked at has definite possibilities." He arched a brow, wondering at the tiny, wistful smile that quirked her lips. "I'm ready for my coffee now."

"Of, of course, I forgot," she said, sliding her chair back and rising. "What's for dessert?" she asked, moving to the automatic coffee unit set on the countertop.

"You'll see," Justin answered, puzzling over her odd expression as she prepared the coffee. His puzzlement deepened as she filled a red enamel teakettle then put it on to boil and took a flower bedecked porcelain china teapot from the back of the stove and a box of teabags from the cabinet. She placed a couple of bags in the pot.

"You're not having coffee?" He didn't try to hide the surprise in his voice; he had firsthand knowledge of her passion for coffee…among other passions. He had to turn his mind to something more mundane when he felt his body stir in reaction to the sensual direction of his thoughts. "What's with the teapot?"

Hannah gave a careless shrug of her elegant shoulders. "I've developed a liking for green tea lately," she said, not looking at him as she concentrated on pouring the now boiling water into the teapot. "It's supposed to be very good for you, you know."

"Not for me," Justin said dryly. "I'll stick with my coffee…and beer."

"Well, here's your coffee," Hannah said, in a strangely choked voice. She set the steaming mug on the table, before going to the fridge for milk.

"Thanks," Justin said, pondering her odd behavior; Hannah had held the mug out in front of her as if she was afraid it would attack her. Weird. He took the carton of milk she handed him, and watched her as she returned to the countertop for the teapot and a mug.

"I don't understand," she said, obviously avoiding his gaze, as she carefully poured the pale tea into the mug. "Why would Adam be interested in another horse farm for the company, when you already have the ranch?"

"At the ranch, we breed and train Morgans, primarily for the rodeo circuit. And, as I already mentioned, we're thinking about branching out, breeding and training Thoroughbreds."

She took a delicate sip of her tea, grimaced, set down the mug and added sugar. "How many more farms are on your schedule to look at? Any other states?"

"No more states, no more farms," Justin said, singeing his tongue. "Damn, that's hot, I felt it burn all the way down," he added, reaching across the table for her half-full water glass. "Do you mind?" His hand hovered above the glass.

Hannah shook her head. "Help yourself."

Justin did, soothing the sting with a gulp of the

cool water. "I'm scheduled to fly out of Baltimore on the red-eye tomorrow night."

"Oh, I see. Are you flying home to Montana, or to Wyoming to report to Adam?" Hannah's expression didn't alter by even a shadow. She looked as she had the first time he met her, mildly interested but cool and composed. Detached.

Justin felt a wrenching disappointment. He knew, better than anyone, that beneath her facade of cool, composed detachment, a spark lay in wait to blaze into roaring flames of passion.

Dammit to hell! Why was she in hiding from him? For she was in hiding. He had sensed it the minute she had stepped from the elevator and had seen him by her door.

"To Wyoming to confer with Adam, then back to Montana," he said, working hard to control the anger and frustration building inside him.

"So you're driving back to Baltimore tonight...or have you booked a hotel here in the city?"

Justin couldn't read her expression, as she had raised her cup to her mouth, concealing the lower half of her face from him. But her voice was even more detached, cooler. The distant sound of it fanned the flame of his anger. What was she playing at, looking, speaking as if they were nothing more than casual acquaintances, when it had been less than a month since they had been passionate lovers?

Well, Justin decided, getting to his feet and circling the table to her, he wasn't about to play along. He had been missing her something fierce from the moment she had driven away from him in Deadwood.

Hell, he had tossed and turned every night, even dreamed about holding her, caressing her, kissing her. Damned if he was going to walk away without tasting her.

Coiling his hands around her upper arms, he drew her up, out of her chair, pulling her body against his.

"Justin…what…" Hannah began, her voice no longer cool, but surprised by his action.

"I think you know what," he murmured, sliding his arms around her to bring her to him, and lowering his head to crush her mouth with his.

He had meant it to be a forceful kiss, but the instant his lips made contact with hers, he gentled, drinking in the taste, the scent, the feel of her. It was like coming home, where he belonged.

The alien sensation rattled Justin deep inside.

After the blow Angie had delivered, he'd never believed he would feel such a way again.

Justin was on the point of lifting his head, breaking his near-desperate contact with her mouth, when Hannah curled her arms tightly around his neck and speared her fingers into his hair.

Needing to breathe, Justin raised his head just far enough to gaze into Hannah's eyes. "No, I am not driving back to Baltimore tonight, nor have I booked a room here in the city," he said between quick indrawn breaths. "I was hoping you'd let me spend the night here. With you. In your bed."

"Justin, I…I…"

Her eyes were warm, almost misty, the way they had looked every time she was aroused. Hannah wanted him, maybe almost as much as he wanted her. Justin knew it. Relieved, he silenced her with the brush of his mouth, back and forth over hers.

"Hannah," he whispered against her parted lips, into her mouth. "I'm on fire for you. Come to bed with me."

"Justin…"

He silenced her again, damn near terrified she was going to refuse. He ached, not only from the steadily growing, hardening of his body, but inside. He stifled a groan when she pulled her head back.

"Justin, wait, listen," she pleaded, her fingers tangling in his hair, hanging on as though she was afraid he'd let her go. "We haven't cleared the dinner things away—or had dessert."

He laughed, because it sounded so…Hannah. And because the exultation filling him had to escape.

He smiled and rested his forehead against hers. "It wouldn't be the first time, sweet Hannah. As we did before, many times before, we can clean it up later. And we can have the dessert for breakfast."

"Dessert for breakfast?" She pretended shock.

Laughing softly, Justin began an exploration of the fine, satiny skin of her face with his lips. "What I brought will do fine for breakfast, or for dessert after breakfast."

Laughing with him, in a sure sign of her surrender, she tickled his ear with the tip of her tongue. "I have never heard of dessert for breakfast."

Justin's body nearly exploded at the moist glide of her tongue into his ear. "Errr…Hannah," he said in a rough croak, "You'd better lead me to your bedroom before I lose control and take you right here and now."

"As if," she retorted, grinning as she pulled away from him, grabbed his hand and started through the living room to a short hallway. "You've never lost control."

"There's always a first time, sweetheart," he said, raising her hand to his mouth to press his lips to her fingers. "And I'd sure hate to embarrass myself in front of you."

Entering her bedroom, Hannah turned her head to give him a wry glance. "That…or are you possibly afraid your loss of control would give me a sense of womanly power?"

"Oh, sweet Hannah, you have no worries in that department," Justin said, shutting the door behind him and twirling her around into a tight embrace, letting her feel her power in his hard body. "You've got womanly power to spare."

Minutes later, their clothing tossed in all directions of the room, Hannah lay naked, eager, in the center of the queen-size bed that had felt so large, cold and empty for weeks. Also naked, Justin stood next to the bed, tall and proud and magnificent, his turbulent gray eyes watching her as she watched him sheathe himself in delicate protection.

The image would haunt her after he was gone. She knew it, would pay for it, but for now, Hannah could think of nothing except having him beside her, inside her, loving her…if only for this one more night.

She held her arms up to him in invitation. He came to her, stretching his long body next to her own. His mouth hot on hers, his hands implements of exquisite torture.

He couldn't wait, and with a murmur of need he slid his body over hers, settling between the thighs she parted for him. She couldn't wait, either. Wrapping her long legs around his waist, she raised her hips in a silent plea.

Justin's possession of her was fast and hard, exactly as she needed it to be. Their zenith was reached in shuddering, spectacular unison. Though Hannah wouldn't have believed it possible, the climax was more intense, more thrilling than any previous one she had experienced with him.

She loved him, loved him with every living cell within her, as she would love his child, their child, after Justin was gone. For then, weeping silently,

Hannah decided she would never again be a receptacle for his convenience. She just couldn't bear to be one of the women "the bad boy" visited every so often.

Holding him to her, inside her utterly satisfied body, Hannah drifted into the deepest sleep she had known since leaving him in Deadwood.

Ten

Hannah woke up at her usual time. A creature of habit, she needed no alarm. She was still tired. She really hadn't slept very much. She ached, but pleasantly so. Twice more during the night, she and Justin had made love.

It had been wonderful. No, it had been more than wonderful. It had been heavenly. Between periods of short naps and long, slow indulgences of each other, they never found time to venture out of the bedroom to clear away the dinner clutter.

Yawning, Hannah pushed back the covers Justin had haphazardly drawn over them after their last romp, and moved to get up. A long arm snaked out to curl around waist, anchoring her to his side.

"Let me up, Justin," she said, trying to pull back. "I still have to clear the kitchen table, eat something and get ready to go to work."

His arm held firm, and he rested his cheek on the top of her head. "Take the day off." His voice was low. "Stay with me until I have to leave for Baltimore."

Hannah was tempted. Lord was she tempted. But mindful of the vow she had made to herself after their first frantic bout of sex—for that's all it had been, at least for him, she reminded herself— she steeled herself against his alluring suggestion. "I can't." She shook her head and pushed his arm away. "I can't leave my assistant on her own today."

"Why not?" His sleepy voice threatened to undermine her resistance. "You did when you went to Deadwood."

Taking advantage of the momentary easing of his hold, she slipped out from under his arm. "I know, but then I had laid out all the upcoming projects, explained my ideas in detail. There are things pending that need my personal attention."

While speaking, she had collected her clothes as she made her way to the connecting bathroom.

"Hannah, wait." Justin jumped from the bed, attractive as sin in his nakedness. He reached for her.

Dodging his hand, she stepped into the bathroom, locking the door before calling out to him, "You can have the shower when I'm done." She turned on the water full blast to drown out the sound of his muttered curses.

Exhausting every curse word he knew, Justin stood stock-still next to the bed, staring at the locked bathroom door. Hannah was closing him out, exactly as she had tried to do last evening. Frustration, anger and an emotion too similar to fear to be acknowledged burned inside him.

He didn't get it. He just didn't get it…or her. One minute she was cool and remote, the next sensual and hungry for him. During the night Hannah had freely displayed how badly she wanted him, again and again.

So what happened between the last time they made love and this morning? And, dammit, they *had* made love, not merely had sex, whether or not she wanted to admit it, either to him or herself.

Shaking his head in bewilderment, he moved

around the room picking up his clothes. They'd have to talk about it, about their relationship, for, like it or not, that's what it was shaping up to be, not a one-night stand, not a slam-bam-thank-you-ma'am, but an honest to God relationship.

It scared the hell out of him. Nevertheless, an in-depth discussion was definitely called for here. He would have to make another stab at convincing her to take the day off.

Hannah had never showered and dressed so fast in her life. Her hair still damp, she twirled it all into a loose twist at the back of her head and anchored it with a few well-placed hairpins. Sighing in longing and regret for what might have been, she turned with steadfast determination and went to the kitchen. Justin stood by the kitchen table, and with a nod she indicated that the shower was all his.

She had the table cleared and wiped, dishes stacked in the dishwasher, the coffee brewing, the tea steeping, bacon sizzling and eggs whipped, ready to pour into a warming frying pan by the time Justin walked into the room.

"We forgot to say good morning." His soft voice crept across the kitchen to slither up her spine.

Gritting her teeth against a shiver, Hannah returned his greeting. "You're just in time," she said with calm detachment, dumping the egg mixture into the pan. "If you want to help, you can set the table." Without turning to look at him, she dropped four slices of bread into the toaster. She jumped when he plucked the spatula from her hand.

"I'll do the eggs," he said, his voice and his body too close for her comfort. "Since you know where everything is, it's better if you set the table."

"Okay." Hannah was glad to escape, if only to the wall cabinet a few feet from him. After setting two places at the table, she went to the fridge for orange juice and milk. "Do you want jam for your toast?"

"Do you have peanut butter?"

"Yes," she said, surprised that he also liked the spread on his morning toast.

"Natural or sweetened? I don't like the sweetened stuff."

"Neither do I," she said, removing the jar from the fridge.

Other than the odd remark here and there about the food, they ate in silence, each into their own thoughts. Feeling edgy, Hannah saw him raise a brow when she glanced at the clock for the third time. But he didn't comment on it…until after he had his coffee and she her tea.

"I think you should take the day off," Justin said, his voice laced with determination.

"I already told you I wouldn't do that," she retorted, her voice equally determined.

"We need to talk." Now his eyes were cold as gray ice.

Getting up, Hannah carried her barely touched tea to the sink, dumped it and rinsed it before replying. "No we don't. I need to leave for work." She walked from the room to the coat closet. "And you need to drive to Baltimore." She pulled on her coat and grabbed her purse.

"Dammit, Hannah," Justin said, his tone bordering on a shout. "Listen to me." He reached out to take her arm, to prevent her from walking out the door she'd opened.

Her nerves and emotions raw, her mind screaming at her to get away before she succumbed to agreeing to be one of his now-and-then women, Hannah avoided his hand as she spun around to confront him. "I won't listen to you, Justin." She was hurting, and wanting to hurt him back, if that was possible, she lashed out at him. "I have to thank you for giving me so much please," she said sarcastically. "But it's over now. You belong in Montana, and I belong here. Whether or not Adam sends you back here, I don't want to see you again."

"Hannah, you don't meant that." He sounded genuinely shocked. "You can't mean it."

"I do mean it," she insisted, fighting tears and a desire to punch him…hard, for hurting her so much. "I've got to go now." She backed out through the doorway. "I'd appreciate it if you would lock the door as you leave." With that last parting shot, she slammed the door on his stunned face.

Justin was mad. He was more than mad, he was furious. He just couldn't decide who he was more furious with, Hannah for cutting him dead, or himself for getting too deeply involved with her in the first place.

Dammit, who needed her, anyway? Certainly not him. The last thing he needed was a haughty, overly independent woman. Hell, there were plenty of warm, eager and willing women out there.

Justin repeated the assurance to himself all the way back to Montana and throughout the following three weeks. He repeated it to himself while he was working, when conferring about the horse farm in Pennsylvania they had decided to invest in, but mostly when he prowled the house at night, unable to sleep for thinking about her, aching for Hannah.

Why the hell had he been so stupid as to fall in love with her? Why had he allowed himself to fall for the Hannah that was not always cold and haughty, but sweet and hot, a tiger in his arms.

Justin knew when he was beaten. To his amazement it didn't even bother him that he'd finally fallen in love—real love. He decided he'd have to do something about it, something more than he had originally planned on back in February.

Going to the phone, Justin placed a call to Adam, his fingers tapping an impatient drumbeat as he waited for his brother to come on the line.

"What's up?" Adam said.

"We need a family meeting about this horse farm in Oley, Pennsylvania."

"Wait a minute, we've already bought the property," Adam said. "And it was your idea to begin with. Don't tell me you changed your mind and want us to back out of the deal when we're just days away from settling it."

"No, no, I haven't changed my mind about the property," Justin reassured him, "only about who we send east to manage the farm."

"Not Ben?" Adam sounded shocked.

"Not Ben," Justin concurred. "I know for a fact that Ben really doesn't want to relocate and that Karla doesn't want to move so far from her family."

"Then who the hell do you have in mind?" Adam demanded. "One of the men on the ranch?" Before Justin could get a word in, Adam added, "Is there another one of the men capable of running a Thoroughbred farm?"

"Yeah. One," Justin drawled, thinking the answer should be obvious to Adam, of all people.

"Who?" Adam snapped impatiently.

"Yours truly, brother mine," Justin said, grinning when he heard Adam sigh.

"I'll call a meeting," Adam said. "Of course, Beth will send her proxy, as usual."

Justin was now chuckling. "To me, as usual."

"Goodbye, Justin." Adam hung up.

Justin laughed out loud, inwardly praying for success in the East Coast endeavor. Not with the farm—Justin felt confident he could succeed with that. Hell, without conceit he knew he was nearly a damn genius when it came to horses. No, the challenge was convincing Hannah that he was the man for her. His plan had to work; he'd make it work...somehow.

It was the middle of March. The days were growing milder. Instead of taking the bus as she usually did, Hannah had begun walking the two-plus miles back and forth from her apartment to her office. The exercise and fresh air were good for her.

Without conscious thought, Hannah's hand slid down in a protective gesture over the small rounded mound of her growing belly. Her pregnancy had been confirmed by her doctor. Her due date was in mid-October; another season, another life.

A thrill shot through Hannah at the thought of the tiny person awakening inside her body. She hadn't felt any movement from her baby yet, but she knew it would not be long before she did.

Hannah had told Jocelyn the day after she had seen the doctor. Over a month ago.

"Does the father know?" her assistant asked, her expression a mixture of stunned delight.

"No," Hannah admitted, shaking her head. "I don't think he'd want to know."

"Not want to know?" Jocelyn said indignantly. "What kind of a user is the son—"

"Jocelyn," Hannah interrupted her, unwilling to hear her curse Justin. "I knew what I was getting into. What Justin and I had was just a fling." She managed a wry smile. "One might say a close encounter of the sexual kind. He never asked for anything more and I expect nothing from him. This is my baby. I'll take care of it."

"And I'll be right beside you," Jocelyn said staunchly, giving Hannah a reassuring hug.

Although Hannah had taken full responsibility for her pregnancy, she still had nagging doubts about not telling Justin. Not to seek financial support for his child—she didn't need his money. She just felt that he had every right to know he was to become a father.

Justin loved children. He would make a good father…if he cared to do so. That was the dilemma Hannah was feeling.

Arriving home refreshed from the brisk walk, Hannah kicked off her shoes and went straight to the phone. She had to tell him, she'd never be able to live with herself if she didn't.

After getting his ranch's number from information, she punched it in and forced herself to breathe normally. It was difficult, especially with the phone continuing to ring. Finally, when she was about ready to hang up, an unfamiliar voice answered.

"Yes, is Justin there, please?" she asked, wondering why Karla hadn't answered.

"No, he isn't," came the brisk reply. "Would you like to leave a message?"

Declining the offer, Hannah pressed the disconnect button, then stood staring at the instrument in her hand, unsure what to do next. Blinking against a sting of tears, she hung up the phone just as the doorbell rang.

Doorbell? Her doorbell never rang without her being notified by the security guard in the lobby.

Hannah hesitated, puzzled by the oddness of the situation. The bell rang again.

Hannah went into the living room and looked through the peephole. She went absolutely still.

Justin.

The bell rang once more, quick, sharp, as if punched by an impatient or angry person.

Drawing a deep, steadying breath, Hannah disengaged the lock and pulled the door open. She backed up as he aggressively stepped forward.

"Justin…" She had to swallow to moisten her bone-dry throat. "What are you doing here?"

Dropping the same bag he had carried before,

he walked right up to her and caught her face in his hands, holding her still.

"Dammit, woman," Justin said, his voice rough. "I love you, that's what I'm doing here. I didn't want to love you. I didn't want to love any woman, ever again. But I do love you." His voice softened to a gentle purr. "Oh, sweet Hannah, I love you. I want to marry you." His stormy gray eyes grew bright with that heart-melting devil light. "And if you don't say you love me, too, want to marry me, live with me and have my babies, I'm going to curl into a ball of misery on the floor and cry for a week."

"Only a measly week?" Hannah was already crying, and laughing.

"Well, maybe two," he conceded, lowering his head to hers. "But I'd rather not. Hannah, sweetheart, say it. Say you love me before I go completely crazy."

"I love you. I love you. I love you." Tears poured down her face. "Oh, Justin, I love you so much I could die from it."

"Don't you dare. We've got a lot of living and loving before us. And there's no better time than now to get started."

Holding her tightly to him—as if he'd never let her go—he kissed her, deeply, lovingly, reverently.

Pure joy bursting inside her, Hannah flung her arms around his neck and kissed him back with all the love and longing she had tried so hard to reject. She moaned in soft protest when Justin lifted his mouth from hers.

"We'll get back to that in a minute," he murmured, gliding his tongue over her lower lip in silent promise. "But I have to ask you something."

Hannah reluctantly opened her eyes. "What?"

"Will…you…marry…me?" Justin asked.

"Oh." Hannah felt a tingle do a tango down her spine. "Well, yes, of course. Was there any doubt?"

"Oh, boy," he groaned, in feigned dismay. "I have a feeling I'm in for trouble with you."

"Yes, you are," Hannah replied happily. "And I with you, but…won't it be fun?" She pulled slightly away before saying, "I said I'd marry you, Justin, and I will. But there is one possible problem."

He arched a brow. "Like…what?"

"Like…you run a ranch in Montana," she said. "And I run a business in Philadelphia."

He shook his head. "No problem."

"But…" she began in protest, afraid he'd ask her to give up the business she had worked so hard to get up and running, and even more afraid she'd agree to do so.

"Honey, let me explain," he interjected. "When I was here a few weeks ago, I didn't just stop in to visit you for a quick bout of sex at the end of my business trip."

"You didn't? Tell me more. Spill your guts, Grainger."

He laughed. "You're something else, sweetheart, you know that?"

"Yeah, yeah." Hannah flicked a hand at him. "Get on with the explanation."

"The idea of our company buying a horse farm in the East wasn't Adam's, it was mine."

"Really?" She frowned. "Is that important?"

"I think so." Justin smiled, pulling her over to the sofa where they both sat. "At my suggestion, the company bought the farm in the Oley Valley. We made settlement yesterday." He paused.

"Go on." Having an inkling of what was coming, she held her breath.

"I'm going to manage it."

"Oh…oh," she cried, almost afraid to believe it. "You're relocating?"

"Yes."

"I can keep my business? Commute?"

"Yes, sweet Hannah." His smile grew a bit shaky. "You can keep me, too, if you want."

"If? If?" Hannah exclaimed, moving into his waiting arms. "Try to get out of being kept."

Holding her tight, as if afraid to set her free, he pressed his forehead to hers. "Oh, sweet Hannah, I love you so much, so very much."

"Oh, Justin. I…I have something I must tell you, something I think is wonderful. I'm pregnant."

"You're pregnant?" Justin asked, his gray eyes starting to gleam. "You're pregnant!" He whooped, laughing. "I'm going to be a father!"

"You're not angry?" Hannah asked.

"Of course I'm not angry. I'm thrilled." He frowned. "Did you know about this when I was here before?"

She nodded. "I knew how you felt about marriage," Hannah defended herself. "I was afraid to tell you, afraid you wouldn't care or that you would think I was trying to trap you."

"Wouldn't care?" Justin appeared stunned, as though he'd taken a blow to the head.

"I…I did finally call you," she said softly, trying to placate him. "You weren't there."

"No one said I had missed a call," Justin said. "When did you call?"

Hannah wet her lips and lowered her eyes. "A couple of minutes before you rang the bell."

"A couple of—" Justin broke off, shaking his head. "You know, sweetheart, I don't know whether to kiss you senseless or shake you senseless."

"You'd better kiss me," she advised demurely. "You can't shake me in my delicate condition."

"Okay." Lowering his head, he took possession of her lips…and her heart.

* * * * *

HOT TO THE TOUCH

by
Jennifer Greene

JENNIFER GREENE

lives near Lake Michigan with her husband and two children. Before writing full-time, she worked as a teacher and a personnel manager. Michigan State University honoured her as an "outstanding woman graduate" for her work with women on campus.

Ms Greene has written more than fifty category romances, for which she has won numerous awards, including two RITA® Awards from the Romance Writers of America in the Best Short Contemporary Books category, and a Career Achievement Award from *Romantic Times* magazine.

One

Respect was a touchy issue for Phoebe Schneider. She'd been a skilled physical therapist for several years, and since no one had twisted her arm and forced her to become a masseuse, it was pretty crazy to complain. Maybe a lot of guys assumed that being a masseuse meant she was loose as a goose, but guys, by their hormonal nature, always indulged in wishful thinking.

At twenty-eight, Phoebe knew perfectly well how the world worked. She just had a little hot spot about the respect thing…say, the size of a mountain.

Today, though, was one of those rare, fabulous days when Phoebe felt so great about her job that any price she had to pay was worth it.

From the windows of the Gold River Hospital conference room, the Smokies loomed in the distance. The mountains were still shawled in snow, the wind still February sharp, but inside, the temperature was toasty. The pediatrics neurologist, pediatrics head and ICU nurse rubbed elbows at the table. Phoebe wasn't just the youngest of the group, but distinctly the only masseuse.

What tickled her pride bone most, though, was that they were all listening to her. Of course, they'd better—because when the subject was babies, Phoebe was known to fight down and dirty.

"We've been through this before. The problem," she said firmly, "is that you're all looking for an illness. A pathology. Some kind of disease you can fix. But when you've ruled out all those possibilities, you have to look at other choices." She clicked her mouse, which changed the screen image on the far wall to that of a three-month-old baby. "George isn't sick. George is cold."

"Cold—" Dr. Reynolds started to interrupt.

"I meant emotionally cold." She clicked the mouse again, showing a picture from the day the baby had been brought into the hospital. A nurse was lifting George from a crib. The baby was indistinguishable from an inanimate doll, because his little arms and legs were as rigid as stone. "You already know his history. Found in a closet, half-starved. A birth mother incapable of mothering or even basic care. This was simply a baby who was born into a world so hostile that he had no concept of emotional connection."

She showed the next series of slides, illustrating the changes over the last month since she'd started working with the baby. Finally she ended the presentation—which ended her consulting job for this group, as well. "My recommendation is that you not place George in a regular foster care situation for a while yet. We think of bonding as a natural human need, but George's situation is more complex than that. If you want this little angel to make it, we need him connected 24/7 to a warm, human body—and I mean that literally. We have to force him to trust, because even at this young age, he has learned to survive by tuning out. He simply won't take the chance of trusting anyone—unless we put him in a situation where he's forced to."

Halfway through the meeting, the social worker tiptoed in late. Phoebe saw skepticism in the neurologist's face, dubiousness in the social worker's. She didn't mind. The docs wanted to be able to prescribe medicine that would promptly fix the baby. The social worker wanted to foster the baby out and get him off her hands.

Everybody wanted easy answers. Phoebe could only seem to come up with time-consuming, expensive and inconvenient answers, which not only regularly annoyed everyone, but also tended to go down harder because they came from an upstart, redheaded, five-foot, three-inch baby masseuse.

No one ever heard of a baby masseuse when she came to Gold River. No one ever heard of it in Asheville, either, where she'd started out. Heaven knew, she'd never wanted to create a job that didn't exist. But darn it, she'd kept running across throwaway babies that the system had only lazy, lousy, inadequate answers for. It wasn't her fault that her unorthodox ideas worked. It wasn't her fault she fought like a shrew for the little ones, either.

When it came down to it, maybe she'd just found her calling. Yelling and arguing seemed to come to her naturally.

When the meeting broke up around four, the powers that be tore out as if released from prison. Phoebe started humming under her breath—she'd won the program for Baby George—further proof that it paid to be a shrew. And now, because the meeting ended early, she could get home and give the dogs a run before dinner.

She pushed on her shoes, grabbed her black-sashed jacket, but she couldn't take off until she put on some lip gloss. Talking always made her lips dry. She found at least a half-dozen glosses and lipsticks in the dark depths of her bag, but she wanted the raspberry gloss that went with her sweater. And then…

"Ms. Schneider? Phoebe Schneider?"

She spun around, the tube of raspberry gloss still open in her hand. Two men stood in the double doorway—in fact, the two of them blocked the entrance with the effectiveness of a Mack truck. Positively they weren't hospital staff. For sure Gold River Memorial Hospital had some adorable doctors, but she knew none with barn-beam shoulders and lumberjack muscles.

"Yeah, I'm Phoebe."

When they immediately charged toward her, she had to control the impulse to bolt. Obviously they couldn't help being giants, any more than she could help being undersize. It wasn't their fault they were sexy lugs, either, from their sandy hair to their sharp, clean-cut looks to their broody dark eyes…any more than she could help having the personality of a bulldog. Or so some said. Personally, Phoebe thought she was pretty darn nice. Under certain circumstances. When she had time. "I take it you're looking for me."

The tallest one—the one in the serious gray suit—answered first. "Yeah. We want to hire you for our brother."

"Your brother," she echoed. She got the lip gloss capped,

just in time to drop it. The one in the sweatshirt and jeans hunkered down to retrieve it for her.

"Yes. I'm Ben Lockwood, and this is my brother Harry."

"Lockwood? As in Lockwood Restaurant?" The town of Gold River had lots of restaurants, but none as posh as Lockwood's. For that matter, the Lockwood name had an automatic association to old money and old gold, which was probably why Phoebe had never run into them before.

Ben, the one in the suit, answered first. "Yeah. That's Harry's place. He's the chef in the family. I'm the builder. And our youngest brother is Fergus. He's the one we want to hire you for."

Phoebe felt a familiar wearisome thud in her stomach. Guys. Looking to hire a masseuse. For another guy. One plus one invariably added up to someone thinking she hired out for services above and beyond massaging.

Still, she didn't waste time getting defensive, just gathered her gear and headed out. The men trailed after her down the hall toward the east entrance. Harry grabbed her box of slides—which tried to tip when she pushed open the door. "I don't know why you two didn't just call. I'm listed. And then I could have told you right off that I only work with babies."

Ben had a ready answer. "We didn't call because we were afraid you'd brush us off. And we know you work with little kids and babies now, but the hospital said you were a licensed physical therapist, the best they'd ever seen. Fox is in a special situation. So we hoped you might consider making an exception for him."

There was no way she was taking on an adult male. None. Phoebe wasn't short on courage, but her heart had been smashed too hard from a close encounter with the wrong kind. She would take another chance. Sometime in the next decade. But for now, the only risks she willingly took were for babies.

None of that was any of their business, of course. She just told them she was booked up the wazoo for months—which had the effect of swatting a fly. Ignoring her protest completely, they trailed her through the parking lot like puppies—giant, overgrown puppies—carrying her bags and boxes, picking up the stuff she dropped, flanking her like bodyguards.

Typical of February in North Carolina—at least in the mountains—evening was falling faster than a stone. The afternoon's brisk wind had turned noisy and blustery, and the clouds were puffing in hard now. In another month or so, magnolias and rhododendron would furiously flower on the elegant hospital grounds, but right now, even the sentinel oaks weren't gutsy enough to leaf out yet. The wind shivered through her long auburn braid, teasing at the ribbon wrapped through it and threatening to unravel it.

The guys were starting to unravel her, too—but not for the reasons she'd first feared. By the time they reached her old white van in the third row, she had the ghastly feeling that she'd fallen totally in love with both of them. They looked at her as if she were a goddess. That helped. They treated her as if she were a hero. She liked that, too. Mostly, though, she had a strong sixth sense about predators. These two were just plain good guys. How was she supposed to resist that?

"Ben, Harry...look. I don't know if the hospital misled you, but I don't do any regular physical therapy anymore. I just don't have time. And besides that, if your brother has some kind of special problems, I have no qualifications to help him."

"Yeah, well, Fox has been to tons of people with blue-ribbon qualifications. Doctors. Psychiatrists. Specialized physical therapists. Hell, we even brought in a priest and we're not Catholic." Ben made the joke but then couldn't pull off a smile. "We have to try something different. We're losing our brother. We need some fresh ideas, a different outlook. If you'd just take a look at him—"

Sometime over the next ten minutes. Phoebe picked up that the Lockwood brothers regularly referred to themselves as animals. Ben was Bear. Harry was Moose. And they called their youngest brother Fox.

She loved animals. Wild or tame. And the Lockwood brothers had clearly dropped their jobs and lives to come here and gang up on her, which said something about how much they loved their brother. "Honest to Pete, I'm telling you straight, I can't help you. I would if I could."

"Just come and meet him."

"I can't."

"We haven't explained what he's been through yet. At least listen. And then if you can't help, you can't. We're just asking you to *try*."

"Guys. *I can't*."

"Just one shot. A few minutes. We'll pay you five hundred bucks for a half hour, how's that? I swear, if you decide you can't help him after that, we'll never bug you again. You have our word."

My God. They wheedled and whined and charmed and bribed. Phoebe rarely met anyone who could outstubborn her, but these two were beyond blockheaded. Still. If she took on one adult patient, it would open the door to being asked again. And that wasn't worth the risk.

"I'm sorry, guys, but no," she said firmly.

At seven o'clock that night, Phoebe flipped the gearshift in reverse and barreled out of her driveway. "I don't want to hear any grief," she told the dogs sharing the passenger seat. "A woman has a right to change her mind."

Neither Mop nor Duster argued. As long as they got to ride in the van with their noses out the window, they never cared what she said.

"You two just stick by me. If something feels hinky, then we'll all take off together. Got it?"

Again, neither mutt responded. Even after two years, Phoebe wasn't dead positive who'd rescued whom. The two pint-size dirty-white mop heads had shown up at her back door when she first moved to Gold River. They'd been scrawny and matted and starved. Throwaways. Yet ever since they'd acted as if she was the throwaway and they were the benevolent adopters. It boggled the mind.

"The brothers really were okay. I know, I know, they were men. And who can trust anyone stuck with all that testosterone? But really, the situation isn't what I first thought. Their brother sounds as if he's in rough shape. So even if I can't do anything, it just seemed heartless to keep saying no."

Again the mutts offered no input. They were both hanging out the open window, their bitsy tongues lolling, paying her no attention whosoever.

Before the sun completely dropped, lights popped on all down Main Street. Wrought-iron carriage lamps lined the shopping district. If she hadn't agreed to this darn fool meeting, she could have been suckered into the shoe sale at Well

Heeled, or accidentally slipped into TJ Maxx. Well, it was hard to slip into TJ accidentally when the store was two blocks away, but the principle was still valid.

Worry started circling her mood. She loved her work. The bank claimed she was a long way from solvent, but money wasn't that important to her. Doing something that mattered was. She'd found a touch therapy for babies with unique problems that really worked. Babies were her niche.

Men weren't.

She liked guys. Always had, always would. But she'd met Alan even *before* she'd hung up the masseuse sign, when she'd still been a physical therapist. He'd been a patient recovering from a serious bone break. Right off he'd judged her as a hedonist and a sensualist—a woman who loved to touch. And he'd loved those qualities in her.

He'd said.

He'd also claimed she was the hottest woman he'd ever met. He'd even said that as if it were a compliment. In the beginning.

Edgily she gnawed on a thumbnail. She'd moved to Gold River to obliterate those painful memories and start over. She'd done just that. Her whole life was on an uphill track again—but she also had good reason to be careful.

Those darn Lockwood brothers had sabotaged her common sense by painting a picture in her mind. A picture of their brother. A picture she just couldn't seem to shake.

Apparently this Fergus had volunteered to serve in the military and came home with a medical discharge because of injuries sustained from a "dirty bomb." The Veterans' Hospital had patched him up and eventually released him. Both Ben and Harry agreed that their brother had initially seemed fine, weak but definitely recovering. Only, he'd increasingly withdrawn after coming home. The family tried bringing additional doctors and psychologists into the picture, but Fergus had basically shut the door and shut down. No one could get through to him.

The brothers claimed they'd heard about her through a doctor friend—a woman who'd said she had the touch of a healer with babies. That was an exaggeration, of course. Phoebe couldn't heal anyone. Certainly not anyone as damaged and traumatized as this Fergus sounded.

She'd lowered her defenses when it became obvious the guys weren't looking for sex, surrogate sex, or any of the other ridiculous things guys assumed masseuses really were. But now she felt unsure again. Their brother had been through something terrible. He likely had post-traumatic stress syndrome or whatever that was called. It was sad and it was awful—but she had no knowledge or skills to help someone in that kind of situation.

When it came down to it, she'd only agreed to come because she was a complete dolt. The brothers had been so darling that she just couldn't find a way to say no.

She suddenly realized that the slip of paper with the address was no longer on the seat, but had been stolen. "Damn it, Mop! Give it!"

Mop coughed up the damp, chewed piece of paper. Thankfully the number on the address was still legible. At the next right, she turned on Magnolia, left three blocks later on Willow, then followed the hillside climb. In theory she knew where the rich lived. She just never had an excuse to dawdle in their neighborhood.

A handful of mansions perched on the cliff, overlooking

the river below where their grandfathers had once scooped up fortunes in gold. The homes were hidden behind high fences and wrought-iron gates. Still, the hardwoods were stripped bare at this time of year, so Phoebe could catch fleeting glimpses of the gorgeous homes. Most were built of the local stone and marble, with big, wraparound verandas and lush landscaping.

The Lockwood house was tucked in the curve of a secluded cul de sac. Feeling like a trespasser, she drove past the gates, past the two-story house and five-car garage—as instructed—and pulled up to a smaller home beyond. The brothers had called it the bachelor house, which was apparently a historical term—a place where the young unmarried men hung out before they were married, where they could sow wild oats away from their mother's judgmental eyes. The concept sounded distinctly decadent and Southern to Phoebe, but the point was that Fergus had been living there since he got out of the hospital, according to his brothers.

Close up, the main house didn't look so ritzy as it did sturdy and lived in, with cheerful lights beaming from all the windows downstairs. By contrast, only a single light shone from the bachelor house, making the place look dark and gloomy and ghostly.

She *liked* ghost stories, she reminded herself, besides which it was too late to chicken out now. Before she could open the door and climb out, the back porch light popped on, so the brothers must have been watching for her. Mop and Duster bounded off her lap and galloped for the shadows, promptly peed and then zoomed straight for the guys in the doorway. Phoebe followed more slowly. The same Lockwood brothers who'd charmed the devil out of her were already giving the girls a thorough petting, but they stood up and turned serious the instant she approached.

"I'll pay you up-front," Harry said quietly.

"Oh, shut up," she said crossly. "I told you that five hundred dollars was ridiculous. I don't do bribes." She added firmly, "I don't do miracles, either."

"That's not what we heard."

"Well, you heard wrong. This is so out of my league. Your brother's going to think you're nuts for bringing in a masseuse. And I do, too."

Neither brother argued with her—they'd already been over all that ground—Ben just motioned her in. The dogs frisked ahead.

It wasn't her kind of decor, yet right off the place drew her. The kitchen was cluttered with plates and containers of food—none of which looked touched—but beyond the debris were lead-paned glass cupboards and a slate sink and a clay-tiled floor. She had to identify things by gleams of reflected light, since apparently no one believed in turning on lights around here.

Beyond the kitchen were doors leading to a utility room and bathroom and eventually a bedroom or two, she guessed. But off to the right was the living room. She caught a glimpse of stuccoed walls and an arched fieldstone fireplace before she heard a gruff, *"What the hell?"*

So. Not hard to guess that the dogs were already introducing themselves to Fergus.

She trailed after them, finally locating the one light source—a single reading lamp outfitted with a nominal fifteen-watt bulb. Still, even in the gloom, she easily identified the living room as a testosterone den. No frou-frou had ever crossed this threshold. From the dark wood to the shutters to the hardwood floors, it was a guy's place all the way. The couch and chairs were upholstered in a deep claret red, the coffee table chosen to tolerate boots and glass marks. The room smelled of dust and last night's whiskey and silence.

She heard the brothers talking in the kitchen, guessed they wouldn't lag behind more than a few moments. In those spare seconds, though, the lonely stillness of the room tugged at her…and yeah, so did the body on the couch.

At first look, if her hormones had perked to attention, she just might have turned tail and run. That was the threat, of course. That she'd care about a man who would hurt her again—who'd form preconceptions about her and her profession, who'd judge her based on surface impressions. But that wasn't going to happen. Not with this man.

Fergus was clearly so safe that her defenses dropped faster than a drawbridge for a castle. He wasn't going to hurt her. Or care about her. Those were absolute "for sures."

Aw, man.

Just one look made her heart fill up with blade-deep compassion.

She'd assumed he'd be good-looking because Bear and Moose were such studs. Instead, he was longer than Lincoln and scrawny. Dark eyes were deeply set in a sharp boned face with a slash of a mouth and a square jaw. He had his brothers' barn-beam shoulders, but his jeans and shirt hung on him. His brothers both had charm in their smiles, creases in their cheeks from laugh lines. Fergus, damn him, had so much pain in his eyes that Phoebe had to suck in a breath.

She only had that brief moment to study him—and to realize that her two fluff balls were curled on his chest—before he spotted her in the doorway.

He didn't acknowledge her. He just said, "Bear. Moose. Get her out of here."

He didn't yell it. His voice wasn't remotely rude. It was just dead cold and exhausted. Both brothers emerged from the kitchen fast and barreled in. "Take it easy, Fox. We were just getting some drinks from the kitchen. We just wanted to have a talk—"

Maybe Fergus was the youngest of the three—and for damn sure, the weakest—yet somehow he came across as the family CEO. "Forget it. I don't know what you two thought you were setting up, but it's not going to happen. All of you, just get out of here. Leave me alone."

Phoebe found it fascinating, watching the two big, brawny guys try to bully their prostrate brother. That flower just wasn't gonna bloom. Who'd have guessed the skinny, surly, mean-eyed Fox could express authority, much less win, against the powerful good guys?

But that wasn't the reason her heart was suddenly pounding like a manic drum.

Phoebe took another quiet step closer. The longer she studied him, the more she realized that he'd never actually looked at her. Or his brothers. She doubted he was seeing much of anything. His eyes were smudged with weariness, and his skin wasn't just gray because of the dim light. He was shocky from pain. Even trying to speak in that dead-quiet whisper seemed to sharpen the fierce, dark light in his eyes.

Worse than that, she saw one of his hands on Mop. They knew. Both her mutts always knew which humans to avoid and which humans needed attention from them. They were hell on wheels and nonstop nuisances, but they somehow responded instinctively to people in pain.

Now she understood why the place was so dungeon dark. Light undoubtedly made the hurt worse.

Phoebe told herself that her pulse was rushing hard for the obvious reason. She cared. She could no more stop herself from responding to someone suffering than she could stop breathing. It wasn't a response to him as a *man.* She didn't have to worry about that, she was positive. But just as positively, she could no more walk out on a human in pain than she could quit breathing.

She started by pushing between the two brothers. "You two, head outside for a few minutes, okay? Let me talk to Fergus alone. Mop. Duster. Lay down, girls."

The dogs immediately obeyed her, but the boys weren't quite so easy to order around. Harry—Moose—looked uncertainly at Bear. "Maybe we were wrong," he said unhappily. "I don't think it's a good idea for us to completely leave you alone with—"

"It's all right," she assured him, as she herded them both toward the door.

Of course, it wasn't quite that easy. The brothers warily agreed to leave her alone for a short stretch with Fergus, but the instant the back door closed, the house was suddenly silent as sin. A goofy little shiver chased up her spine—until she returned to the living room.

From the doorway she caught the gleam of Fergus's broody, angry eyes and almost immediately relaxed.

Phoebe was only a coward about one thing.

This wasn't it.

Nice guys she had to worry about. But a tortured, mean-tempered crabby pistol like Fergus, she could handle in her sleep. The poor guy just didn't realize who his brothers had brought home to dinner.

Two

"Fergus…my name is Phoebe Schneider. Your brothers asked me to come here."

He heard the voice and he saw her as a shadow, but it was like trying to process information through a fog. Trying to focus hurt. Trying to talk hurt. Hell, trying to breathe seemed to set off new knives in his temples. "I don't care who you are. Just go *away*."

There seemed to be a dog—or two—on his chest. A wet nose had snuffled under his palm. It was odd, but he didn't mind. Maybe it was the surprise of feeling the pups' warmth, their thick scruffy fur under his fingers. But then the woman quietly ordered them to the ground, and they immediately obeyed her.

"Honestly, I'd love to take off, Fergus. I never wanted to come here to begin with. This is crazy, right? Why would you want a stranger around when you don't feel well? But your brothers are rock-headed bullies. They got it in their minds that I can help you, and they're just going to badger both of us unless I at least *try*."

The headaches always seemed to come with memory flashes. The little boy with the dark hair and beautiful, big, sad eyes. Shyly coming up to him. Taking the candy bar. Then…the explosion.

Over and over the headaches repeated the same pattern, the explosion in his memory echoing the explosions of pain. Sometimes, like now, he literally saw stars. Ironically they were downright beautiful, a dazzling aura of lightning-silver lights that would have been mesmerizing if a sledgehammer hadn't been pounding in his temples. And, yeah, he heard the woman talking. Her voice was velvet low, sexy soft, soothing. Most of her words didn't register, because nothing was registering in his brain right then. But she was still there. *That* got through.

He heard a small plop of sound, like a jacket or sweater being dropped. And there were suddenly new, vague scents in the room—camellias, strawberries, oranges. And through the scissor-slashing pain, he thought he caught a glimpse of long, dark-cinnamon-red hair.

When the headaches got this bad, though, he was never sure what was reality and what was hallucination.

"I don't want you to waste energy talking," she continued quietly. "But I need to know what these headaches are about. Your brothers told me you were recovering from injuries. So, did you get hit on your head or your neck? Is that the cause of the pain?"

He tried to answer without moving his lips. "No. I've got

dirty bomb parts sticking out all over my body. But not my neck. Not my head. Hell." He squeezed his eyes closed, clenched his teeth. "No more talking. Go away."

"I will," she promised him blithely, but then didn't. "So this is a migraine?"

He didn't answer, but that didn't seem to deter her.

"If it's a migraine, you've surely had a doctor prescribe some serious pain medication for you...."

It was like ignoring taxes. It didn't work. So he tried answering her again. "I have buckets full of pills. Ergotamine. Beta-blockers. Calcium channel blocker. Codeine—" Hell. Even talking this quietly jostled new razor-edged nerve endings. "Quit taking them all. Don't help. Only make me throw up. Then it's worse..."

Alarmed, he realized she was coming closer. She definitely had long, cinnamon-red hair. Other impressions bombarded him—that strawberry scent and hint of camellias. A wide, sensual mouth. Snapping clear eyes. Blue eyes. Too blue.

"Get out," he said. If he had to throw her out, he would. He'd undoubtedly hurl if he tried any real physical movement, end up shaking and sick from the exertion, but this time he meant it. He'd had enough.

Finally she seemed to get it, because she obeyed and turned around. He heard the soft footfalls, heard the distant sound of the back door opening, his brothers' voices, then the door closing again.

The sudden silence should have given him peace, but it wasn't that easy. He concentrated on closing his eyes, not moving, not thinking, not breathing any more than he had to. But the little boy's face kept showing up in his mind. A child.

A young child. Like all the young children he used to teach. And the drum thudding in his brain sounded like a judge's gavel, as if he were being accused of a nameless crime, as if he'd been found guilty without ever having a chance to defend himself.

He was sinking deeper into the pain when he heard her voice again—her voice, her sounds, her presence and, yeah, her dogs. One leaped on his stomach, tried to nuzzle under his hand.

"Down, Mop," she whispered, and again the scruffy pup immediately obeyed. As if she thought he could conceivably be interested, she started chitchatting in that velvet-low voice. "Normally I work at home, so the dogs are used to being with me. And I do leave them sometimes. They've got a dog door and a big, fenced-in backyard. But the thing is, they just hate it when I leave in the evening, so I tend to bring them if I possibly can."

"No." This had gone on far enough. He got it now—the purpose of the casual chitchat had been to distract him from whatever the Sam Hill she was doing. He heard rustling sounds behind him, smelled more odd, evocative fragrances, then heard the strike of a match. When she turned off the lamp, the only light in the room came from the teardrop flames of a few candles. The darkness was much easier on his eyes, his head, only the rest of the smells and sounds made no sense. They weren't bad sensations. They were just alien to the house and him.

"Close your eyes," she repeated.

"No. Why? For God's sake, do I have to get up and throw you out of the house to get you to leave?"

"Fox," she said gently, "close your damn eyes and quit

fighting me. I'm nobody you need to worry about. Just shut up and let go."

That was such a ridiculous thing for a stranger to say that momentarily he was too startled to respond. Even the memory flashes disappeared. He tried to concentrate, because he was determined to push past the pain and get up. She was leaving. He figured she had to be some kind of medical do-gooder his brothers had brought in, but it didn't make any difference. He was a pinch away from losing his cookies. His only hope was staying so still that the pain got no worse.

Except that he had to get rid of the redhead first. "You're all done, lady. I don't know what the hell you...I...oh. Oh. Oh, God."

She touched him.

She was behind him, out of sight, must have knelt down right at his head, because he felt her hands on his temples. Cool, smooth fingers whispered on his temples and forehead. There was a substance on her hands—something slippery that smelled like Creamsicles. She stroked the narrow spot below his eyebrows, then the vee above his nose, then soothed that light-scented oil into his forehead, into his hairline.

He opened his mouth to swear at her again, even got out the 'f' sound of the word he furiously wanted to express...only he forgot.

He meant to swear, he really did, but nothing came out but a groan.

A weak, vulnerable groan. Exasperated, he tried to do the cussing thing again, only to repeat the same problem. He forgot.

Her fingers sifted into his short, coarse hair, fingertips

gently massaging the skin, the pads of the fingers soothing, smoothing. The slick, soft stuff went into his hair, into his scalp. He didn't care.

"I can't make a migraine go away," she said quietly. "But if we can get you to relax, you'll have a shot at sleeping it off. You're so tense with the pain, it's making it worse. But it's hard to work on you while you're lying on this couch. Especially with all your clothes on. If you could just shift forward a little, the couch arm wouldn't be in our way so much…"

He stopped listening to her. He couldn't listen. He was too busy feeling.

She couldn't physically move him—hell, he had to be twice her size. But somehow she made the couch pillow disappear, so that she could lean over and contact him more directly. She worked, and kept working, behind his ears, down the sides of his neck.

She stopped to get more of that smelly Creamsicle stuff, came back, shivered it through his hair, scraped it through his scalp, rubbed it, kneaded it, soothed it, caressed it.

The more she worked, the more he felt a deep, sexual pull in the pit of his belly. Nothing she was doing was sexual. She never touched him below the neck and, hell, she was getting that gooey slippery stuff all over his head.

But it seemed as if she pulled the pain right out of him.

His headache didn't instantly disappear. But the sensations she invoked seemed bigger than the pain, big enough to distract him, big enough to suck him under a sleek, silent, shimmering wave of sensation.

She started humming under her breath, an old song. "Summertime." About how living was easy and the cotton was high. She couldn't hum. Her voice was so off-key it should have grated on his nerves—and God knew, his nerves had been in shreds for hours.

But not anymore. The soft pads of her thumbs stroked his closed eyes, so lightly it was like being stroked by a skein of silk. She brushed his cheekbones, remolded them, scrolled down to his jawline, pushed, stroked, pulled.

He suddenly went hard—which was as impossible as a phoenix rising. No man could get a hard-on with a migraine. The thought was ludicrous.

But damn…he'd never had a woman touch him this way. He'd never had a woman *own* him this way. He'd never felt this…connection. As if someone else really were on the other side of the dark abyss and he wasn't alone, not anymore, as if she knew intimate things about his feelings that no one else ever had.

It was petrifying.

He didn't let other people in. Or he hadn't, since coming back from the Middle East. His life had irrevocably changed. He just wanted to be left the total hell alone—and he didn't want her near him, either, but hell.

He felt himself slipping and then slipping further. Into her spell. Under her spell.

She could have done anything, said anything she wanted— as long as she kept touching him. All the P.T. and rehab and rebuilding he'd been through over these last months—yeah, he'd survived it all, willing or not, but nothing had dented the pain. Nothing had come close.

Until her.

His eyes were already closed, but he could feel sleep coming. Real sleep. Not the kind where he'd wake up in an hour, soaked in sweat, heart pounding, screams and explosions and the indelible face of a little boy relentlessly in his head. But the other kind of sleep. The kind where you sank into a deep, safe stillness and felt free enough to…just…let…go.

Mop and Duster lifted their heads when Phoebe snuffed out the candles. She waited a moment for her eyes to adjust to the darkness and then quietly picked up her jacket and gear. She tiptoed through the silent house, trying to make no sound until she stepped foot outside.

Ben and Harry were still there, waiting for her, pacing back and forth the length of the veranda.

"I'll be damned. He didn't kill you."

She thought that was a particularly perceptive comment of Ben's. "He's sound asleep."

Both brothers shook their heads. "He can't be. He doesn't sleep anymore. In fact, that's part of the problem—he's so damn surly because he can't get any rest—"

"Well, he's out for the count now. And hopefully he'll stay asleep until he can clock up some serious rest." Phoebe took a moment to inhale a deep, long breath. She had no idea how long she'd been inside, but the sky was now blacker than pitch and the bushes covered with a fresh coat of rime. She let the dogs chase off into the darkness to do their business. It gave her another moment.

Right then she seemed to need about fifty moments. Typically her hands could tremble for a while after the intense, hard work of a serious massage. Tonight, though, she knew there was another reason for her shakiness—a reason that badly unsettled her. Complicating her concern, the Lockwood brothers were looking at her as if she were a goddess.

"It wasn't anything special I did," she told them promptly. "I can't cure anyone's migraine. It's just that the best 'fix' for people who have headaches like that is to get them to sleep, any way and any how you can. At least, that I've found. Anybody could have done what I did."

"But no one else has. And you can't imagine all the people who've seen—"

She wasn't going to argue with the two big lugs, not after an impossibly long day. Right now, besides, her knees were moaning and groaning from kneeling so long for Fox. And her hands…her hands still felt him. "Look, I'm pretty sure he'll be better when he wakes up—as long as he gets a few hours of solid sleep—but does he live here alone?"

"Yeah." Harry motioned to the big house. "Our mom has been living there alone since Dad died. We all moved out after we grew up. Normally Ben has a place in the country and I live over my restaurant. The bachelor house was empty for years. But Fox gave up his apartment when he went into the military—didn't make sense to pay rent when he figured he was going to be gone for several years. The point, though, is that when he came home all beat up, the bachelor house seemed an ideal place for him to hole up, close to family."

Ben filled in more. "We've been hanging close for the last two months. Fergus won't let anyone stay with him, but the idiot is in no position to take care of himself, and for darn sure, mom can't cope with him alone."

"Hell, we can't cope with him, either," Harry said. "I can't believe you got him to sleep—"

"Don't." They kept looking at her as if she were an angel, which was funny and fun but too ridiculous to tolerate any longer. "I just got here at the right time, that's all. He was probably on the other side of the headache, ready to sleep."

"The hell he was," Ben said peaceably.

"Yeah, well, I won't be coming back, so don't even try going there. He made it more than clear that he didn't want me around, so this was definitely a one-shot deal."

"But you'd come back if he asked?"

"He won't ask." She opened the van door. The pups leaped in.

"But if he did ask—"

"Yeah, then...*maybe.* If I could make it fit with my schedule. If I thought he was asking, and not you two pushing the idea on him. If..." She dug in her purse for her keys. Not that she carried a big bag, but she could probably have survived for six months in Europe on what she considered emergency supplies. Eventually her fingers emerged with the keys—and when she looked up, suddenly the two giants were descending on her, grinning ear to ear. She got a smooch on both cheeks before she could stop them.

"*Thanks,* Phoebe. We love you."

Color bloomed in her cheeks. "You guys," she began, and then just shook her head and climbed into the van.

Until she turned out of the driveway and disappeared into the dark night, her shoulders were knotted up with tension. Slowly, though, she felt her muscles—and heart—start to simmer down.

Touch was erotic. That's just the way it was. She couldn't touch someone—intensely touch, the kind of touch required if you really wanted to help the person—without responding herself.

So. Helping Fergus had turned her on. Nothing new about that. Nothing interesting.

Nothing she needed to be afraid of.

"Right, girls?" she asked the pups.

The dogs looked up, as if trying to reassure her, yet she still seemed to need to take in heaping gulps of fresh air.

It was Alan who'd made her feel cheap and immoral. Sleazy. As if sexuality and sensuality were a weakness in her character that made her less than decent. She knew that was crap. She *knew,* but, damn, the residue of hurt was harder to shake than a flu germ, even after all this time.

In her head and her heart, she'd believed forever that touch was the most powerful sense. Almost everyone responded to being touched—the right kind of touch. People could go hungry, could go without sleep, could suffer all kinds of deprivation.

But people who went without touch for a long period seemed to lose part of themselves.

Phoebe understood perfectly well that touch in itself couldn't heal anything. Touch just seemed to enable a body to *want* to heal itself. It seemed to help a body rest. It seemed to remind even the lost souls that there was wonder on the other side of loneliness—the wonder of connecting, of finding someone else who reached you emotionally.

She pulled in her driveway, past the softly lit sign:

BABY LOVE
Phoebe Schneider, Licensed PT, Licensed LMBT, ABW, MP
Infant Massage Therapy

She docked the van in the narrow driveway, turned the key and leaned back. The sign was the key, she realized.

She just had to quit thinking of Fergus Lockwood as a man—and think of him as if he were another one of her baby clients.

Actually, he struck her very much like one of her lost babies—as if he'd been deprived of touch. As if he'd lost touch with himself because he'd become so isolated from human contact. In fact, as if he needed touch so badly that he'd responded fiercely and evocatively to any contact.

In other words, he'd never been responding to her as a woman.

She climbed out of the van, only to suffer a traffic jam at the back door with the pooches trying to barrel in ahead of her. It was after bedtime, after all. "So that's the deal, girls," she told them. "He's not likely to call again, but in case he does, that's how we handle it. We just think of him as one of our babies."

She flipped on the light and plunked down her purse. A vision immediately filled her mind of rolling smooth muscles, sleek warm skin, fierce dark eyes. She swallowed, and thought babies—yeah, right.

By Sunday afternoon, when she pulled into the parking lot for Young at Heart, Gold River's home for the elderly, she'd totally and completely forgotten about Fergus.

A domineering, macho wind was hurling down from the mountain, throwing handfuls of confetti snow here and there and burning her lungs. It was the kind of afternoon when she just wanted to snuggle in a down comforter with two dogs, a book, a chick flick and a mug of hot chocolate—with melted marshmallows.

She wondered—just idly, since she'd completely stopped

thinking about him—whether Fergus might be tempted by a small, sizzling fire on a cuddly cold afternoon.

There was a lot more wrong with him than the debilitating headaches, Bear and Moose had told her. He'd been home from the hospital for two months, yet except for short grocery runs, stayed locked in. Didn't see people. Didn't return calls. Didn't *do* anything.

She had no idea what he'd done before—for a living or for hobbies or anything else—but obviously they were describing a problem with depression. Maybe the depression was a result of his experience in the military. Maybe it was from injuries that refused to heal—chronic pain could cripple the strongest optimist. The thing was, it was hard to help someone without knowing specifically what was wrong with them. You had to have some clue what motivated the individual.

Not that she was thinking about what might motivate Fergus.

She wasn't thinking about him at all.

"Hey, Phoebe!"

"Hey, handsome." Typically she was effusively greeted the instant she walked into the rest home—as were the dogs, who were as welcomed here on Sunday afternoons as she was. In principle she had her hands full with her baby clients, but the manager of the rest home had somehow conned her into regular weekend visits. She hadn't said yes because she was a sucker or weak-willed or anything like that. She just hadn't quite known how to say no.

Barney—who she invariably called Handsome—was ninety-three and skinnier than a stick, but he still had a full head of fluffy white hair. He could walk with a cane, although he couldn't stop his hands from shaking anymore. The

dogs piled over to greet him, as did Phoebe, who enthusiastically—if carefully—pecked him on the cheek.

"I swear," she whispered, "you're so good-looking, I think
we should run away from this place and have a wild, crazy
affair."

"Go on with you. You're young and beautiful—"

"And you're not?" She raised her eyebrows and patted
him on the fanny—which he loved—and then she moved on.

The bad wing was on the west side. She always started
there. No one seemed to touch the end-stage patients but the
nurses. The staff offered necessary care and caring, but no one
had time to express affection or gentleness.

Mop and Duster were allowed on the beds—encouraged,
in fact. Even the Alzheimer's group roused to pet a dog. She
brushed hair, rubbed shoulders and necks, massaged cheeks,
patted, soaked feet and hands. Some didn't respond. But
some always did.

An hour later she hit the east wing—which was definitely
more of a kick-ass crowd. They fought over the dogs, chat-
tered nonstop, bent her ear with their endless array of health
complaints.

She couldn't help loving them. They made her feel so
needed.

Most had lost the spouse who would have still touched
them, and other living family seemed afraid of their brittle
bones. They were so hungry to hold hands, to feel a cheek
against theirs, to stroke and hold and hug.

The manager at Young at Heart had repeatedly begged
Phoebe to go on retainer for them as a regular. He claimed
the whole place perked up after one of her visits; she made
that much difference in health and morale.

That was nonsense, of course. But for the next couple hours, she was busier than a one-armed bandit. She washed Willa's hair—not because the rest home didn't have a regular hairdresser, but because Willa adored the head massage. Who didn't, Phoebe thought....

Which reminded her again of how Fergus had responded to even the most basic massage techniques. The Lockwood brothers had confused her by intimating Fergus was unreachable. Cripes, he'd melted faster than a sundae in the sun.

It kept coming back to her...the feeling of his scalp in her hands, the short hair shivering through her fingers...but the best had been that one moment when she finally felt the tension in his muscles let go, let go, slow as a shadow, the pain in those beautiful eyes finally easing.

"How come some nice man hasn't snapped you up?" Martha always asked, invariably, like now, when Phoebe was soaking her feet in a baby oil and clove mixture. "I just can't understanding it. You're so pretty, with all that gorgeous red hair—"

"I came close to marriage one time." She gave the standard answer, standard smile, standard laugh. "But thankfully I escaped that fate worse than death by moving here."

"You won't be singing that tune forever," Martha said shrewdly. "He just wasn't the right one. But it just makes no sense. The men should be pounding on your door."

"Nah. I think word's spread that I'm a mouthy, bossy troublemaker."

Gus, who only asked one thing from her every week—to sit in the TV room holding hands for ten minutes with a dog on his lap—piped in, "I'll marry you, Phoebe. You can have all my money."

"I'd marry you for love anyday, you sweetie pie. I don't want your money."

"A looker like you should be more greedy. Nobody can survive in this world without a little selfishness in their soul. You gotta think about taking care of yourself. Looking out for number one."

It was funny, she thought, how easy it was to fool people. She'd never have done this kind of work if it didn't give back to her tenfold. The truth was, she was selfish and greedy and she always put herself first. And she proved it when her cell phone sang on her way home.

It was Harry Lockwood. "Could you come for Fergus again?"

"Can't." Her answer came out sure as sunshine.

"He asked for you."

She believed that like she'd believed at fifteen when her date swore he'd stop, promise, hope to die. "Look, if Fergus calls and asks me to come, I'll set up a time with him. But it's Sunday night. I haven't had any dinner. I have to wash my hair, get my stuff together for the week, groom the dogs. Sunday nights are sacred, you know?"

"This is about hair?"

"No. It's about my not believing your brother asked for me."

"Okay," Harry said, and hung up.

The cell phone rang again just as she was pulling into her driveway. "Phoebe? Did I mention the last time I saw you that I'm deeply and hopelessly in love with you?"

She laughed even before she recognized Ben's voice. "I swear, the two of you are bad to the bone. But the answer is no. Absolutely no. I'm not intruding on Fergus again unless he specifically wants my help."

Ben went on as if she'd never spoken. "I've never been tempted to marry, but then I saw you. I've always been a fanny man, and your darling little butt is really the best I've ever—"

She shook her head. "Hey! That's fighting really dirty."

"We have to fight dirty, Phoebe. Fox is in real trouble. He was doing fine for a couple days after you left, most of the week, in fact. But now I don't think he's slept a wink in the past forty-eight hours. If you'd just known him before this all happened—Fergus was always full of the devil, never sat still a minute in his life. He was interested in everything, active in sports and hobbies and the community. And kids. God, he loves kids. You can't even imagine how good he is with kids. So to see him sitting in that dark room, doing nothing, not wanting to do anything—"

"Come *on,* Ben. If you brothers are close and he won't listen to you, why on earth would you think I could do anything? I can't just go over there and bully him—"

"You did before."

"He had such a bad headache before that he'd have let in the devil if it could have helped him."

"We tried the devil. We've tried everything. You're the only one who even dented that pain of his." Ben cleared his throat. "Harry said you had to wash your hair."

She knew that tone. It was one of those male "I'll be understanding about this ridiculous female thinking" tone.

"Harry also mentioned that possibly you might want a year's worth of free dinners. And I was thinking—I don't know where you live—but I told you I was the builder in the clan. I never met a woman who didn't want her kitchen redone—"

"Oh, for God's sake. This is ridiculous."

"And while I was fixing your kitchen, you could eat at Harry's restaurant—"

"Stop! I don't want to hear another word!"

"Does that mean you're coming?"

Three

Fox closed his eyes and stood absolutely still under the pelting-hot shower spray.

Maybe he'd given up sleeping and eating and couldn't get his life back for love or money. But nothing kept him from showering once a day and sometimes twice.

Even after all these weeks, parts kept coming out of him. The doctors claimed that's how it was with dirty bombs. Something new needled to the surface of his skin every once in a while. In the beginning he'd been horrified, but now he found it amazing—if not downright funny—what terrorists chose to put in dirty bombs. Bits of plastic. Hairpins. Parts of paper clips. Anything. Everything.

Some of the parts hurt. Some didn't. Some scarred. Some didn't. Mostly Fox was grateful that nothing had hit his face or eyes—or the cargo below his waist, not that he anticipated having sex again in this century. You had to give a damn about someone to get it up. He didn't. Still, it mattered fiercely to him that his equipment still functioned normally. Go figure.

His obsession with showers, though, had evolved from a terror of infection. He didn't fear dying, but damn, he couldn't face the risk of another hospital stay if any more sores got infected.

When the water turned cool, he flicked off the faucets and reached blind for the towel. He moved carefully, because sometimes his left leg gave out. Technically the broken wrist and thigh bone were both healed, but something inside still wasn't totally kosher, because one minute he could be standing or walking, and the next his left leg would give out.

Tonight that wasn't a problem—but apparently the fates couldn't let him get off scot-free.

The first step out of the shower, he found himself teetering like an old man, dizzy and disoriented. The same child's face swam in front of his eyes, drifting in the foggy steam of the bathroom—real, then not real, clear, then not clear. Sometimes the boy turned into one of the students he'd had; sometimes it was the boy in the dusty yellow alley on the other side of the world. He leaned against the glass shower doors and tried taking a long, slow breath, then another.

A headache was coming. A headache always followed one of the flashbacks to the kid. If he ever got his sense of humor back, he'd think it was funny for a guy, who used to dare anything in life, to be this scared of a headache. Of course, that was then and this was now. Before the pain attacked, he had to get himself out of the bathroom and settled somewhere safer.

Abruptly he heard something…the sound of a door open-ing? Either he imagined the sound—which would hardly be headline news—or it was Harry, coming to restock the refrig-erator with another set of dinners he couldn't eat. Whatever. He leaned over, hands on his knees, waiting for the soupy feeling to pass. Beads of water started drying on his bare skin, chilling him. His hair dripped. The towel…it seemed he'd dropped the towel. He'd get it. In a minute.

"Fergus?"

It was Bear's voice. Ben's, not Harry's. "In here." Damn, he hoped his oldest brother wouldn't stay long. Bear hovered over him like…well, like a bear. All fierce and protective. All angry at anyone and anything who'd hurt him. All willing to do anything to make it all better.

Fox had told his brothers a dozen times that nothing was going to make this all better. The wounds'd heal. They were almost healed now. But whatever was broken inside him seemed like the old Humpty Dumpty story. Too many pieces. Not enough glue.

"Fox?"

He tried denying the dizziness, pushing past it, repeated, "In here."

The denial thing seemed to work. He forced himself to pluck the towel from the tiled floor and straighten before Bear saw him and got the idea again that he was too sick to live alone.

"Hey, Fox, I brought…"

Oops. He'd assumed it'd be his brother standing in the doorway, but his brother was six-three and a solid 220. The intruder had thick, straight, long red hair, almost as long as her waist. Small, classic features. Blue eyes that snapped with attitude, a few freckles on the bridge of a bitsy nose, pale eyebrows arched just so. And a soft, wide mouth.

He remembered that soft, wide mouth. Actually, he remembered every detail of her features. It wasn't that he wanted to remember her, but she was one of those rare women who no guy could possibly forget.

God knew why. She was no angel. That was for damn sure.

Even if her eyes and posture didn't indicate excess attitude, she was wearing a red top again today—a red that screamed next to all that thick red hair. She must have bought the jeans in the boys section, because they bagged at the knees and drooped on her nonexistent butt. Then there were the boots—which were beyond-belief girl shoes and not real boots at all—three striped colors and a high heel. She'd kill herself if she walked far in them.

He caught all of her in a glance. One glance—that no amount of dizziness seemed to blur.

Obviously, finding him in the bathroom doorway had stalled her in midsprint. She'd apparently been heading for the living room, where she'd found him last time. Even if she'd guessed the location of the bathroom, she wouldn't necessarily expect to find anyone standing there, naked as a jaybird.

Her gaze met his, then dropped below his waist, then shot right back up to his eyes faster than lightning.

"Aw, damn. Aw, shoot. Aw, beans," Bear said behind him. "Phoebe, Fox, I'm sorry. Fox, I should have told you I was bringing Phoebe—I never heard the shower, just assumed you were in the living room—"

Fox took his own sweet time, wrapping the towel around his waist. Hell, she'd already seen the main event, and there was no way to hide all the bites and gouges and scars with one lone towel anyway. Besides which, if he tried moving too fast he'd likely end up falling on his nose. "I'll be darned. Did I forget calling for a physical therapist?"

"Now, Fox, you know I brought her. And I told you before, she's not like the other physical therapists you tried. She's more a masseuse."

"Oh, yeah, now I remember that masseuse thing." Fox met her eyes square. "It's okay then, you can go home. That's the one part on my body that I know is still working just fine."

She sighed, but instead of looking insulted—as he'd hoped—she seemed to look amused. "Sex'd probably be the best thing for you, but you're out of luck, I've had no training in that. For the record, I do have a PT license from Duke. And as far as body work, I'm licensed in Deep Tissue, Swedish, Shiatsu, Rolfing, Reflexology, PNF, and NautThai—"

"PNF?"

"Proprioceptive Neuromuscular Facilitation—"

"Forget it. Let's go back to why you've had no training in sex—"

"You're sure feeling peppier today," she announced, which lifted his spirits like nothing else had in ages.

The thing was—if he could fool her, he could fool his brothers. Down the pike, he might even be able to fool himself. In the meantime, she'd itched his curiosity. "Why in hell would you throw out a degree from Duke in physical therapy to do massage work?"

"So I can get my hands on naked men. Why else?"

He saw his brother making frantic hand-motion signs behind her back—Ben was acting increasingly weird. But Fergus couldn't take his eyes off her.

It wasn't that she appealed to him exactly. She couldn't, when no woman was yanking his chain these days—and the kind of woman who always appealed to him had boobs and a butt. She had neither, but damn. She was just so…zesty. Who'd have guessed she'd laugh when he tried to insult her?

Obviously, he had to try harder to annoy her.

"I'd think you could get your hands on a lot of naked men without having to bother guys who aren't interested."

"You're so right. Getting men naked is amazingly easy. On the other hand, easy guys never turned me on. I like a challenge."

"A challenge to you is barreling into a guy's house who never asked you?"

She should have bristled for that one at least. Defended herself. Fought back. Instead she just said, "Not usually. But I'm making an exception because you're so darn adorable that I'd probably break all the rules to get my hands on you. What can I say? You really ring my chimes, cutie."

That was such an outright fib that she darn near rendered him speechless. His eyes narrowed. Nobody, but nobody, rendered him speechless. "You're so full of bologna, I can't believe it."

"What makes you think I'm full of bologna?"

"Because you're not remotely promiscuous." God knew how such a personal comment flew out of his mouth, except it somehow bugged him, her talking about all those naked men. In spite of that luscious mouth and her wearing those absurdly sexy high boots, she just didn't come across to him as easy—not any kind of easy. Beneath that whole frisky act, there was just something vulnerable about her.

Once the comment came out of his mouth, though, he had

no chance to take it back. Her hands immediately formed small fists and arched on her hips. "How do you know I'm not promiscuous?"

"All right, all right, of course I don't *know* it. I don't know you from Adam. But twenty bucks on the table says you've been celibate for the last year." *There.* It was gone faster than a flash, but for that quarter of a millisecond he caught something in her eyes. Never mind the big talk and the long, gorgeous hair and all that sensuality reeking from her. She *had* been celibate.

"For all you know," she said, "I'm happily married and have been having sex three times a day with my darling."

"Yeah? So, are you married?"

She rolled her eyes with exasperation. "No, I'm not married—but for all you know I sleep with ten men a week—not that it matters either way. How on earth did we wander so far from the point? And the point, Fox, is whether you would or wouldn't like another head rub. You've got another bad headache coming on, don't you."

Hell. He not only had a bad headache coming on; the buildup felt like the mother of all earthquakes warming up in his skull. But for an instant he'd almost forgotten. He'd almost forgotten his head, his injuries, his depression. That he was standing there naked except for a towel. That his brother was right behind her. That the life he'd once known seemed to have clicked its heels and taken off for Kansas, because he didn't recognize himself or his life anymore.

She'd distracted him. Something about her seemed to reach in him like no one else had in a blue moon—and it shook him up good. He dropped the teasing tone and said quietly, "You're right. I've got another headache coming on. But

I don't need anyone's help to handle it." And without skipping a beat he turned to his brother. "Bear, leave her *alone*."

He wasn't exactly sure where that directive came from, except that both his brothers seemed unusually taken with Phoebe—not that he cared. But he just kept getting some instinct that she wasn't as tough and full of pepper as she let on. On that first night she'd said something like, "Fox, I'm nobody. Nobody you need to worry about"—as if she thought of herself as no one consequential—and it had gnawed in his memory ever since. How ridiculous was that?

Hell, the thought that she needed protecting—that he could even consider himself a protector—boggled his mind. And his mind was already too damned shredded to need any more boggling.

Without another word he stalked down the hall to his bedroom, where he firmly closed the door. There was no lock, but there didn't need to be.

No one called after him. No one tried to get in. He figured his rudeness got through...which was exactly what needed to happen. Fergus knew his brothers meant well. He knew his brothers were trying to help him—including their bringing in that little redhead.

He didn't mean to—or like—taking his surliness out on her, but something about Phoebe really bugged him. Really, really got to him. The problem was weird and unsettling...but not complicated.

All he had to do was stay away from her. Piece of cake.

Phoebe barely glanced up at the rap on her door. Saturday mornings half the neighborhood popped over—a tradition she'd started when she first moved here, stemming from a trick her mom had taught her. She set a fresh-baked almond cinnamon coffee cake on the porch to cool.

That was it. The whole trick. Even the meanest neighbor or the shyest stranger couldn't seem to resist the smell. Which was all well and good, but usually the group waited until eight before showing up. Her hair was still down, her feet still bare, her terry cloth shorts and tee on the ragged side of decent, when Gary stuck his head in.

"Hey, Phoebe."

"Hey, you. Mary still sleeping in?"

"Yeah. It was the same when she was pregnant before. Sleeps like the dead." He ambled over, plucked a fresh piece of coffee cake, no plate, no napkin, and then chose a place to sprawl. Her other neighbor, Fred, had already settled at the head of the table. Traditionally he galloped over with his walker at the first smell coming out of the oven.

"You're going to burn your fingers," she warned Gary.

"And this is news how?" The mutts immediately took root on laps—one on Fred's, one on Gary's.

Phoebe poured the boys coffee, but then went back to the counter where she was slicing a grapefruit. Her cooking specialty was the almond cinnamon coffee cake—and not that she was bragging, but it was even better than her mother's, and her mom's was the best in the universe. Unfortunately and ironically, she seemed to be a grapefruit addict herself— for which the neighbors teased her mercilessly.

The back door whooshed open again. "Hi, sweetie," Barb greeted her. Within seconds she was battling with Gary for the coffee cake spatula. "Give it. My God, you guys already leveled a coffee cake on your own. How could you be so greedy?"

Phoebe ignored the fight and concentrated on her grapefruit. Her neighbors, thank God, could take anyone's mind off their troubles. It was the first time in days she hadn't thought about Fergus.

Barb seemed to relish the role of the neighborhood bawd. Even this early on a Saturday, she was wearing a low-dipping top, slick spandex pants, and a full arsenal of makeup. She'd been married to a plastic surgeon. It showed.

"So what's new around here?" Barbara won the coffee cake piece she wanted, sashayed over to the coffee and then went prowling down the hall carrying her cup.

"Nothing," Phoebe answered.

"Oh, yes, there is. I'll find it. You're always doing something new around here." A moment later Barbara called back, "I'll be damned. You cleaned."

"I did not." Phoebe was offended she'd been accused of such a thing.

"You did. There's no dust."

She'd only cleaned because she was worried about that damned man. That wasn't the same as compulsive cleaning, now, was it? It was just something to do at two in the morning when she was pacing around, fretting whether that rock-headed jerk was in pain and alone. Before she could invent a respectable reason for the lack of mess and dust, though, Barbara let out a shriek from far down the hall.

"Oh, my God, what kind of gigantic construction project have you got going on in here?"

"What, what?" That got both Fred and Gary out of their chairs, Fred leading the charge with his walker through the house.

Phoebe sighed mightily and traipsed after them. It confounded her how such a private person—such as herself—

could end up with such nosy neighbors. They seemed end-lessly fascinated by everything she did to the house, partly because they thought she was unconventional and artistic.

That was hooey. Reality was that she'd only bought the house because she couldn't find a rental that worked for her setup, and the only house she could swing had to be a major fixer-upper. The location was unbeatable, three blocks off Main Street, so it was an easy walk for customers. The struc-ture was a basic two-story saltbox built in the sixties. There were balconies on both floors and no termites—those were the positives.

Then came the fixer-upper part. The windows hadn't been caulked in a decade; the drive could have starred in a jungle movie, and the yard resembled a wildlife sanctuary. When she tried selling her neighbors the sanctuary theory, though, someone loaned her a lawn mower. Pretty clear what the neighborhood standard was, and weedy wasn't it.

The neighbors were more fascinated by what she did with the inside. From the beginning she realized the house was going to suck in millions to make it habitable—only she didn't have millions. Cripes, she didn't even have furniture. So she'd headed for Home Depot and bought paint. Lots of paint.

The kitchen cabinets were mint green, the walls a bright blue. Beyond the kitchen was a dining room she'd turned into an office, and painted those walls a light lavender. An arched doorway led into a long narrow vanilla-yellow living room. All in all, the downstairs pretty much covered every possible ice cream cone color.

In some rooms, she even had furniture now.

In the back of the house, where Barb hustled the breakfasters, was her business. Customers—usually moms—entered from the back door.

A bathroom and curtained-off changing area took up the north wall; the massage center dominated the room's center. The counters, sink, stand-alone tub and massage tables were all white—not shiny, in-your-face white, but an ultra-soft clean white.

All, that is, except for one corner, where dusty bags of cement, heaped stacks of stones and long boxes of plumbing parts looked as out of place as mud in a hospital. Further, the sledgehammer in front of it at all was almost bigger than she was. She may have overbought there, just a tad.

"What in God's name have you gotten yourself into, girl?" Gary questioned, hands on hips.

Phoebe was still carrying her bowl of grapefruit. It was impossible to explain that once she'd cleaned the place stem to stern—even the windows—she still couldn't get her mind off the damn man. He was hurting, she just knew it. Not letting anyone help him, she knew that, too. But it wasn't her problem—and wasn't going to be her problem—so she'd searched for a project that would force her to think about something else.

"I'm going to build a waterfall," she told the group.

"A waterfall," Barb repeated. "Honey, you barely have a pot to pee in, and you give away half of what you do have. And you're going to build a waterfall? Inside the house?"

"Now wait. Just wait. It's not as impossible as it sounds. I saw it in a magazine…" And then she mentally pictured it. The south corner of this room really had nothing in it, so there's where she wanted it—a sensual, warm, indoor waterfall at shower height, leading to a small pool surrounded by tropical plants. "If I used tile inside, stone outside, it would look almost like the real thing. And I could use it with the babies, either by sitting in there by myself, or just have the parent sit with their little one. It wouldn't be too different from a hot tub, just more…sensual. And natural. And restful."

Gary and Fred took one look at the bags of cement and piles of stones and started guffawing.

"Hey. It can't be that hard to find a mason who can show me how to mortar in the stones. And I figured the pipes for the sink are already here, so there has to be some way to tap into them for the water source. I mean, I know it'll take some work—"

"Some work?" Gary hooted. "You're going to need a crew of fifty to pull this off!"

"So, it'll take a lot of work. But I really think it's a practical idea—" Since that sent Gary and Barb into new gales of laughter, she appealed to Fred. "Don't you think it'd be beautiful?"

"I think you're the prettiest thing this neighborhood has seen in decades, sugar. And if you want to build yourself a waterfall, then that's what you should do."

But then he caught Gary's eye, and the two of them started cackling all over again.

At that precise moment she spotted the man in the doorway—not *any* man, but Fergus. Her Fergus Lockwood. He had his arm raised in a fist, as if he'd been knocking and was going to try yet again to gain someone's attention.

The pups spotted him first and beelined straight for the newcomer. Her neighbors all spun around and gaped, then gaped back at Phoebe, then offered hellos and we're just

Phoebe's neighbors and everybody was just leaving—although no one left.

Phoebe dropped her bowl of grapefruit. The bowl cracked. The grapefruit skittered across the tile floor, leaving seeds and grapefruit juice in its wake. Obviously the world as she knew it hadn't suddenly ended, yet, for just a few seconds she couldn't seem to move. Her heart went woosh, the way it had a nasty tendency to do around Fox the other two times she'd been near him—only it was worse this time.

It was all his fault she'd come up with this ridiculously impossible waterfall idea. All his fault she'd cleaned house. It was the woosh thing. His brothers were adorable, so at least if they caused that thigh-clenching heart-thumping response, she'd have understood it. She recognized those guys as hot, but not a problem.

Why did she only feel that woosh and zing for the wrong guys? And, darn it, one short glance at his long, lean bones and her hormones were all a dazzle. Where was the fairness in life? The justice?

"Phoebe? I didn't mean to barge in, but the bell didn't seem to work, and no one seemed to hear me knocking. When I heard all the voices, I—"

"It's okay," she said swiftly, and zoomed forward—almost putting her bare foot in the broken porcelain but getting smart at the last second. A little smart, anyway. "These are my neighbors—Barb, Gary, Fred, this is Fergus—"

"We're leaving," Barb said again, as she pumped his hand. Fergus went rigid.

Phoebe saw his response and recognized that he was hurting. Thankfully that slapped a little sense in her head. "Y'all can take the rest of the coffee cake on your way out. And I'll catch up with you later," she said firmly.

It took a minute to clear them out, clean up the broken bowl, have a heart attack because she'd had no chance to brush her hair or put on makeup or real clothes, get Mop and Duster to quit behaving like puppies on speed, and then get back to him.

He was still standing exactly where she'd left him, looking around her massage room setup. "Phoebe, I really am sorry about interrupting you."

"You didn't. That was just a Saturday-morning neighborhood free-for-all. They eat me out of house and home. What's wrong?"

He answered her slowly, quietly, his gaze directly on hers. "I was rude before. I wanted to apologize. When I go through one of my bad pain stretches, I can't seem to…think. My foot was so deep in my mouth, I'm amazed I could even get it out again. I'm sorry if I hurt your feelings."

"You didn't. And it's not a worry. I understand about pain." She cocked her head curiously. "But you could have called to say you were sorry. Instead…you're here."

He tugged on an ear. "Yeah, well. Nothing I tried ever helped those headaches. You did. And if you'd consider taking me and my sometimes big mouth on as a client, I'd appreciate it."

He obviously hated eating crow. She couldn't very well hold a grudge when she hated sucking up after making a mistake herself. "I take it you're having one of those headaches right now?"

"I've got one coming," he admitted. "But that's not why I came now. The headache isn't that bad. And I didn't expect you'd be working on Saturdays. I just came to apologize, and I figured Saturday morning you might not have clients, so it'd be a good time to ask if you'd consider taking me on down the pike—"

Before he could finish, she said, "All right."

"All right, you'll take me on?"

"Yes. If we can come to terms." She perched up on a counter and crossed her bare feet. "If you want me to work with you, Fergus, my idea would be to sit down together with a whole program. Not just deal with those headaches when they're tearing you in two, because that timing is way too late. You need to practice some techniques to make them go away for the long term."

"Like what techniques? What kind of program?" he asked warily, but her attention was diverted when she saw him starting to sway.

"Strip down," she said swiftly.

"Beg your pardon?"

"You're on my turf now, Fox. Go behind the curtain, strip down—I don't care if you keep on your underwear or go buff—but take off most of your clothes. I need two minutes to heat the sheet and prepare. When you're done, come back in here, get on the table, cover up."

"I—"

"Do it," she ordered him.

She wasn't going to think about it—about how or why he rang her chimes. Or about that stupid euphoric feeling she got around him, either.

It had cost him to come here, particularly for a man who had a hard time leaving the house these days. And though he may not have been in serious pain when he started out, he was obviously getting more miserable by the minute. She kicked her speed up to high gear. The pups were sent outside, the phone put on no-ring. The massage table was automatically dressed with a clean white pad, but it was baby-size. She scouted out an adult one, then threw a sheet in the dryer to heat on high for a few minutes.

Minutes before, she'd worried about looking like something a cat wouldn't drag home, but any thought of vanity disappeared now. Impatiently she pushed up her long hair, twisting and clipping it, while she considered which oils she wanted. She decided on lemon balm, sweet marjoram and calendula. She clicked on the CD, then strategically placed several small towels where they'd cushion his neck, the small of his back, under his knees.

She heard him cough—and easily guessed he was on the other side of the dressing room curtain, ready, just not sure what to do next. She didn't look up, just said, "Climb on the table and lie down on your back. I'm going to pull the shades, darken the room so it won't be so bright, Fox. There's a cover you can pull on, if you're too cool."

She used her bossiest voice, yet she still momentarily held her breath, unsure if he'd try giving her a hard time. But he said nothing. Once he settled on the table, she turned around and immediately smoothed a cool compress on his forehead and eyes until she finished setting up. On the CD player she clicked on madrigals. She'd never liked that kind of music, but this wasn't about her. Somehow even the most rowdiest babies seem to quiet down when she used that disc.

The details were done, then, and once she moved behind his head, she concentrated as fiercely as a brain surgeon. This was work. It wasn't about *him;* it wasn't about sex; it wasn't about analyzing why such a scrawny, stubborn, contrary man put such an impossible zing in her pulse.

It was just about a man who was hurting…and about her, hoping to find a way to help him.

She worked for fifteen solid minutes, but his headache was almost as stubborn as he was. He just couldn't seem to relax. The pain had a grip on him with wolf teeth. She leaned forward, closing her eyes, feeling his heartbeat, feeling the heat of his skin, feeling his pain…and then going for it. Temples. Eyes. Frontal lobe. The sides of his neck, under his chin, his whole face. Then into his scalp.

Two minutes passed. Then five. Seven more minutes passed before he even started letting go…but then he was hers. Her heart suddenly quickened with a rhythm she couldn't shake. She never got that feeling with her babies. Never got it with her elderly clients. Touch was sensual and healing and fulfilling, and she needed—liked—to help people. But it wasn't sexual.

It was so, so sexual with him. Intuiting where to touch, how to move, wasn't just about evaluating his pain. It was about sensing what he wanted. What he liked. What moved him.

Even though the pain finally eased, he didn't open his eyes for a long time. Silently she pulled up the sides on the massage table so he wouldn't accidentally fall, but still she stood there, knowing he wasn't totally asleep yet. His body fought sleep, naturally wary that if he let go completely, the pain could steal up on him again.

At one point he murmured, "I just want you to know…I'm not marrying anyone. But if I were…it'd be you."

"Yeah, yeah, that's what all the guys say," she quipped easily, but her voice was still a careful whisper.

He fell silent again, but not for long enough. "I almost forgot. You warned me before about all those men you have in your life."

She hadn't warned him. She'd just said what he was undoubtedly already thinking because of her being a masseuse, but she let it go. Seconds ticked by. Then minutes. Finally his breathing turned deep and even. She watched his chest rise and fall, watched the thick furrow between his brows smooth out, watched those tightly muscled shoulders finally ease completely.

The idle thought sneaked into her mind that this had to be the craziest thing that had ever happened to her. The guy hadn't touched her. In any way. She was the only one who'd done the touching. Yet she was somehow more drawn to him than any other man she could remember.

It was downright scary having to worry that she was losing her mind this young.

And it was scarier yet to realize that this fierce, wonderful pull she had for Fox was so dead wrong. He was a man whose wealth and background was bound to make him look down on her and her profession, a man who had shown no interest in her. A man as inappropriate for her as Alan had been. A man who had the potential to hurt her, she feared, even deeper than Alan had.

Four

The dream stirred Fox into waking. In the dream a sizzling-hot sun fried his back—just like every other day. For months he'd wondered if that incessant sun had ever driven anyone mad. Yet he wanted to be here. Wanted to do this.

The last few days, they'd been clearing debris, starting the work of rebuilding a school. It was more than good work. It was exactly the reason he'd felt driven to enlist. Back home the honor thing had bugged him. He couldn't teach kids history every day and discuss what it took to be a hero and an American without realizing that it was damn well time for him to actively show instead of tell. The other reason was the kids. Having the chance to rebuild hospitals and schools made him believe that his kids, his students, just might have a better world to grow up in.

And that was exactly why he didn't hesitate to crouch

down when the little brown-faced squirt shyly approached him. He offered the tyke some candy, a yoyo. He knew the language, which was partly why he'd ended up there. And the child with the big brown eyes and hollow cheeks looked hungry and desperate, as if somehow, some way, somebody had to do something to make his life better.

That the child had a bomb wrapped around his belly never crossed his mind. Never. Not for a second. Not even when it went off...and he was blown back a dozen yards, scissors and shards of God knows what spearing every surface on his body that wasn't covered by gear. And the kid, that damn kid, that damn damn damn baby of a kid...

And that's when Fox woke up. When he always woke up. But this time he was as disoriented as a priest in a brothel.

Something was really, really screwy.

This wasn't the leather couch where he always fell asleep. Instead he seemed to be lying on some kind of cushioned surface, wrapped in a soft warm sheet. Everything around him was saint white, except for a bunch of bosomy plants hanging in windows, spilling leaves and flowers in crowded tangles. For some goofy reason there was a bathtub in the middle of the room, and yet the far corner was heaped with stones and construction and plumbing parts. Goofier yet, his nostrils picked up the most wonderful smells—the sharp tang of lemon and a minty herb fragrance, and then another scent, something he couldn't quite identify, something vague and fresh and brisk and just a bit flowery....

Her.

The minute he turned his head, he saw Phoebe. As always when he woke after a crash-deep, crash-dark sleep, the headache was completely gone and his senses ultrasharp. He could feel every ache, every fading stitch and bruise.

He also promptly realized that he was naked as a jaybird under the sheet—and hard as a jackhammer. One look at her seemed to do it.

She was curled up in a white rocker. All the blinds in the room were drawn, except where she'd opened them several inches in the south window above her. Sunshine beamed down—as if just for her. Her bare legs were swung over the chair arm, and the shape of her naked calves was enough to inspire another jolt of testosterone. Her bare feet were dirty, and she was wearing what he called Saturday clothes, sweats, shorts and a big old voluminous shirt that completely concealed her body.

She held a mug of something steaming in one hand, a book in the other. He vaguely remembered her hair all pinned up and out of the way, but she'd let it loose at some point, because now those long red strands shimmied down her back like a gush of water, catching claret and cinnamon and tea and amber colors in the sunlight. The freckles on her nose were naked.

He wished she were.

He'd never met a more sensual woman. In looks, in touch, in everything. He felt both defensive and suspicious about that weird magic thing when she touched him. He just didn't get it…how she could possibly induce so much feeling in a guy who *didn't* feel, didn't talk, had cut himself off from life for months now—and wanted it that way.

But none of that aggravation seemed to dent his fascination for her. Fox conceded that the issue might be a lot simpler than he was making it. Probably any man'd have to be dead not to respond to a two hundred percent handful of a woman like her.

She startled, as if suddenly realizing something was different in the room. When she turned her head and saw he was awake, she immediately plunked down her mug.

"What time is it?" he asked her.

"Almost three."

Couldn't be. "You're *not* telling me I've been here all day."

"You were sleeping so soundly that I didn't want to wake you. And there was no need. I was just puttering around here. No clients on a Saturday."

"I'll pay you for the time I was here."

"Yeah, you will," she agreed. "But if you feel up to it, I'd like to ask you some questions." She pushed out of the rocking chair, came closer.

"What kind of questions?" he asked suspiciously.

"A massage shouldn't be able to dent the kind of serious headaches you're getting, Fergus. Migraines and cluster headaches and stuff that bad…they're medical. Physiological."

"Yeah, so I've been told." She was close enough to see the tent in the sheet, but she seemed to be looking straight in his eyes. He willed the mountain to wilt, but damned if it didn't seem to be getting harder instead of softer.

"It just doesn't make sense. That I've been able to help you with headaches as bad as you get them. Do you have any idea at all about what brings them on?"

He closed his eyes, opened them again. "The docs said, after ruling out a bunch of medical reasons, that the headaches had to be some kind of stress response."

"Stress I can work with you on."

"Work with me," he echoed.

"I mentioned it earlier. I'll work up a program, then send it over to you and your family, so you can look at it on your own time, see if you're willing to give it a shot. The thing is, what we're doing now is shutting the barn door after the horse is already loose. Trying to beat pain when it's already sucked you under is like trying to reason with an enemy who's already won. What you want, ideally, is to get power over the pain ahead of time. Before it's gotten bad."

"Okay. Makes sense." He was unsure why she sounded so tentative and wary. He hadn't been very nice to her, no. But there was something in her voice, her face, as if she were braced for him to dismiss anything she said.

Again she said carefully, "That's all I can really do. Teach you some techniques to work with stress and pain. I can also give you some strength- and stamina-building exercises, both to help give you some ammunition against the pain and to help you sleep better."

"That's a joke. I don't sleep." He also wasn't usually this chatty, but damn it, the more she looked at him with those big, soft, blue eyes, the more his hormones felt giddy with wonder. Goofy, but there it was.

To slap some reality into his head, he tried to move. She didn't leap to help him, just watched him struggle to push himself into a sitting position. It took forever, which royally ticked him off. He'd had it with the recovery business in every way. Eventually, keeping the sheet bunched around his waist, he managed to angle his long hairy legs over the side and sit up straight.

"Fox," she said quietly, "could you give me a bigger picture here? Your life isn't my business, I realize, but it'd still help if I understood more about what you normally do, what you want to do. Your brothers filled me in a little. They said that you left a full-time job to join the military. That you got a military discharge from the service—so that's off the table now. That you're only temporarily living in the bachelor house, close to family, until you're fully recovered."

"So far you're dealing aces."

"Okay, but what's the rest of the story? Are you planning on living in Gold River long-term? Planning on going back to work soon, and if so, what kind of work? What kind of physical activities or hobbies do you normally do or want to do?"

He scraped a hand through his hair. There was a smell on his skin, in his hair, all around him. A softness. That lemon balm scent thing. It wasn't exactly girly, but it sure as hell didn't go with hairy legs and a torso full of jagged scars.

"Before I joined the service, I was a teacher. A history teacher." At her look of surprise, he said, "Yeah, I get that same look from everyone. My brothers chose businesses that make money hand over fist, and somehow I elected for the do-gooder career. Anyway. I taught middle school. The hellion ages, when the kids are all dripping hormones and getting big mouths and give their teachers grief nonstop. Teaching was kind of like juggling dynamite every day. Probably why it appealed."

"So…are you hoping to go back to teaching this fall?"

"I'm never going back to teaching," he said curtly. "Do you answer questions, too, or just ask them?"

She blinked. "What do you want to know?"

"How you happen to be living in Gold River."

"I'd been doing physical therapy work for a hospital. I liked the work, but there came a point when I wanted to concentrate on babies—and I wanted to work independently, make my own business. So I started the *Baby Love* massage thing. And I just like it here. The town, the people, everything."

"Originally you came from—?"

"Asheville."

"And where's the guy in this picture?"

"What guy?"

"That's what I'm asking. You left Asheville for a small town like this, there was a guy involved," he said with certainty.

"Okay," she said cheerfully, and whipped around. "You're obviously feeling better. I've got groceries to buy, dogs to run, and I'm going to the movies with friends tonight. So, I'll let you get dressed in some privacy so you can take off. I'll drop a program plan at your place. Then you can call if you decide it's something you want to do...."

He didn't know he was going to do it. Ease off the table, twist the sheet around his waist toga fashion and go after her. It wasn't as if she charged out of the room at gallop speed. He easily caught up with her by the hall, looped his hand around her wrist.

She startled at the contact, turned her head.

Fox was aggravated at that moment. It wasn't a rational feeling, just an awareness that something was...out of kilter. She gave off heavy, warm caring vibes one second...and bristly defensiveness the next. She wasn't his problem, so her being confusing shouldn't matter. But it did. Somehow it did. There was something building between them...like ashes that could turn into white-hot coals if they were stirred.

He couldn't pin down his own intentions. Somewhere, though, he'd started worrying that she had feelings for him. Sexual feelings. Real feelings. And that couldn't be, because for now and the whole indefinite future he was in no shape to care for anyone. So maybe he intended on scaring her. Or annoying her. Hell, who knew? He hadn't had a functioning brain in a blue moon.

He just knew when he touched her arm, when she whipped toward him, when he saw the look in her eyes…that he was going to kiss her.

That she knew a kiss was coming.

And then…

Then he just did it.

Took that soft, crushable, sexy mouth.

Who could guess he'd set off an explosion? Maybe she hadn't been kissed in a while. Maybe her body was going through some kind of hormone overdrive. Maybe she really did like him—well, that last theory didn't seem likely. The Lockwood men used to be women magnets, himself included, but he'd thrown out any ability to charm when he'd taken on a body full of scars.

But damn.

She *did* seem to be igniting for him, even if he couldn't explain it.

Her skillful, sensual hands slid up, looped around his neck, clung. That mouth molded under his, melted under his, moved under his, communicating yearning and longing. Communicating desire. Her tongue suddenly whispered against his. Her soft, full breasts suddenly ached against his chest. Her throat suddenly let out a sweet bleat of helplessness.

The sheet wrapped around his waist gave up fighting gravity and fell to the floor in a woosh. He knew he'd never manage to stand upright long—not just because his injured leg lacked strength—but because all the oxygen in his head had dropped heavier than thunder to below his waist.

His hands framed her face, holding her still as he grappled to understand how a single kiss could become Armageddon. He tried another kiss to find out, since the first one only raised giant-size questions and answered absolutely none. After that he took her mouth a third time, his reasons getting fuzzier. But the silky soft exploration of her lips and tongue and teeth seemed totally necessary. It wasn't that he was looking for trouble…

His conscience nicked him for the fib. All right, all right, he was looking for a *little* trouble. He'd righteously ducked away from thinking about women since his injuries, telling himself that love—and sex—simply had to be taken off his table indefinitely. How was he supposed to know that deprivation had been haunting him? Or that he'd been *damn* worried about whether his body was still able to function normally.

It was.

Charlie, let loose, wagged around like a happy puppy tail, poking and pressing against her abdomen with uninhibited enthusiasm. Phoebe was short. Impossibly short. If he'd just had the strength, he could have lifted her, but as it was, his body creaked and groaned the longer he leaned down, crunching his neck, his spine.

The pain nagged at him, but only like a pesky mosquito. Tasting her, touching her, sipping her, made him feel like a man who was offered a drink of cool, clear water after weeks in the desert. She was so like water, liquid, flowing around him, her kisses drowning the drumbeat in his ears, his head. He immersed himself.

There was no wasting time dipping his foot in the water to test the temperature. He dove straight in, all of him engaged, mouth, elbows, brain, heart—and for damn sure, Charlie. It wasn't as if he were the only one acting insane.

She kissed him back and kept kissing him back. Her throat kept making those yearning, lonesome sounds. Her breasts kept tightening, swaying toward him, into him. Her soft hands held on as if she'd fall if he let her go.

Okay. Fox finally got it. What the deal was.

She wasn't real. She wasn't normal. She was a witch. A conjurer of men's fantasies. Real women just didn't respond to a guy like this—as if she wanted him to do anything he wanted, as if all her inhibitions blew away when he touched her, as if he were the hottest, sexiest guy ever born. As if she'd never lived until he touched her.

Fox remembered that whole fantasy from when he was sixteen. That's how he daydreamed it'd be with a girl—but then of course he grew up. Real women took manners. Real women took finesse and care to ignite. They had to know a guy before they could trust him, and it took serious trust for sex to be good. Well—any sex was better than no sex. But the best stuff was worth taking the time to do right.

With her it was as if someone had created her only for him. She knew just how to taste. Just how to sound. Just how to touch to make his world go dizzy and his mind go daft.

It was so weird. He'd been weak as a kitten for months, yet suddenly he felt powerful enough to move a couple of mountains. For a long, black time, he'd shut off emotion, yet this damned impossible redhead had him thinking about love again. About waking up next to somebody. About being able to weave his fingers through that, long, long silky red hair every night, any night.

"Hey."

It seemed to be his voice, coming out thicker than molasses, interrupting them. Not hers. He lifted his head. She didn't lift hers. He was the one stuck doing the honorable thing and inserting a little sanity into this madness. Where the Sam Hill was her common sense? She was giving him five million *yes* signals. It was the middle of a Saturday afternoon, for Pete's sake. Her dogs were sitting there with cocked heads as if they were trying to comprehend the totally strange behavior of the humans. The sun was beating in like a benediction. He was hurting. And God knew, pain wasn't new, but he hadn't experienced hurt coming from massive sexual frustration until two minutes ago.

"What's going on here?" he demanded lowly.

"Huh? Weren't you the one who suddenly came on to me?"

"But you didn't stop me."

"Like that makes you less guilty for starting this?"

"No. It just makes me completely confused about why you let me kiss you. And why you kissed me back." He couldn't take his eyes off her. Her cheeks were punched with color, her eyes hectic bright. Her hair had been tumbled before, but man, now he'd really made a wreck.

Had she been this breathtaking the first time he'd met her? How come he hadn't noticed it then?

She averted her eyes. "Fox…I feel bad for you. You've been through so much. And you're still going through a lot of pain."

"Ah…so the only reason you kissed me back is because you felt sorry for me?"

She wrapped her arms under her chest, tight. "I know…no guy wants to think that a woman pities him."

"You've got that right."

"But *pity* isn't the right word, Fergus…it's more like compassion."

"So this is all about compassion?" Fox wondered if she'd ever considered selling heaters in the Amazon.

She gave a little laugh. "Okay. There was more to it than that. I'll let you in on a problem I have."

"Sure."

"Guys often seem to think that I'm really into sex because I'm a masseuse. For me, that's been a real conundrum. Obviously, I care about people or I wouldn't have chosen this line of work. But when I touch someone as a masseuse—like I have been with you—it really is about compassion and nothing else. There's no sexual component at all."

Fox struggled to get his mind completely off Charlie. He sensed she was trying to tell him something serious, something critically important, but it was hard to concentrate past his hammering need and her handing out this total nonsense. "I'm not sure what you mean here. Are you saying that you didn't feel anything sexual?"

"It's not personal," she assured him. "I'm just trying to be honest. I'm just not a very sexual person. I'm more maternal, I guess."

"Maternal," he echoed.

She nodded vigorously. "Which is why I work with babies."

"Because you're maternal but not sexual."

"Exactly," she said.

* * *

Wednesday evening Fox still couldn't get that conversation out of his mind. He picked up a glass of water, yet quickly forgot to drink, forgot the buzz of his brothers' conversation in the next room, forgot the homemade lasagna steaming as his mom lifted it from the oven.

What on earth had Phoebe been trying to sell him? That she didn't like sex? That she wasn't a sexual being? That she was just into compassion? Was he supposed to just nod his head and say, oh, sure, horses fly?

Memories kept swirling back. Except for mouth-to-mouth kisses, he'd barely touched her in any intimate way…yet he felt as if he had. And even though he'd been stark naked, she'd only physically touched him above the neck—yet she seemed to touch every emotional chord and hormone he'd ever owned.

So.

He'd already figured out that she was a frightening woman. Unsettling. Unnerving. Unfathomable.

But unsexy?

How could Phoebe conceivably believe that about herself? Why would she want to?

"Fergus, would you pay attention," his mother said irritably.

Fox mentally jerked himself awake, but still knew that this was a precise measure of what a mess that woman had made of him. His mother was right here, carrying her world-famous lasagna, and yet all he could think about was sex and Phoebe.

That was power.

No wonder he was scared of her.

"I was listening," he assured his mother. His brothers loped into the kitchen, undoubtedly driven by the same addictive smell of the gourmet dish.

"I was just trying to tell your youngest brother," his mother said to Bear and Moose, "that people with means simply don't teach school. And since he doesn't seem inclined to teach again, this is an ideal opportunity to reconsider other career choices."

"Okay," Fox said patiently, "what is it you think would be a better career than teaching?"

His mom's eyes lit up, thrilled to be asked. Bear and Moose took the far chairs and slunk down low and quiet. They'd been in the hot seat. They didn't like it. It didn't get better with age. "Something that involves making serious money. And more participation in the community."

"Well, actually, Mom, I make a ton of money. I've been investing for years." Fox shot his brothers a look. How fast the traitors dove into the lasagna. Next time *you* need help, I'll be in Tahiti. "And as far as participating in the community, I'm working directly with kids. Or I was. How else could I possibly participate more productively?"

"You could be a senator," his mother said firmly.

"You would wish that on me? A life in politics?" He added, *"No."*

"Well then…if you haven't got any other plans on the burner, *are* you thinking about teaching this coming fall? As far as I know you still have an active contract, don't you?"

God, she was sly. Other moms were, well, sweet. His was trickier than a con artist. She wanted him to rejoin life again. She wanted him to care about work and life and himself again. Except that even for his mother—and God knew he loved her—he couldn't imagine going back into a classroom.

When he failed to answer, Georgia Lockwood pounced on the reason they were all together. "Furthermore, you haven't told me anything about this woman Bear and Moose keep talking about. I don't understand why she's coming here, and I don't understand why you're involved with her."

"She didn't have to come here. She just offered to explain the whole program thing to the family. And I'm not involved with her."

His mother looked at him over the top of her delicate gold-wire rims. "Fergus, don't think I just fell off the turnip truck."

Neither brother, on the other side of the table, even breathed. They just kept shoveling in the lasagna. "Trust me, Mom. I never thought that."

"A masseuse." Georgia rolled her eyes. "Come *on*. I realize that you're an unmarried man, that you have…needs. People don't wait like they used to. I may not agree with how things have changed, but I can at least understand it. I would be perfectly happy to hear you have a young woman in your life on *any* basis."

"Mom—"

"I won't be judgmental. You don't have to ever worry about that."

"Mom—"

"I would like grandchildren. I admit it. None of you seems to be moving in that direction. I blame your father for making you all so independent and…rowdy." She sighed. "But never mind that. The point is in principle, I'd prefer grandchildren coming from a two-parent family and our last name—"

"Mom!"

"—however, if there's no other way I can get them, you can just bring them home in whatever form they come. I won't say a word. Not a word."

Fergus shot his brothers a look that would have fried an ice cube. They'd blackmailed him into this whole deal—setting him up with Phoebe, then conning him into being there when Phoebe presented this program thing. And now where were they? Taking in mom's lasagna like vultures but not helping him worth beans. "Mom, get it out of your head. She's *not* a date. Not anyone I'm seeing that way—"

Precisely at that moment they all whipped around at a knock on the door. And there was Phoebe—who'd obviously poked in her head when she couldn't rouse anyone's attention any other way. When she stepped in, shock numbed his tongue. She looked nine months pregnant.

A second later, of course, he realized that it wasn't her stomach, but something *on* her stomach making that huge lump. A baby. A real live baby. All swaddled in some kind of papoose carrier that was strapped to her tummy.

Fox recovered his breath and started to stand up and greet her, but never had the chance. His mother took one look at the baby and surged toward Phoebe like a human tidal wave, her eyes suddenly brighter than diamonds. "Well, you obviously have to be Phoebe! You didn't tell me she liked babies, Fox. Isn't that nice? Come right on in, dear, and I'll get you a plate. I'm Mrs. Lockwood, but you feel free to call me Georgia. If you don't want lasagna, could I talk you into some coffee or sweet tea? I was just telling the boys, how wonderful it was that you'd involved Fergus's whole family in this, um, program…"

Fox took one look at Phoebe's face and felt his heart sink. Her friendly smile looked forced and frozen. She must have heard what he said—about not being a date, not being anyone he was seeing. She'd probably even heard the deprecating comment his mom had said about masseuses. Hell and double hell. She had no way of knowing that he'd just been trying to divert his mother from giving her the third degree…and now, she ignored him completely as she walked in. She greeted his mother and then crossed the room to give each of his brothers a kiss.

His brothers.

Both of them.

Got the kisses.

Not him. She ignored him as if he were a puppy puddle.

"Why, no one told me you were bringing a baby, dear." Her mom descended on Phoebe as if a long-lost relative had suddenly shown up. So much for a prejudice against masseuses. Put a baby in the picture, and Georgia was now happy to treat Phoebe like a goddess.

"Actually, she isn't mine. But I work with babies, and I've got this one for the night. I didn't think anyone would mind if I brought her. I mean, I only needed a few minutes to—"

"Are you kidding? Of course it's all right that you brought her." More beaming smiles from Georgia. "So you work with babies, do you?" A fierce look at her three boys. "No one told me that, either. Sit down, sit down."

Phoebe shot him a look then, but what that flash-gash of a look was supposed to mean, he didn't have a clue. A knife suddenly ripped into his side. It had started this morning. Another teensy bomb part, working to the surface, this one above the kidney on the right side. He could see it under the skin. Metallic. Small. In a day or two, it'd wedge to the surface, break through, and then he could try plucking it out like a sliver. But right now, it just plain hurt.

Which ticked him off. He didn't have time for any damn

fool weakness right now. He needed to look normal. He needed to be normal. It was one thing for his family to pester him and another for them to pester Phoebe.

"...baby's name is Christine," Phoebe was saying to his mom. By then she'd been settled in the kitchen rocker and looked like a mythic earth mother, with her arms loosely cuddling the snoozing baby on her stomach. "She was brought to the hospital several days ago. Abandoned, somewhere in the mountains. She'll go into the system—in fact, there's a foster mom already waiting for her. But I've been working with Social Services for a while now on babies like this."

"You mean, baby-sitting them?"

"No, not baby-sitting exactly. More providing a kind of interim care before they're placed in a normal home situation. Abandoned or neglected babies often fail to thrive or fail to bond or both. If they've been hurt that young, they develop an instinctive fear of touch. So I do touch therapy. Love therapy, the social worker calls it—"

"Oh, I love that term," Georgia said delightedly. "What exactly is involved?"

"Different things, really, because every baby's different. But in Christine's case, we're doing what I call a connecting technique. Except for eight hours at night—when I've got an aide to take over—I'll literally keep her attached to me for a solid three days, either directly carried or in the front carrier like this."

"And you do this because?"

"Because we're not sure if she ever learned how to bond. This basically forces the human connection. A real foster or adoptive mom can't do this, of course, but if the ability to bond is there... Mrs. Lockwood, you don't have to go to all this trouble." Phoebe looked stunned at the sweet tea and fresh sugar cookies and apple slices and lasagna being heaped on the table beside her.

"I'm fascinated," Georgia insisted. "In fact, I'd love to hear more. So you—"

Fox cleared his throat. It was nice that the two women were getting along, and that his mom had completely dropped the judgmental kick about Phoebe being a masseuse. But it looked as if the women could talk through the next millennium without coming up for air.

Phoebe immediately looked up at him. There was something...shifty in her eyes. "You're hurting, aren't you?"

Damn woman, kiss her a few times and she thought she knew everything. "No, but—"

"I know, I know. I came to talk about a program for you, and so far all I've done is tie up everyone's time." Phoebe gently rubbed the baby's back as she kept up a soft, steady rocking motion. "The reason I suggested your family listen to these ideas is so they could provide input. You may not go for this at all, Fox. But your family knows more about your health and life issues than I do. And we all need to be on the same team to figure out what motivates you."

Fox frowned. She sounded real sweet, real sincere. Her voice alone aroused every suspicious bone in his body. Something sneaky was coming. Something he didn't want to hear. He just knew it.

Five

Phoebe braced for an explosion. Judging from Fox's thundercloud expression, he definitely hadn't liked the idea that he needed to be motivated—much less that anyone had the power to do it. And if that teensy idea had him already bristling, the rest of her suggestions definitely weren't going to go over well at all.

Phoebe directed smiles at her allies—Bear and Moose and, for sure, Georgia. Fox's mom was adorable. Although her clothes were expensive, she was still wearing a tie-dyed shirt and jeans. And money or no money, she obviously still ruled the roost over her sons, as well.

Phoebe had suffered knots in her stomach when she first walked in here...because, yeah, she'd overhead Mrs. Lockwood's opinion of masseuses. Georgia didn't have a mean bone; she was just expressing the stereotypes Phoebe had heard a zillion times. Masseuses were fine, just not someone you'd want your son to marry. You were happy to go to them for a sore neck, but they made a living touching people, for heaven's sake, so naturally they were on the frayed hem side of respectability.

For two seconds it had hurt Phoebe to hear Fox and his mother talking—but that was foolish. It was one of the main reasons she'd wanted to include his family in Fox's health discussion—so he'd see how a man's mom was likely to treat her.

Christine let out a peep—a little breathy baby snore—and Phoebe rubbed and cuddled her. She'd also brought the baby deliberately. She could have asked her night sub to take over, but truthfully, she figured Fox seeing her with a baby would give him a big, fat, healthy jolt. Babies were a fabulous terror technique for bachelors. Just in case he'd harbored the idea of having wild, uninhibited sex with her, there was nothing like a baby to wilt the *W* right out of that wild. At least for men.

And for herself, she wanted to give up wild, uninhibited sex forever, anyway.

That embrace the other day was still haunting her mind. She simply had to give herself a slap upside the head. It was time to quit mooning over the darn guy and concentrate on her work. She didn't heal well from heartache. Ergo, she needed to stay away from guys who were especially likely to hurt her. Her attraction and pull toward Fox—toward yet another guy who wasn't likely to value or want her long-term—had to be put to bed. Pronto.

And tonight was a terrific chance to make sure he lost interest—assuming he ever had any.

"Okay, now," she addressed his mom and brothers, "these severe headaches Fox gets so regularly…"

"I'm right here," Fox mentioned.

"Uh-huh. They're not exactly migraines or cluster headaches—they couldn't be or I wouldn't be able to dent them with the basic massage techniques I've been using. So we're talking the cause being stress, which one of Fox's doctors already suggested."

"Yeah," Bear and Moose both nodded from across the table.

"I kind of have an unusual view of stress because of my work with babies. In a sense, the babies are suffering from massive stress. They've either been deprived of touch or associate touch with pain—so much so that they've withdrawn from wanting contact. What I do with the babies is a kind of touch therapy to force them—gently—to accept touch. To try to get them to see human contact as something wonderful and helpful."

"I love what you do," Georgia enthused, looking as if she wanted to launch into another round of conversations about babies. Phoebe persevered.

"From everything I've seen…Fox is actually suffering from the same kind of stress. He was hurt. So to protect himself, he's withdrawn. In a way, his headaches function to protect him. So does the rest of his behavior. If he stays in the house, holes up, allows the headaches, he's essentially put himself in a position where he can't be exposed to more pain. You get the concept?"

"Sure," Bear said.

Moose hesitated. "Well, I sure don't. You mean he feels safer if he's hurting? Like those headaches of his are a choice?"

"No. God, no. No one would volunteer for those awful headaches—and all his other injuries are real, besides. But when an animal is hurt, he holes up in his den, right? He rests. He stays away from risk until he's able to handle it again."

"Yeah, I totally get that," Moose said.

"So. Now we have to get Fox out of his den. We have to motivate him to want to get out—which means that we want to supervise his exposure to pleasant and nonrisky experiences."

"Okay, okay, this was cute for a couple of minutes," Fox said irritably. "But enough's enough. I'm not one of your babies. I don't need someone to give me 'pleasant' experiences. I'm not an animal holing up in a den. Phoebe, if you've got some program you want me to do, talk to me, not to them."

Phoebe deliberately tried to make herself sound like a teasing sister. "Now, I can't do that, darlin', because you'd just argue with me. Bear, Moose, I need you on my side if we're going to make this work. You, too, Mrs. Lockwood—"

"Oh, I'm all for whatever you suggest," Georgia said brightly. "This is exactly what Fox needs. To get out of the house, pick up his life again. He's been so depressed."

"I have *not* been depressed," Fox snarled.

The baby stirred again. Phoebe knew the infant would need feeding soon, so she pushed on. "Okay. This is the program. Two times a week I'll do bodywork on Fergus. Some of that'll be massage, concentrating on building strength and stamina. But I also want to teach him de-stress and relaxation techniques—before those headaches get the better of him."

"Sounds like a plan," Moose said.

"Then Moose, Bear…I'm counting on one of you to find the time to take him fishing once a week."

"Fishing?" Bear perked up.

"Fishing? How'd that get into this conversation?" Fergus said disbelievingly, and was ignored.

"I want him out of the house, outside somewhere. I know it's still pretty cold to go out on a boat, but I still like the idea because he couldn't just walk off, go home, you know? He'd have to sit there. And the sun and water could have a real shot at relaxing him."

"You got it. I'm your man," Bear said, and added, "in all the ways you want."

She chuckled at his innuendo. "Thanks, you sweetie. Then, Moose, if you could take him for one evening a week—"

"*Take* me. Like I need a baby-sitter?" Fox snapped.

She honestly didn't want to keep ignoring Fergus, but she still had information to cover, and the baby wasn't going to stay good forever. "Moose, I want Fox doing something stress free, but still something that requires him to get out of the bachelor house. So it'd be a good idea if he went to your place—or any other safe place that would force him out of his rut—"

"I'm sure as hell not in a rut," Fox informed the entire room.

"I was thinking…poker," Phoebe mused. "Something you could do with some guy friends? But if you brothers aren't into cards, I don't care what you choose to do. The point is just getting him out of his den."

"I'm on it," Moose agreed enthusiastically. "Phoebe, I think you're absolutely brilliant."

"I am," she agreed with a chuckle.

"You're not giving me anything to do!" Mrs. Lockwood wailed.

"That's because she's fired," Fox told his mother.

"Now, Fox. You can't fire me because I was never hired. This is just a program plan. Georgia, ideally I'd like you to spend two times a week with Fergus, making him cook."

"Making *him* cook? Instead of me cooking?" The idea was obviously new to Georgia.

"Yes. I want you to have the ingredients and the recipes for his favorite foods around. You do the food shopping so he isn't forced into public quite this fast. But make him do the cooking and preparing, whatever his favorites are. Just supervise. Do it with him."

"What a marvelous idea. Phoebe, it's easy to see why my boys are so in love with you."

Fox raised his hand. "One of your boys is not in love with her. In fact, one of your boys would like to take Phoebe in the backyard for a little personal discussion. No one needs to call the cops or worry if they hear screams. It'll just be me, killing her."

Phoebe refused to laugh, no matter how funny he was being. To his family she said, "I'd like to start this whole program immediately. I know it's late tonight, but I'd still like to take Fox over to my place…give him his first class in pain management." Finally she glanced at Fergus. "Unless you don't need any help with pain control tonight?"

She had him.

She knew she had him.

Something was hurting him. Bad. She knew it from his eyes, from the stiffness in his neck, from his surliness. He wasn't going to turn down help, not when he was this miserable, no matter how much he wanted to.

"I've still got Christine right now...." She patted the pink-blanketed baby again. "But if you'd head over to my place in a half hour or so, Fox, I'll be ready. I was expecting to keep the baby all night, but I have a night sub, Ruby, so it'll take me a few minutes to call her and set that up. After that..." She turned back to his family, not waiting for him to give her any more glares, grief or bologna. "You three can work out your schedules, how and when you can take Fox. But if it's amenable to everybody, I'll take him Thursday and Monday, late afternoon and evenings, all right?"

Bear and Moose heartily agreed, and a few minutes later they walked her out to the van, helping carry her stuff and approving all her ideas with exuberant thumps on the back. They treated her so easily as an honorary sister that Phoebe couldn't help loving them. They were so easy to be with.

So was their mom.

It was just Fergus who made her uneasy.

Just Fergus who itched all her nerves—and hormones, too.

But she'd gained on the problem, she thought tonight. Coming over to his mom's house to discuss the plan for Fergus's recovery had been totally the right thing to do. Meeting his mom, being with his brothers, had helped her get a grip on her emotions, put the whole problem of Fergus in perspective. She needed to stick with a goal she could handle. Helping Fox heal. If she didn't stray off that course, she couldn't possibly get in trouble.

By the time she left she was humming up a storm. Bear

and Moose kissed her cheek goodbye and left her with a chorus of "I love you, darlings" and "Take care of yourself" singing in her ears.

Fox was still scowling when his brothers came back in. He'd seen the guys walk her outside. Seen how their hands were all over her.

"I'm thinking about asking her out," Bear admitted.

"Whoa. I thought you were tight with that teacher in town. Heidi. What's-her-name."

"Yeah, she's nice. But there's no real spark, you know? She's as comfortable as chicken soup. Now, Phoebe, on the other hand—"

"If you don't ask her out, I am," Moose announced.

"Wait a minute." Fox didn't wonder why he was suffering from intense stress—and it had nothing to do with his injuries. Moose was the guy magnet in Gold River, had women climbing all over him—but those relationships never kept his attention more than a few months. Bear was the opposite. Bear was actually looking for a life mate. He'd done the wild oats, done the partying, was starting to look for someone to be with seriously. "Neither one of you is going to ask her out."

"Why?" Both of them asked, and damned if his mother wasn't peering over their shoulders, curious why they couldn't, either.

"Because," he said furiously.

They waited, gaping at him, but he'd said everything he had to say in that single word. And since his side was killing him, he felt completely justified in hightailing it out of there—after thanking his mother for dinner, of course.

He stumbled back to his place and started a shower, hid

under the hot spray, hoping his side would fix—it didn't—hoping the hot water would splash some sense in his head. Which it did. Sort of. He climbed out, pulled on a fresh sweatshirt and jeans and headed out.

He wasn't going to Phoebe's because *she'd* arranged the time, but because he needed to see her. Even if she was using witchcraft or ooga-booga and was a scary, scary woman, the reality still was that no one had fixed his headaches but her. There was nothing wrong with seeking her services.

The problem was that he needed to set up a fair payment schedule for her so they were totally on a business basis. And the other problem was…she bugged him.

In her driveway, Fox slammed the door of his RX 330. Damn woman. How could she possibly know enough about him to get under his skin? When it came down to it, what did she really know about him?

Nothing.

She was bossy. Domineering. Cute. Trouble by any man's definition.

Why did it have to be *her* that made the pain go away? Five million drugs out there, why couldn't one of them work? All the doctors and physical therapists and tests he'd been through and to—none of it had been worth spit. He'd stopped believing anything could help him

He stomped up her gravel drive, scowling at her place. Even in the dimming light, he could see the whole place needed repair. The lawn was a weedfest. A shingle hung crooked from the roof—and if he could see one, there had to be more. And, yeah, he'd seen the inside of her house earlier.

The wild color scheme inside had taken him aback initially…until he'd studied it, figured out what she was doing.

The colors were so striking and interesting that they drew the eye. You noticed the walls instead of what wasn't there, such as furniture. Carpeting. All the stuff that people filled rooms with.

It wasn't Fox's problem if she was living on a financial shoestring, but hell, the whole damn world was greedy today, so why couldn't she be? Instead she was feeding the neighborhood on Saturday mornings. Donating her time weekends, and on nonpaying customers—like him.

That kind of generosity was a disgusting character trait. Who could live with a saint like that?

He barged up to the front door, rapped hard enough to crack his knuckles and then waited. Hissing in air under his breath.

Only…then she opened the door. And there she was, fresh and barefoot, wearing something that looked like pajamas—kind of a pale green, made out of a fabric that made him think of a soft, snuggly rug. Her feet were bare, her hair looped up with some kind of wooden pin holding it together. There was no baby in sight or sound. Somewhere she'd switched a light on, but the light barely trailed as far as the entranceway, creating only enough illumination to make her skin look impossibly soft. Softer than moonshine. Softer than petals. Softer than silver. And then there was the other stuff. She was wearing colors and smells that soothed. Her bare mouth aroused him, so did those sassy-bright blue eyes.

Suddenly it was easy to remember that he was pissed off. He didn't waste time on hello, just went straight for the punch. "This isn't going to work."

She didn't waste time on hello, either. "Yeah it is. Or it can."

He started to walk toward her massage room, but she said swiftly, "Wait, Fox, we're going to the living room."

"Why?"

"Because we're not doing a massage. We're going to do an exercise to help you work with pain. Where is the pain, by the way? It's not a headache this time, is it."

She didn't phrase the comment like a question, which further ticked him off. Damn woman knew things about him that no one could know. "My side's giving me a little trouble. The left side. *Not* something you can help with, and not why I'm here." He aimed his trigger finger at her. "You used my family against me."

"Yup."

"That's unethical. Mean. Underhanded."

"It sure is," she agreed. "Whatever works, huh?"

He wasn't buying into that smile. Not this time. "Don't do it again. If I've got a problem, I solve it. I don't involve family or anyone else."

"Well, of course you don't, you're a grown man. But in this case, your family's pretty frantically worried about you. So now we've given them something to *do*. That may not help you, but it sure helped *them*. Think about it, Fox. I'll bet the bank they'll let up on the heavy-handed caring if they have a constructive way to feel they're helping you."

He thought about that and then scowled. "If you say one more wise thing, I may just put a fist through a wall. There's *nothing* more annoying than a woman who's always right."

"Got it. Heard it before. Let's move along." She motioned to the fluffy rug on the living room floor. "What I want you to do is sit down—any way you want, cross-legged, with a pillow, lying down, whatever's the most comfortable for you."

He sat. Both her pooches beelined for him the instant he

crossed his legs. He'd have scooped them onto his lap if she hadn't crooned, "Mop. Duster. Lie down."

She knelt down across from him—which gave him a binocular shot of the round swell of her breasts, the dip of white skin at her throat. Although her sweater was bulky, it *was* loose at the neck. He wondered if she really believed the cumbersome fabric concealed anything. He also wondered if she ever wore shoes, and how in God's name she'd found a pistachio color to paint her toenails. Her toes were damn near as cute as her—

"Fox," she repeated sternly.

"Pardon? I didn't hear you." He heard the courteous hint of apology in his voice and damned his mother for raising him to be polite to women. "Phoebe, I really didn't come here for any damn fool exercises. I came here to argue about—"

"I understand. You don't like me. You don't want to be here. You're ticked off that I've been able to work with your pain so far, when you'd rather not be asking help from anyone." She said all that smoothly and swiftly, as if to get it out of the way—and as if the damned woman had been reading his mind. "We can fight about all that later, though, can't we? Let's just get this exercise out of the way first. Then you can take all the time you want to rip me up one side and down the other. Take my hands, Fox."

He *knew* she wasn't coming onto him. There was absolutely nothing about her attitude or dress or expression that let on she even remembered the heat of those kisses a few days ago. But for an instant... Fergus mentally corrected himself. It wasn't even an *instant*. Maybe it was a milliinstant. Or a micromilli-instant. But for that micromillisecond of an instant, when she said "take my hands," the image whooshed through his mind of the taste of her mouth.

Of his touching her again.

Of her coming apart for him again.

Of him forgetting the whole damn world with her again.

Naturally that micromillifantasy was absurd and he immediately squelched it…only, it was already too late. The redheaded witch had done it to him again. Forced him to take her hands, forced him to close his eyes, and the next thing she knew, Charlie was stiff as a poker, and Phoebe was forcing him to do ludicrous things.

"Now, Fox…don't talk…don't think. I only want you to do one thing. Imagine. Put a picture in your mind…of the safest place you can possibly imagine. It's a place where nothing can hurt you. Where no one can hurt you. Where you have absolutely no fear of anything."

"Phoebe, I—"

"No. Don't talk. You can in a little bit, but right now—just for a couple minutes—I want you to do this with me. Concentrate. Concentrate with everything you are, on imagining a safe place in your mind." She waited. "Can you invent someplace like that? Imagine it? A place where you know you'd feel completely safe?"

"Yeah."

"Okay. Now keep that picture in your mind and explore it. Look up. Look down. In your mind, pretend you can smell the smells there, hear the sounds there. Know every part of it." She waited. "Are you doing that?"

"Yeah."

"I want you to feel how safe this place is."

"Okay, okay, I feel it." Eyes still closed, he scratched his knee, then stopped, because her voice was flowing over him like music.

"No one can touch you in this place. It's yours and yours alone. No one else has the same safe place you do. No one knows where your place is. And no one can ever take it away from you."

Her voice kept doing that hypnotizing thing—and, yeah, of course he figured out what she was doing. But that didn't seem to be able to stop him from putting this picture in his mind. The picture wasn't anything special. Just a rolling field, a meadow with wildflowers and tall sweet grasses, swaying in a spring wind. Aspens and poplars hemmed the far edge of the field, rustling and shivering in that same breeze. The sun beat down, softer than a balm and healing warm. A bird soared overhead. A fawn cavorted in the grasses. It was a bust-ing-gut happy kind of scene. Nothing hurt. For some crazy, totally insane reason, nothing hurt.

His eyes snapped open. And found Phoebe, still sitting cross-legged across from him, her eyes on his face, her smile on his smile, her scruffy pups snoozing on both sides of her. He said heavily, "This is beyond weird."

"What's weird?"

"Nothing hurts."

"That's great."

"No. You don't understand. I *mean* it. Nothing hurts. Even my *side* doesn't hurt."

"Great."

Before, Fergus thought he'd had enough. But now he'd had *enough*. "This is *not* funny. It's impossible. What'd you do to me?" he demanded suspiciously.

"You did it, not me, Fox. And the exercise won't always

work, but it's always worth a try. So when you feel stress or pain coming on, give it a shot. Go to your safe place."

"That's a pile of hooey," he informed her succinctly.

"Actually, Mr. Skeptic, it's not hooey at all. It's plain old physiology. When you feel pain or stress, your body tenses up. Those tense muscles and tendons essentially cause more pain—whereas when you feel safe, your blood pressure and heart rate both calm down. That helps your body loosen up. Which helps ease the pain. Any exercise that helps you relax would work the same way."

He understood what she was saying. He'd just quit believing in Santa Claus almost three decades ago. Determined to jolt himself back to sanity, he yanked up his sweatshirt on his right side to above his ribs. There, in plain sight, was the needle-size fragment that had been working its way to the surface of his skin for hours now. As Fergus well knew, there was pain and then there was pain. This wasn't bad pain. It was barely mentionable compared to the serious injuries he'd had. But it was what it was—an annoyance. It hurt just enough that he couldn't get it off his mind, the same way it was impossible to ignore a sharp sliver.

Phoebe sucked in her breath when she saw the injury. "What on—"

When he made to poke the spot, she grabbed his hand.

"Are you nuts, Fox? Don't touch that, for Pete's sake! It's an open sore!"

He was speaking to himself more than her. "I *can* still feel it. It's just…*damn.* You were right, Red. Who'd believe it? It's not gone, but it really is nothing compared to how much it was bothering me before."

"That's what I was trying to tell you. That 'safe place' exercise is one way to physically slow down your breathing and pulse. If you can do that, then you're always going to win some over pain. It's not a magic cure. But there are more exercises I can—" She gulped. "Look. Can I take that out? Or do you want to go to a doctor?"

He couldn't twist well enough to see the spot very well— but enough to notice the sliver had broken through the skin. "If you've got tweezers, I can deal with it."

She had tweezers. She had first-aid cream. She had red stuff to wash the spot. She kept him talking while she ran around, accumulating her little tray of supplies, making him explain about the dirty-bomb thing, how parts kept coming to the surface, how that was likely to happen for a while, how it wasn't the end of the world, just disconcerting, and occasionally…gross.

"It's not gross, Fox. That's ridiculous. It's just a sore. But how come no one ever tells us this kind of thing on CNN?"

"Beats me—what are you doing?" He was conscious that for all the touching she'd done to him before, she hadn't actually put her hands below his neck. Not on bare skin. And, yeah, she'd seen him bare that day in the shower, but it wasn't the same thing as having her eyes an inch away from his ribs. Her mouth, her eyes, her face, so close to his heartbeat. So close to his damned ugly scars. "Ouch," he said.

"Darn—did that hurt?" she asked cheerfully, and bent closer with the tweezers again. He could see all that wild, thick red hair of hers, but not her face just then, not the sore. And out of nowhere she suddenly started singing the national anthem.

He forgot the sensitive spot where she was probing. Anyone would. "My God. Is there a cat in heat in here?"

"Fox. This is one long sliver. Are you sure you don't want to go to the emergency room?"

"Hell, no. I can do it myself."

"No, you can't. You can't reach it on your own. It's too far under your arm. Okay, turn a little more this way." When he failed to, she picked up the lyrics. "…what so proudly we hailed…"

He used a cuss word. The big one. And promptly shifted his arm over his head promptly. "I heard you hum before. It was bad, but not this bad. I'll sit as still as you want if you just don't sing again, all right?"

"You promise not to move?"

"I'll promise anything. If you swear you won't sing again."

It was a weak attempt at humor. Very weak. So weak that suddenly neither of them was moving. Somewhere a pup was snoring. Somewhere a faucet was dripping. But the only thing he was really aware of was her face, inches from his. She was looking at him with this…expression. Of caring. And compassion. And something more. Something so gut personal, so intimate, so about her and him, that he couldn't seem to breathe for a whole long second.

And then she said, "It's gone, Fox."

"No, it isn't. It's there every damn time we're in the same room together. Every time you look at me. Every time I look at you."

"No. I mean…it's out."

"I wish I could believe that, but I swear to God, that feeling's coming after us like a freight train. Damn it, Phoebe. I'm not totally sure I planned to have sex again for the rest of my life. I came home not expecting to feel anything for the rest of my life. And then you came along."

"*Fox*. All I'm trying to tell you is that the long metal sliver is out!"

Oh. The sliver. But when he looked at her face again, that fierce, soft look of longing and desire and closeness was still there—real as moonlight. As real as the pulse drumming in her throat. As real as her parted lips.

Six

Phoebe saw him coming, saw him aiming for a kiss, and knew perfectly well he intended trouble—and not a little trouble, but a major-meltdown type of trouble. Yet she couldn't smack him. Not after having seen all those scars, all those healing wounds, all those hurts, so close up. She couldn't do anything to further hurt Fox. It was unthinkable.

Yet when her body bowed toward his—when her lips parted for his—it wasn't exactly because she *wanted* to kiss him. It was just that she recognized his soul needed healing far, far more than his body. And, of course, she had no power to heal his soul or anyone else's. But she couldn't be so mean as to reject Fox.

That was her excuse for kissing him as if she'd die without another taste.

It wasn't because she was a wanton, red-hot mama. It

wasn't because she let her senses rule her sense. It wasn't because she was the kind of woman who'd kick out her morals when a guy turned her on. Phoebe wasn't worried about all those insinuations Alan had implied about her character. She wasn't.

She didn't have time to worry about nonsense like that just then. Her brain was scrambling too hard trying to figure out how to tactfully, carefully, extricate herself from Fox without hurting him. She was fiercely considering that problem. Or trying to—only, by then he was kissing her again. And again. And again.

She fought for a breath. "You're not up for this," she whispered worriedly.

"Oh, trust me. I am."

"I don't want to touch you in the wrong place. Risk hurting you—"

"Phoebe. You couldn't conceivably hurt me in the wrong way. It's the first time I've hurt this good in a lifetime and then some." His hands sieved through her hair. Even in the dusky light, she could see his eyes, fiercer than fire. "Don't stop me. You can stop me later. I swear, I won't go further than you want, not now, not ever. But…don't stop me from kissing you a little more right now, okay?"

If any other man tried that ridiculous line on her, Phoebe would have laughed…but Fox, damn him, wasn't any other man. He sounded as if he really meant it—that he truly believed they'd stop, that he'd stop, that he wasn't just beguiling her into being seduced. And because she believed he was telling her the whole truth—as he knew it—her heart helplessly lunged again.

He'd locked the door on his feelings for so long. It meant

something huge that he'd opened himself now, for her. Yeah, it was sex—she knew it wasn't for more—-but that didn't make his trusting her with his wary emotional state any less. The man was in so much pain. She *had* to respond to him. Anyone would have. Her heart wasn't involved. Not really.

Not exactly.

Oh, hell. Maybe she was falling so deep, so hard in love that her heart was going to get ripped apart and shredded…but right now, holy kamoly, could he kiss.

Since she'd kissed him before, she should have realized how flammable he was. She knew how potent those narrow lips were. How tasty. But he got these terrible inventive ideas this time. His tongue dipped and swirled and teased. His mouth tucked and ducked and tilted and found a hundred new ways to claim hers.

She never took off his sweatshirt, yet somehow it handily dropped to the ground. She swore she never volunteered to touch him, yet somehow her hands were freely running over his chest, his back. She'd touched him before, but she'd touched him as a masseuse.

Now she learned him with a woman's hands, inhaled him the way a woman breathes in her lover. Her fingertips chased over muscles and tendons, over the flat of his stomach, the ridges of ribs, up to the column of his neck—not to chase away knots this time, but to inspire some. Not to ease away sore spots, but to ignore other tactile sensations entirely.

The skin on his shoulder had the vague scent of soap and the naked scent of him beneath that. She caught the hint of musky sweat as he struggled with the heat rising between them, as shocking fast as the gush of a volcano…but that hint of sweat was an aphrodisiac for her. It wasn't work or stress sweat, but simply man sweat, him sweat, the scent of a man on fire.

And still he kissed her. His lips trailed her neck, making necklaces with his damp tongue. His rough, long fingers pushed at her sweater, eased it up and over her head, and on the way back, slowly tugged at her hair. A clip tumbled, then another and another, until her coiled-up hair came apart. So did she.

Mop suddenly clawed at her side. Duster stayed snoring, but Mop tended to worry that her mistress needed rescuing at odd times.

"Lie down, baby," Fox said, in the same tone she used for the dog. Mop obeyed as if she immediately recognized it was okay, it was Fox, not a danger…although he was a danger, Phoebe knew. She'd opened her eyes at the pup's interruption. Now she could see Fox's expression. He stopped moving for that instant, stopped touching her, just took a long, long moment to just look at her.

The last she remembered, they'd both been sitting up, facing each other. Now they both seemed to be lying on the scratchy rug, face-to-face, both of them bare from the waist up. Her yoga pants were tied at the waist, but the ties had loosened and the waistband had dipped below her navel—not revealing anything but the swell of her hip—but he saw that promise of nakedness. He looked. He savored.

He desired.

And so did she. She passionately wanted to be the one who healed Fox. Who made him feel. Who made him *want* to feel again.

She pulled his hand to her breast, encouraged the palm to shape her, to own her. At the same time she pushed at the snap of his jeans, then chased down the zipper. She'd have low-ered the zipper a ton slower if she'd known ahead that the wicked man wasn't wearing underwear. His jack popped out of the box so fast it risked being clawed with the zipper teeth—but she quickly protected him by wrapping her palm around his long, smooth shift. The flesh was warm and sleek and pulsed violently inside the circle of her palm.

He hissed in a breath. "Don't."

"Hmm…is that one of those no's that really mean yes?" she murmured.

"Don't tease."

"You know what, Fox? If there was ever a man who needed some teasing, I think it's you." As if to prove her point, his shaft released a single drop of warm, soft moisture. "Oh, yeah, you like this fine," she whispered, and then suddenly froze.

In seconds she went from tropic heat to icy Popsicle. The trigger was hearing her own throaty chuckle, seeing his re-sponsive lunge to pay her back with the same kind of explo-sive caresses. Only…she didn't want to be a seducer. Didn't want him thinking of her as an inhibited easy lover.

The conflict shot anxiety in her pulse with the speed of a bullet. She wanted him. She totally wanted to make love with him, to invoke wonderful and healing emotions with him, to share those feelings together. Only, she didn't want to…give in, surrender. She could. But she was afraid of feeling ashamed, the way Alan had made her feel ashamed. She knew Fox wasn't Alan. Knew it wasn't the same situation at all, but…

"What's wrong?" Fox whispered between kisses, tracing the shell of her ear.

She couldn't think when he was touching her. Not like that. Not *really* think. "Fox. You want to make love?"

"You bet the bank I do. With you. Now. If you're willing."

"I am willing. In theory."

"I'm happy with theory," he assured her, as he forged another trail of kisses down her throat.

"But I just don't want you to expect…"

Finally he lifted his head. "Is this that deal from last time? That you don't like sex?"

"I didn't say I didn't like sex. I'm just not a very sexual person, so if you build up a whole bunch of expectations— especially since we barely know each other—"

"Phoebe. You know me better than anyone ever has— whether I want that to be true or not. I may not know you half as well. But how you've gotten through my defenses—my brick walls—tells me this is right. That something is totally right between us. Maybe crazy. But still right." He hesitated. "I can't promise you any kind of future."

"I'm not asking for one."

"It's not you. It's nothing I have against commitment. It's…my life right now."

"I'm not asking for a future," she repeated.

He frowned suddenly, swiftly, as if he were determined to pursue a serious conversation on this. Only, it just wasn't going to happen. Nothing less than a tornado was likely to dim the bright, fierce light in his eyes—the need—not at this moment. "So. You're just not a sexual person," he said in a soft patient tone, as if he were talking a climber down from a perilously tall cliff.

"I'm *not*." At least, she was determined not to be. For him.

"Okay. I'll tell you what. Anything I do that doesn't ring

your chimes, sing out. Will that work?" When she didn't immediately answer—it didn't seem as if he were really expecting an answer—he dove straight for the gold. From those kisses he'd branded on her throat, he worked down, between her cushioned breasts, down into the dip of her navel, then up for the plateau of her white, smooth tummy.

His hands chased down her yoga pants as his tongue and lips continued the same inexorably wicked path. She had no time to tighten up, prepare, brace herself to freeze. She just couldn't make it happen. The breath ached out of her lungs on a lonesome, hungry sigh. Her hands reached for him, needing to touch, to care, to share. To unite.

She tugged the rest of his jeans off as he stole her sanity and inflamed need inside her hotter than a devil fire. She desperately wanted Fox to think she was a good woman. A responsible woman whom he could respect, whom he could count on. He didn't have to love her, but his regard, his respect, mattered more to her than she could even explain.... But this passion between them mattered, too.

She didn't remember ever feeling a burning this hot before. Frustration clawed at her pulse, made her heartbeat go begging. The connection to him...there was just no way to explain, even to her own mind, why she felt so compellingly connected to him....

But it was as if she understood his pain.

It was as if he understood hers.

They rolled off the carpet, back on. Rolled under the soft yellow pool of a lamp's glow, then back in the shadows. It was a good thing she'd been living relatively frugally, because there wasn't much furniture to collide with—still, she would have been more careful with him if he had just let her. For a man who needed no more bruises, he seemed singularly un-interested in anything but greedily sipping up every tactile sensation, every sound, every taste, every cry from her she could earn or cause.

You'd think the guy had just figured out what was worth living for.

She had fears. She had seriously sound fears and worries. But she simply had to give them up. When he loomed over her, her bare legs wrapped tightly around his waist, she could no more have denied him than stopped breathing. There was joy in his eyes. Intense frustration, need sharper than a knife—but joy, too. That life-shouting zest that only sharing with another could conceivably inspire....

She took him in. Closed her eyes, lifted her mouth for his, lifted her hips for his and shimmied until he was seated inside her like in a tight, smooth glove. He let out a growl like a lion just freed after years in the zoo. She let out a murmur like a kitten thrilled with her own power.

For an instant they hovered, holding that moment when he was deep inside her and they were meeting each other's eyes.

And then they flew. Both rocking to the same rhythm, beating to the same music, riding the same emotional mountain crest. Sweat gave a sheen to his skin, gilded hers. A phone rang somewhere. A car backfired. The refrigerator ice maker clattered a new round of ice cubes.

But not in their world. She held on, eyes squeezed tightly shut, feeling release pulse through her like a jolt of sweet, hot electricity. Feeling Fox pulse through her…like a jolt of love so hot, so sweet, that it sucked her in and under to a whole new emotional place.

And then she sank back. As he did. Both tried to remember how to breathe normally again.

Minutes ticked by.

She didn't fall asleep, she didn't think, yet it seemed when she opened her eyes, time must have passed, because there was a sweatshirt covering her and Fox was lying on his side, one arm anchoring his head, his other hand drifting through her hair. His eyes had lost that fierce hot intensity and instead simply looked moody dark and fathomless.

"I let the monsters out," he said.

She glanced up, to note both puppies—with wet feet—had taken the best seat in the house while the humans were still on the floor. More moments passed while she absorbed a huge, crazy feeling of total well-being and simple happiness. It felt right, his being with her. Felt perfect, their making love together—like nothing in her life before.

"Hey, you," he murmured, and nuzzled a kiss on her temple.

"Hey, you, back," she whispered.

"Phoebe," he said soberly, "I didn't know that could happen."

"Sex?"

"You're laughing...but yeah. Sex. I really, really didn't know if it would happen for me again in this life."

She sobered, too, then touched his cheek. "What happened to you in the Middle East, Fox?"

"I don't know."

"Yeah, you do."

He hesitated. "I lost me. Lost my belief in myself, my judgment, what I valued about myself. As a man."

"Because of...?"

"It doesn't matter why." Again he brushed a strand of hair from her cheek. "What matters is that I honestly wasn't sure if I'd ever be able to make love again."

She flushed from the toes up, on the inside. From the core of her heart, she'd wanted to help heal him. "I hate to tell you this, big guy, but you gave me signals more than once that your body parts were interested and functioning just fine."

"A hard-on is one thing. Following through is another. And feeling—really feeling—is another." His mind seemed to suddenly change directions, because he went still. "But it's bugging me, Phoebe. That making love wasn't exactly...fair."

She swallowed. "We're having a few regrets, are we?"

"This is the South, red. My mom didn't raise any sons to take advantage of women."

"You didn't take advantage of me."

"Yeah, I did." Mop, as if figuring out the humans were finally, finally returning to real life, scooched over next to his bare hip and resumed the napping position. "I hadn't had sex in a long time. You went totally to my head. That's not an excuse. But it *is* what happened."

"I invited what happened."

"You didn't invite getting involved with a guy whose head is screwed on backward. Who has no life, at least temporarily."

"I knew you were on a recovery track, Fox. Nothing happened that I wasn't allowing to happen."

"That wouldn't count worth beans with my mama, let me tell you." He was joking, doing the Southern gentleman thing. But he'd stopped playing with her hair, stopped touching her. Stopped staying in touch with her. "You've got a right to more than I offered you, Red...but it's not that easy for me to come through. At least not yet. I need to think—a ton—before even trying to talk more about this. For tonight…I'm going home."

"Yes. I assumed you would." She didn't freeze inside. She'd never—once—assumed that he'd stay after making love with her. It was just sex they'd had. It wasn't a relationship. It was what it was, and there was no hurt spiking its way into her heart.

"For the record, though…I'm going to try your recovery program."

"Good. I think it's worth trying. It's all stuff that's good for you."

"It may be. You haven't had a wrong idea about my state of health yet—even if you've been aggravating the hell out of me."

"You're awfully easy to aggravate, Fox."

"Then how come other people can't seem to do it? I know you won't believe this, but everyone who knows me thinks I'm the most patient guy this side of the Atlantic."

"You've fooled all of them?" she said with surprise, and made him grin. But not for long.

"I'll do your program. But this is the deal. First, I'm going to pay you by the hour." He mentioned a sum.

"I don't need to be rolling in diamonds, slugger. This is what I charge—"

"I don't care what you charge. That's what I'm paying you. And another thing—"

"What?"

He motioned to the far archway, where the hall led down to the business part of house. "I'll build your waterfall."

"I don't think you're up for that kind of heavy work—"

"If I can't, I can't. But I'll try. When my dad died, he left my mom financially secure enough, but she was still determined that we'd all know how to do things, not be dependent on others. So I know some plumbing and carpentry. Depending on how my body holds out, I can do the work. And that'll be part of my payment to you. Money. But the waterfall, too."

When he left, she found herself standing naked in the dark window, watching the lights of his vehicle pull out and then disappear into the night. All that extraordinary postsex euphoria and closeness seemed to vanish faster than a light switched off…and a sick feeling of fear replaced it.

Mop moaned next to her ankles, until Phoebe picked up the disgraceful whiner and cuddled him under her chin. Still, she stared out the dark window, thinking fiercely that she felt good about making love with Fox. She *did*. Totally good. Really. It was just…

Vague memories zipped through Phoebe's mind, of her childhood. Her mother had been a hard-core earth mom and emotional hedonist. Her dad had adored those qualities in her and valued her in every way. It was so easy to grow up believing that sensuality was healthy and a wonderful part of being a woman. Her dad called her pure female, and meant it as the warmest of compliments.

And every media source in the universe taught a girl that men wanted a sensual woman. A hot, willing, uninhibited woman who freely expressed her sexuality was the ideal, right? Every man's dream, right?

Wrong.

At her feet, Duster suddenly yipped, clearly miffed that Mop was being held and she was being ignored, so Phoebe had to scoop her up and cuddle her, too…but that sick, wary feeling inside kept turning in her stomach. Men wanted a "hot" woman, all right. But only to sleep with, not to keep. Something in a man distrusted a woman who was too open with her sexuality. They feared she wouldn't be faithful. Feared they couldn't trust her. Something deep inside just didn't respect a woman like that.

Phoebe had learned it all the hard way from Alan. The part that really bit was his accusing her of being a hedonist and sensualist—because she couldn't defend those charges. She very definitely was those things. He'd made her feel so dirty that she'd started to think of herself the same way...until she switched her career from PT to massage work with babies.

She hadn't thought of Alan in months...until Fox entered her life. She knew the men were completely unalike. But she still feared ever falling for someone again who didn't, or couldn't, completely respect her.

Abruptly she turned around and aimed for the back door so she could let the pups out one last time before bed. The cool draft of air on her bare skin made her shiver, helped her face more reality.

She refused to regret making love with him. Helping Fox regain his life really mattered to her—no matter what she had to do, no matter what the emotional cost to herself. She just had to remember how this night had ended.

He hadn't wanted to stay all night with her after making love.

And he'd pretty damn violently been insistent on paying her—hugely—for her services.

She got it. If she could heal his wounded soul, she wanted to. She just couldn't kid herself that he valued her as more than the hired help. For a few hours, there, she'd felt such an extraordinary connection to him.... She'd felt like a soft, fragile rose, petals opening inside her that had been sealed shut for so long...but she knew better. Really.

To Fox she was a masseuse. As long as she guarded her heart from wanting to be more in his life, there was no problem.

And she wasn't about to forget that again.

Seven

In a single week, nature had blown off winter and poured in spring. Bright-yellow azaleas bloomed everywhere. The sun shone through sassy-green fresh leaves. Sleepy, sneaky breezes teased the senses.

The earth and grass smelled pungent, as if every spore and root under the surface was having sex and about to burst into life.

Except for him, Fox thought glumly.

Just because he'd had heart-destroying sex with Phoebe once, of course, was no reason to assume they'd have it again. There were compelling reasons why they shouldn't, besides. Only...

Only, he wanted to have sex with her.

Immediately. Regularly. Preferably on the hour. For several weeks nonstop.

Right or wrong had nothing to do with it. His hormones only understood that issues of values were inconsequential. Having had her, he wanted more. He wanted. Her. No one else. Nothing else. And his hormones kept beating that same drum, day after day after day.

"What in God's name are you doing?" Bear asked dryly.

Fox glanced up. It was a Bear day—which meant, according to Phoebe's ridiculous recovery program—that he was supposed to be fishing. For the cause—and fishing was always Bear's favorite cause—he'd dragged him across the border into South Carolina. Any other time, Fox wouldn't have minded. Lake Jocassee was a serious piece of paradise—one of those God's-country kinds of places. The reservoir of cold, clear water was back-dropped by sunlit knolls and mountains, mostly undeveloped—and everyone loved it that way.

Bear had trailered the boat, bought the live bait as well as a box of proven lucky lures, stashed Fox in the bow and puttered off for an ideal fishing spot. Jocassee was known for trophy trout—also for bass, but it was the brown and rainbow trout Bear wanted for dinner. At this time of day and year fishing wasn't ideal, but that didn't deter Bear, who'd already hooked enough to bring Mom two dinners, easy.

Now, though, Bear had unfortunately been distracted. "What are you *doing*?" he repeated.

"What do you mean, what am I doing? I'm sitting here with you."

Bear sighed and then leaned over to grab one of the books from Fox's lap. He started reading the titles aloud. *"Women and the Law of Property in Early America. The Politics of Social and Sexual Control in the Old South."* Bear scowled at him. "You call this kind of reading relaxing?"

"Well…yes, actually."

"And you think you're convincing anybody you'll never be a history teacher again?" His brother's voice dripped humor.

"This has nothing to do with teaching! This is pleasure reading!"

"Yeah, right. The point, anyway, is that you're supposed to kick back and *fish*. Phoebe told you—"

"All Phoebe insisted on was that I get out of the house. So I'm in the incessant fresh air. What she wanted. That doesn't mean I have to like fishing."

"It isn't human to hate fishing."

"How long are you going to hold that against me? Give me a ball—foot, base, basket, soccer, whatever, and I'll whip the pants off you in any of those sports. But sitting here torturing worms on hooks…" Fox shook his head.

"I'll tell Phoebe on you if you don't at least pick up a pole."

"That," Fox said darkly, "is an ugly, ugly threat. Did I tattle on you when you and Moose put the skunk in the school cafeteria? Did I tell Moose when you threw up on his favorite shirt in high school? Brothers never tell."

"That was completely different. This is for your own good. Reading a bunch of history is not *relaxing*. Not the way Phoebe said we were supposed to make you. You're supposed to have *fun*."

"Reading *is* fun," Fox said firmly, and opened a book again. He didn't know which book, because he'd given up trying to concentrate a good hour before. The sun poured on his head, his shoulders. The lake was so clear he could see several mesmerizing feet below. Normally the lake—or reading books he loved—really would have relaxed him. It was just that right now, the only thoughts in his head were about Phoebe.

So maybe they'd only made love once. And possibly it had been ten days, twelve hours and seven minutes since that once, but the entire encounter was still diamond clear in Fox's mind—and not just the naked parts either.

One of the things that bugged him was how—twice now—she'd suddenly upped and claimed that she didn't have a sexual nature. Both times she'd been in the middle of kissing him senseless. It'd be funny if it wasn't so…odd. Since she was obviously a natural sensualist to the core, Fox couldn't fathom why she'd claim something so ridiculous—or want him to believe it.

Of course, all women were impossible to understand at a certain level, so Fox wasn't dwelling on just that one thing. Other details about that night still tantalized and frustrated him, as well. Color was one. She had all those colorful rooms in her house—blue, green, yellow and all—yet he still hadn't seen her bedroom or what color she'd painted it. And then there was the critical issue of panties.

She'd been wearing yoga pants that night. It was typical of her to wear comfortable, easy-moving clothes, but underneath those figure-concealing pants he recalled—in total and exquisite detail—her panties. They'd been thongs. Satiny. They'd been white except for the heart-shaped spanking-red bitsy front patch—which, actually, a guy nearly needed magnifying glasses to see at all.

Still, Fox happened to have been that close up. He *had* seen. And they seemed like a fairly astounding choice of panties for a woman who tended to wear oversize sweaters and pants. Same issue with the house. She'd painted all those sensual, soft colors—yet she freaked if you mentioned that she had a sensual side.

Something was wrong, Fox thought. Well, hell. A lot was wrong, as far as his coming on to a woman when he couldn't offer her a damn thing. But besides that…something was wrong with Phoebe. Wrong *for* Phoebe. She was a life lover, a giver, a hedonist, a dare anything kind of woman who stood up. She understood his heart and his feelings better than he had.

She'd helped him so much with her generous, giving ways that it bugged him all the more that there was this problem. This *something* in her that was off. It was as if she were afraid, or wary. But of what?

"And the other thing that bothered me was her saying she didn't care if there was a future," he said irritably.

"Huh?"

"For Pete's sake, what kind of attitude is that? I mean, it's one thing if people can't work out a relationship—not that I like the *r* word. It's a stupid word. But when it comes down to it, you meet someone, you work at it, and then it either works out or it doesn't, right?"

"I think you're getting dehydrated. There's more ice water in the thermos," Bear said patiently.

"I'm just saying, when things go wrong, it doesn't have to be about *blame*. Usually both people try. Nobody goes into a deal thinking they're going to deliberately hurt the other person. I mean, unless they're complete dolts."

"Okay. Beats me who you're talking to, but I'm for the conversation. If we're going to talk about women, though, I think we should talk about Phoebe."

Fox suddenly jerked his head around and focused on his brother. "What? I wasn't talking about Phoebe."

"I didn't say you were," his handsome older brother said cheerfully, but then didn't speak further because there was a tug on his line. The whole world stopped for a trout. Who could figure. This one was a rainbow, maybe nine inches, fought like a boxer—and won. "Hell," Bear said, when the fish freed itself from the line and took off.

Finally. "What were you going to say about Phoebe?" Fox demanded.

"Well…a couple weeks ago when her name first came up, I was just teasing about asking her out. But April and I quit even playing at making something happen between us. Not like we had a big thing going, anyway. The point, though, is that I really am thinking about asking Phoebe out now."

"No."

"No why?"

"No because."

Bland-faced, Bear tried laying out a few of his dating credentials. "I make good money. Great money, in fact. Got good family genes, can offer a woman security, and I figure I'm pretty close to wanting to settle down. It's been years since I had fun waking up with a hangover and a new woman. Just no interest in catting around anymore. I'd like a couple of rug rats. A woman I could talk to, be with every night—"

"And that's fine, just fine. You're getting really old," Fox assured him. "You need to settle down. But not with Phoebe."

"Ah. I get it now."

"You get *what* now?"

"Moose knows it, too," Bear said smugly. "That you've got a thing for her. We just weren't sure how serious it was."

"I don't—can't—have a thing for anyone. You think I'd

ask a woman out when I don't even have a job? Don't have a clue what I'll be doing even next month?"

"Okay, so right this exact minute you're not on track yet," Bear agreed. "But you only had two of those hellion headaches last week."

And one, Fox thought, that he'd actually dented with that ridiculous exercise of hers—not that he could admit that in public. Even to a brother.

"What I was trying to say," Bear went on, "is that you finally seem to be headed uphill, Fox. You're not completely well yet, but you're definitely on an uphill road. So…"

"So?"

"So, I'll tell you what. I may or may not ask Phoebe out. But I'll wait until you've finished the whole month's program that she created, okay? Until you're better. And that really is the key."

"*What* key?" Sometimes following Bear's conversations was like interpreting politics. You had to weed through the words to get to the meaning. Assuming there was one.

"The key," Bear said patiently, "is that you need to get better. It's the best offense and defense you have. That woman's got you tied up in knots. When you get better, you'll be strong enough to untie the knots, to figure what you really want out of the situation."

Fox opened his mouth, closed it. He wanted to argue furiously that neither Phoebe nor any other woman had him tied up in knots or ever would, but there wouldn't be much point in that. She did. Period.

But that didn't mean Bear had everything right. Fox loved his brother, but Bear was almost always wrong, and this was no exception. He couldn't possibly wait until he was stronger to fix the situation with Phoebe. Truth was, he doubted he could stand waiting even another minute.

A guy couldn't just make love with a woman—not when the emotional connection had rocked his world inside and out. And then just go back to do those pansy "safe place" pain exercises as if he and Phoebe were nothing more than accidental business acquaintances.

He couldn't let her get away with it. Healing him and loving him and giving 300 percent to him at every turn—and then taking zippo in return. The more Fox dwelled on it, the more he realized that he simply had to find out what was bugging her. Either that or risk losing what little mind he had left, because for damn sure, he couldn't think of anything *but* her until they got this settled.

And after they got this all settled, then they'd make love again.

The more Fox thought about it, the more he figured he had a good plan coming together.

He was still feeling confident the next day, when he parked in her driveway and stepped out, carrying an impressive array of tools. The tools weren't totally a disguise. She did, after all, have a waterfall that needed constructing. But as he lifted a fist to rap on her front door, he heard the unexpected sound of crying from somewhere in the house. A baby's crying. And not a little mournful wail, but a full-scale, nonstop scream, as if someone were torturing an infant.

No one could be torturing an infant at Phoebe's place—not if she were alive—so naturally he panicked. Either there'd been an accident or some other crisis must have happened. So he pushed open the door, yelled out that he was here, and charged toward the sound of the crying.

He found Phoebe almost immediately, standing in the kitchen, stuffing some kind of long-stemmed, sweet-smelling, sissy purple flowers in a vase. She was barefoot—no surprise. Wearing a long jeans skirt, and a loose tee in bright red. Something bubbled in a pot on the stove—something with garlic and rosemary and some other unidentifiable saucy smell. It was the kind of mysterious sauce smell that could bring a man to his knees. Easily. Phoebe's back was to him. She was humming softly, moving to an R&B tune played low on the radio as she fixed her flowers and occasionally stirred the pot. The whole scene looked wonderful...except for the shrieking infant in the front pack strapped to her tummy.

She spun around when she sensed him in the doorway. "Well, hey you." Her smile was bright and sexy...but not particularly personal. "Did I goof up the schedule? It's just Wednesday, isn't it? You're not due until tomorrow, are you?"

The cheerful question slugged him straight in the gut. It was her reference to "the schedule." How easily, this whole last week, she'd treated him as a client instead of a lover. He scraped a hand through his hair. "No, but I—"

"It's okay," she said in a normal voice, as if anyone could hear over the infant's caterwauling. "Come on in. You're welcome to visit. It's just that I have Manuel...and the odds of Manuel being quiet are about a thousand to one."

She didn't look shaken by the baby's screams. As busy as she looked, her left hand stayed in touch with the little one, rubbing and loving and consoling. Because of the baby's name, Fox assumed it was a boy; otherwise it would have been impossible to tell. The head was bald, the face all squinched up and red from the screaming.

"Manuel came from Chicago," Phoebe filled in.

"How come you got a baby from so far away?"

"I don't, usually…but I've had contacts with different agencies across the country for a while now. Everybody's got the same problems. What to do with throwaway babies. How to turn a baby around when there's been no bonding or care to start with." She ambled over, carrying a wooden spoon, lifting it for him to taste. "More salt?"

He tasted. "It's perfect."

"I dunno. I think it still needs something. Maybe a little more garlic or more tarragon…anyway. The crime statistics alone could put hair on your chest. Look at a kid in trouble, you'll almost always find a baby who didn't bond, didn't get the nurturing he needed. I don't have this little sweetie for long. Just three days."

"Three days is enough to matter?"

"Yes and no. Yes, loving time—touch time—with a baby always matters. And it'll hopefully be enough to see if we can start him on a different road…"

Fox was interested in the details. The work she did fascinated him. But just then it was hard to concentrate. "You're sure he's not sick?"

"Positive."

"You're sure he's not hungry or dying or anything? I mean, the way he's crying—"

She nodded. "It sounds inhuman, I know," she said softly. "His birth mom was an addict, so this little darling came into the world in agony. He's been through the whole withdrawal procedure, so at this point he isn't feeling the craving for drugs so much as…anger. Misery at being alive. And maybe we can't help him, but you know, we can't just keep throwing babies away—"

No, he didn't know. He also didn't know how Phoebe could think, much less calmly hold a conversation, with a baby crying that relentlessly. But for damn sure, the part of his plan about talking with her—and then making love—fizzled fast.

It was a shocking moment to realize he'd fallen hopelessly in love with her. Not just because the chances of their making love any time in the immediate future were completely annihilated. But she was standing there in her bare feet, with the screaming baby and the spoon, backed by all her candy-colored rooms…and there it was. This overwhelming emotion, when he could have sworn he was no longer capable of any feelings, much less real ones. Yet just looking at her sucked him in so deep, so rich, that he could have died and gone to heaven, thrilled just to be with her in the same damn room for that instant in time.

"You came over for a reason this morning?" she asked, just as if they'd been having a normal conversation.

"Yeah—I didn't know if you were going to need the therapy room, but if it was free during the lunch hour, I figured I'd get some work done on the waterfall."

"Oh! That's great. And the room's free—Manuel is all I'm trying to do today. I do have to wander back there now and then—"

"Well, will it bother him if I'm making noise?"

"Everything bothers him," she said, with a tender pat on the baby's diapered rump. "But it doesn't matter. It's the best thing for him to be exposed to normal sounds, normal life—because that way he finds out he'll be protected no matter what's happening around him. So go for it."

He went for it.

First off, he hunkered down in the corner of her massage room and studied all the supplies she'd bought and her master plan. Good thing he had a contractor for a brother who could railroad the applicable licenses—and double good thing that his mom hadn't raised any sons who ducked hard work. Act One had to be the plumbing, and after that he could move on to the easy stuff—mortar and stone and tiling. Big messes. Big weight. Big work—at least for a guy who could barely bend without creaking and groaning. It was going to take some mighty long hours to build this insane indoor waterfall she wanted.

But it was so like her—to value something sensual and beautiful over something practical. And it was a way to do something for her. A way to give back. As far as Fox could tell, too damn many people took from Phoebe without her letting on that she needed anything—much less took anything—from anyone.

He poured on the coals, knowing that his body would give out quickly from this kind of physical work. He didn't realize how he'd become used to the sound of the baby crying, until there was suddenly silence. Instinctively he leaped to his feet, thinking that damn squirt must have died, and raced back through the house so panicked he forgot about his dusty hands and safety goggles.

He found Phoebe in her odd little mint-green room—the closet turned into an office. She was sitting at a desk, paying bills, the baby sleeping on her tummy.

Actually sleeping. He checked by hunching down and looking.

"It won't last," Phoebe whispered humorously. "But, yeah, he really is napping."

"Any chance he'll do this for a while?" Hell. He was afraid to even whisper.

"I dunno. When a baby's born addicted, one of their problems is that they can't rest. This little one's past that…but he just seems angry all the time. No one got around to giving him a reason for living, you know?"

Fox said soberly, "Yeah. I do know."

Phoebe glanced at him with suddenly sharp eyes. She opened her mouth—he knew she was going to start asking questions—so he swiveled around quickly and headed back to work.

A half hour later he heard the baby start wailing again—followed by Phoebe's slow, ever-patient, soothing voice and her ghastly off-key humming. A few minutes after that she showed up in the doorway.

"Are we going to be in your way if I give him a bath here, Fox?"

"No sweat." He was nowhere ready for power-tool noise yet. He was still interpreting the plumbing instructions, laying out the fittings. And he kept at it, although he watched her from the corner of his eye and became more and more confused at what she was doing. She filled up the big claw-footed bathtub in the middle of the room. The location of the tub didn't surprise him; he'd just figured she used it for physical therapy, but it was huge, hardly baby-size. He'd have thought the sink would be a lot easier way to bathe a baby that little. But he'd stopped talking by then, didn't want to interfere, and truth to tell, he'd sunk into a skunky mood. Her comment had done it, the one about how the baby hadn't found a reason for living.

His mind kept jolting back to the little dark-haired boy—

the one in his nightmare, the one he'd tried to approach. The one he'd tried to show that there were people in this life who could be trusted, who wanted to help, who'd reach out. Everyone in his family and circle of friends had fought him about going into the military. They said it was a crazy choice for a man who hated guns, but they didn't get it. That was the point. That he hated guns. That he loved children. If people didn't stand up for kids, didn't take a risk and reach out, how was anything going to change?

Aw, hell. Whenever his mind crept down those dark alleys, he always seemed to sink like a stone. He could feel the ugliness creeping inside him, the darkness he'd been trying to swim out of for weeks now. Or at least he'd been trying to—since Phoebe.

And there she was, suddenly. When the tub was full, she stripped the baby of clothes and diaper—no surprise—but the surprise when she scooped the baby into her arms again and stepped into the tub.

His jaw dropped.

She wasn't naked herself. She had on a little T-shirt and boxers. But he'd just never expected her to climb in the bath with the baby. The little one almost immediately stopped crying—possibly from shock, possibly because it liked the warm water. Who could guess?

But she laughed with delight, praising him softly, gently. "So is water going to be your Achilles' heel, Manuel? Because if we've finally found out what turns you on, little one, we're going to be wet a lot.…"

Finally he understood what she was doing. She'd already told him that her intent was to stay physically in touch with the baby 24/7 if possible; he just hadn't realized that meant *really* 24/7—that even in activities like a bath, the baby would have her to hold on to, like now. Naked as a newborn, he was lying on her tummy, feeling her security, her hands, the warmth of her heartbeat.

Fox's pulse suddenly drummed, drummed. She was really a damned extraordinary woman. Her confidence with the baby, her endless patience, the love she gave so freely, so generously…God. It was no wonder he couldn't help loving her. What human being could *not* love her?

But it still ripped through his mind that there'd been a time he'd had confidence and patience. A time he'd believed he even had a gift with kids. Kids had always been his calling. He'd really believed it.

But that sure as hell wasn't true anymore.

"Fox?"

He turned around at the doorway, carrying his jacket and tool box. "I didn't want to interrupt the two of you. But I have to go."

"Right this second? You weren't going to say anything?"

"When the kid wasn't crying?" He motioned toward the work corner. "I know I left it a complete mess, but I'll be back later. I figured I'd just cover it up for now." Both theoretically and symbolically, he thought.

"You're due over tomorrow night for your session."

"Yeah, I know." But right then he felt the worst hell-hot headache coming on that he'd suffered in a while. He knew it was bad. The kind that would make him sick as a dog. He just wanted to get out of there and get home.

And right then he was unsure whether he was coming back. Ever.

Eight

Phoebe lit the melon-scented candle and blew out the match. She stepped back with her hands on her hips and surveyed the table worriedly. Mop and Duster both yipped, just in case she'd forgotten they were there. They certainly couldn't forget the fabulous smells drifting from the stovetop, and for some God unknown reason, no one was giving them tidbits.

Phoebe had given the beggars plenty of treats, but right now she was too concerned about Fergus to concentrate on anything else.

The rap on the front door inspired the dogs to race, barking the whole time, to great the visitor. Phoebe had barely opened the door before they leaped on Fergus, but when he looked up from the petting frenzy, his eyes were definitely only on her.

"I *am* due here tonight, right?"

"Right." She *knew* how he could make her feel, yet still had to fight the rush and her zooming pulse rate. Naturally he was surprised to find her dressed differently, because he never saw her in anything but loose-fitting clothes. Form-fitting attire would hardly work for a masseuse. Her soft black sweater and slacks were hardly sexy—she didn't do sexy—but yeah, she'd made a different kind of effort tonight. She still hadn't put on shoes because she never wore shoes if she could help it, but she'd brushed her hair loose and put on a little face goop. Not much. Just some lip gloss, a little blush, a little mascara.

Judging from the dangerous glint in Fox's eyes, you'd think she'd put on major war paint.

She led him toward the kitchen, musing that she *had* strategized a major war effort tonight. From her clothes to the setting, she'd wanted to create something that would startle him—because she had really, really doubted he intended to show up today.

Something had been seriously wrong when he left two days ago. She didn't know what, but in the space of a short conversation, Fergus had changed from a recovering, functioning, whole-hearted guy back into a taciturn shadow again. When he'd left, she'd desperately wanted to chase after him and confront whatever was wrong—but she'd had the baby to take care of. Besides which, she'd realized joltingly that she had no right to chase after him—that she had no personal right to care about Fergus.

Tonight, though, she'd convinced herself that her strategic choices were all strictly professional. His recovery was her business, right? So if she chose to wear a snuggly black sweater and if it happened to catch his attention—as long as it was for a professional reason, that was okay.

He asked about Manuel, and they chatted a few minutes about the baby and how her work was going. Since he was only planning to stay for the usual two-hour session, though, she needed to hustle the dinner along, and motioned him to sit down. "I have another exercise for you to try today."

"Oh, yeah?" He didn't seem to notice the candles, the linen, the setting she'd worked so hard on. The darn man hadn't taken his eyes off her yet. It was downright distracting. "What are those smells?"

"Dinner."

"Dinner wasn't part of the deal," he said.

"It is today. Anything's part of the deal that puts you on a healing track, cookie."

"Cookie?" He almost choked on the teasing endearment, but she just chuckled—and put on oven gloves. Her scarred relic of a kitchen table had been covered with an elegant navy blue tablecloth—alias a bed sheet. She'd dimmed the lights, set up a centerpiece of melon-, peach- and strawberry-scented candles. Scraps of navy velvet ribbon tied the silverware, since she didn't own real napkin holders.

The menu was far from gourmet. Hot buttered, homemade bread. The potato dish everybody made for holidays with sour cream and corn flakes and cheddar cheese. Chicken rubbed with fresh cilantro and island pepper. Fresh cherries and blueberries, and eventually, a marshmallow sundae with double-chocolate ice cream. All easy, basic stuff. All comfort food.

Fox, though, raised an eyebrow as more bowls and plates showed up on the table. "What is this?"

"Like I said—just dinner."

"This is 'just dinner' like a diamond is 'just a stone.' You think I can't tell when a woman's determined to seduce me?"

"What?" She dropped a hot pad. Then a fork.

"Give me a break. You know what the smell of homemade bread does to a guy's hormones, don't you?"

He was teasing with her. Flirting. Her heart soared a few thousand feet—not because he made her feel mooshy inside, but because, darn it, all the risks she'd taken for him really were paying off. For him, if not for her. Even a few weeks ago, he'd still been locking himself in a dark room, unwilling to be around people and, for darn sure, stingy with his smiles.

"The homemade bread was about motivating your hunger," she insisted.

"That's exactly what I said. That the smell of homemade bread is a foolproof way to motivate hunger in a guy. Better than just about anything on earth—give or take that sweater you're wearing."

"It's just a sweater, Fox! I—" The cell phone chimed, forcing her to peel off an oven glove to answer it.

It was her mom, and because it was an unusual time for her mother to call, she motioned to Fox that she'd just be a few seconds, and continued bringing on the food. "There's nothing wrong is there, Mom? You're okay? Dad's okay?"

"Everything's fine." Her mother's magnolia-sweet voice was a little too careful, but Phoebe swiftly learned why. "I just wanted to tell you something, honey. I saw in the paper tonight that Alan's getting married. I know you two are long over, but I just didn't want any stranger springing the news on you...."

The chicken was going to dry out if she didn't get the dinner served, so she promised to call her mom later and hung up as quickly as she could, then hustled to sit across from Fox.

"Sorry about the interruption," she said with a smile. "I talk to my mom a few times a week, but we still never seem to be able to have a short conversation."

"She said something that bothered you?"

"Oh, no. Everything's fine."

"She must have said something or told you something—"

To ward off another direct question, Phoebe served potatoes—no man alive so far had ever resisted those potatoes—and freely offered him some of her family background. "My dad and mom are both from Asheville. Dad's an anesthesiologist. My mom always claimed it was a good thing he made good money, because she was too lazy to work—but that was a complete fib. She's a hard-core volunteerer. Works with sick kids at the hospital. And troubled teenagers at a runaway place. And she's on the board of directors for an adoption agency. She never stops running.... She also paints."

"So that's where all these colors come from?" He motioned around her house.

"Oh, yeah. Mom definitely taught me not to be afraid of color."

"You sound pretty close."

"Couldn't be closer. Same for my dad."

"So what'd she say that bugged you?"

Her smile dipped, but only for a second. "Fox," she said firmly, "this is about you. Your time, your dollar. I don't mind talking about myself, but not when we're working together." She glanced at his plate, though, and realized he was on his second helping. "Forget it. Ask me anything you want."

"Pardon?"

She motioned. "Look at you. Eating like a pig. I'm so

proud." She passed him the plate of warm bread again. "Okay, I forgot, what was it you wanted to know?"

"What your mother said. And I'm *not* eating like a pig."

"Come on, you," she crooned. "Try the glazed carrots. The recipe's so good you won't even realize it's a vegetable, I promise. She was just telling me that a man I used to know was getting married."

"I take it you and this guy were a thing?"

"Yup. Was engaged to him myself, in fact. She was afraid I'd be shook up and hurt when I found out about it."

"So…are you? All shook up and hurt?"

"Do I look remotely shook up?" But over the flickering candlelight, she saw his expression. "Damn. Quit looking at me like that, Fox. Go back to eating."

"How long were you with the guy?"

"Three years. Close to four."

"So he's the one you broke up with. The reason you moved here."

"Yes, Mr. Nosy. If you want the down and ugly, he broke my heart. Bad enough that I couldn't seem to shake it without moving to a new place, totally starting over, physically and emotionally. But that's water way over the dam now. Eat those carrots."

He was. But he was still like a hound with a bone. "How did the son of a bitch break your heart?"

She waved the royal finger at him. "Normally I wouldn't care what language you use. I can do all the four-letter words myself. But not tonight, Fergus. The whole dinner and program tonight is to coax you to feeling calm and relaxed. To help you heal. That's not going to happen if you get yourself all revved up."

"I'm not revved up. I just want to know what the bastard did. Cheat on you?"

"No."

Fox suddenly slammed down his glass of water. "Hell. He didn't hit you, did he?"

She raised an eyebrow. "Did you forget who you were talking to? No one in this life is going to hit me and live to tell it."

He nodded. "Yeah, that was a foolish fear, Red. Zipped out of my mouth before I stopped to think. Any guy who'd try that kind of nonsense wouldn't still be alive. And you sure wouldn't have mourned him."

"You've got that right."

Fergus heaped another helping of potatoes on her plate. "You're tough and strong and can take care of yourself. No question about that. So what exactly did this guy do to hurt you?"

She sighed. "I'll answer that. I'll even give you the long, boring, embarrassing answer—but you'll have to answer something for me first. I want to know what happened. In the Middle East. I know the cover story, how you were hit with a dirty bomb and all. But I want the details. Where were you, what was going on, what was the whole shemola."

It was his turn to hesitate. In fact, he apparently wanted to avoid that question so much he scooped up their empty plates and carted them to the sink, then turned around to give her one of those fierce, glowering looks that always successfully made his two big brothers back off pronto.

It didn't work on her. She just had a feeling this was it— it with a capital *I*. Either they had some kind of breakthrough together or he was going to back off from seeing her—not because she hadn't helped him with the pain, but because something in Fox wasn't sure he wanted to heal.

Surprisingly he ambled into an answer, as if the subject bored him but he was willing to go along with her. At least for a while. "I enlisted in the service because of the kids. Because teachers need to be role models for kids, and history teachers get stuck being role models of a unique kind. Every day, see, I was talking about heroes in American history. What made a hero. Why we studied certain men and women over others. How we defined leadership and courage and all that big hairy stuff."

"Okay." Since he was clearing away the dishes, she stood up, too. The dogs trailed her like hopeful shadows. She slid them scraps, washed her hands, then brought out her ruby-glass bowls and the double-chocolate ice cream. Then waited.

"Okay," he echoed her. "So a part of teaching history is teaching heroes—teaching kids that all of them had the potential to be heroic in the right circumstance. That being a hero wasn't about having courage. It was about finding courage. That everybody was vulnerable and scared sometimes, but that the right thing to do is to stand up for people more vulnerable than you are."

God. He was going to turn her into mush. She heaped five big globs of ice cream without even thinking. Her heart just squished for what he said, how he said it, what he so clearly believed from his heart. But she said just "okay" again as if leading him to continue.

"So…" He fed plates into the dishwasher as if he were dealing cards, whisk, whisk, whisk. "So there came a point when we came to a unit about the Middle East, talking about history there, what had been happening over the last several decades specifically. The problem, as I could see it, was that the grown-ups in their families tend to wring their hands about anything to do with Middle East, you know? Everybody's tired of trying to fix something that nobody thinks we can fix. Of trying to do something we don't have the power to do. We're tired of getting involved, wanting to feel like we're good guys, and then getting kicked in the teeth for it. And because that's what the kids were hearing at home, that's what they brought to me at school."

"And you did what about this?" She sat down with the two ruby bowls of ice cream, then poured on the warmed marshmallow on top.

"God," he said, watching her.

"Now, don't get diverted. Keep talking."

He did, but with a spoon in motion. "So…I didn't see I had any choice but to volunteer for the military—because that's what I'd taught them. That you couldn't just talk. You had to show up. That even weak-kneed, gun-hating, sissy teacher types…such as myself…had the power to change things—"

"Fox. You haven't got a sissy bone in your body."

"Maybe not. But it still tends to be the stereotype for male teachers, that we're lightweight fighters, so to speak. And it bugged me, what the kids were hearing at home. Anyway, I'm just trying to explain. I felt I'd lost the right to talk to them about heroes and leaders, if I wasn't willing to stand up myself."

Phoebe put her spoon down. She was the worst sucker for sweets ever born, especially for this kind of sundae, but she suddenly knew something bad was coming. She *knew*. And she didn't prompt him when he hesitated this time because right there, right there, she changed her mind about whether he should tell her this. She wasn't a psychologist. What was she *thinking,* to be so arrogant to believe she could help?

"So...I got over there," he continued slowly. "And they put me to work, pretty much on the kinds of projects you'd expect them to assign someone like me—rebuilding schools, trying to organize the old teachers, spending time as a sort of liaison with the townspeople. I carried a gun, but I never had a reason to aim it. There were incidents. Plenty. But I wasn't really personally affected. I just did my thing, what I was getting the stripes for, what I really went there to do...."

"Here," she said firmly. "You need cherries on that sundae. And more marshmallow—"

But when she tried to grab his bowl, he hooked her wrist instead. They weren't exactly done eating. They weren't done with dishes, either. But for some unknown reason they went outside, sat on her back steps and sipped in the crisp spring night. The dogs were chasing around the bushes, happy to be out and free. Clouds whispered a promise of rain. He dropped his jacket on her shoulders and picked up his story, his tone still as even as a tailor's hem.

"The local kids started coming around. Nothing odd about that. Kids always know when an adult honestly likes them, you know? And the kids wanted their schools back. So they started hanging with me. And I could speak some of the language, so I'd get them going. I'd teach them some English, they'd teach me some of their language. We talked about rock and roll, and games, and ideas, whatever they wanted."

His jacket was cuddled around her shoulders, when all he had to warm him was a shirt, yet she was the one whose fingertips were chilled.

"So...there was a certain morning. It was hot. Over a hundred. Sun blazing, just like every other day. I'd started work early, gotten up before anyone else—God knows why, probably because I was nuts. Anyway, I'd turned around this corner, was picking up a box of supplies, when a kid came in the alley. A boy. Not even half-grown. Big, dark eyes. Beautiful eyes. I see the way he looks, and think he must have been sleeping in that alley, so my mind's running ahead. I figure he's orphaned, and then that he might be hurt, because he's got that kind of deep, old hurt in his eyes."

Mop and Duster came flying back to flop on his feet. His feet, not hers. Damn it, they knew.

"So I start talking to him, like I always do with kids, same tone, same smile. Bring an energy bar out of my pocket, offer it to him. I'm thinking what I'm going to do if he's in as bad shape as I think he is, because I'm sure as hell not leaving him alone in that alley. I'm thinking, this is exactly what it's all about. Not the guns. Not the bull. But this. Finding a way, a real way, to give a wounded kid a life."

"Fox." There was gravel in her throat now. Gravel in her heart. It came from looking at his face, the naked sadness in his eyes.

"He had the dirty bomb under his clothes. Did something to detonate it."

"Oh my God," she whispered.

"I can't explain the rest. Why I came home so messed up, so angry. I mean, obviously it was tragic and horrible. But it's not as if I could have stopped it. I never actually saw him die, so it's not like that specific memory could be part of the nightmares. I didn't. I didn't see much of anything—I have a real vague memory of being blown against the far wall and knocked out, but that's it. I didn't know anything else for hours. But when I did wake up…I woke up angry. Beside-myself angry. Mad enough to punch walls and cuss out any-one who tried to help me—"

"Fox."

Finally he looked at her. "I haven't told my family most of that. Didn't want to. Hell, I don't honestly know where all the rage came from. But that story better be a good enough explanation for you, red, because that's all I've got. That's what happened. There's nothing else—oomph!"

Maybe he'd intended to say more, but she swooped on that man with the fury of an avenging angel. She knew he still had half-healed wounds and a half-dozen seriously sore spots. She knew it was stone chilly on the back porch steps. Most of all she knew that she'd never again intended for Fox to see her sensual side…but the damn man.

What was she supposed to do? Listen to that terrible hurt of his and do nothing? Listen to how badly he'd hurt for that child, so badly he couldn't stop hurting himself, and pretend it was just a story she was hearing that didn't affect her?

She kissed him and kept on kissing him, thinking he de-served every damn thing she could give him and then some. If he lost respect for her, then that was how the cookie crum-bled. Sex was a way to show love, to give love. To pour on love. It was only one way, but at that very second, she needed to pour five tons of love on the damn man, and she didn't have a zillion other options at her disposal. Sex was too darn handy not to use it for all it was worth.

Still kissing him, still teasing his tongue with hers, she pushed the jacket off her shoulders and then started to pull up her sweater. Both of them needed a second to suck in air, and it was that second when she yanked the sweater off her head and tossed it.

Not a great idea. Mop and Duster promptly took off with it and tore across the yard, but that was an oh-well. Fox's eyes were open at that moment. Dark and deep and confused. He opened his mouth—so she shut it again.

Headlights suddenly glowed from the neighbor's driveway—far enough away that they couldn't really see much. Or maybe they could. She didn't care. She didn't unbutton his shirt because she'd have to kill him if he caught cold because of her. She went directly for the snap on his jeans.

He needed gentle treatment, she thought. He needed tenderness.

Unfortunately, he wasn't going to get either.

At that instant she hated the kind of world that would hurt Fox that way. The kind of world where a child could die that way. It was infuriating and untenable and despairing and awful. She told him, in hot velvet kisses, in angry pressure-cooker kisses, in rubbed-in caresses and kneaded stroking. She told him, with her hands, sliding over skin, touching, owning, claiming every part of Fox she could love. She told him by closing her eyes and concentrating and emoting every ounce of love she could beg, borrow or conjure.

He hissed a swear word. She was pretty sure it was her name.

She gave him her fury…another gift she could offer through the sense of touch and sound and taste. She whispered kisses on him, closing his eyelids with the most precious touch, painting softness with more kisses down his throat. It wasn't fury the way a man would express it, but it was a torrent of feeling all the same. It was all she knew how to do. When something was this unbearable, it was all she could do. There was no fixing his wounds, so all she could try to do was share them.

She whisked more kisses down his chest, over his shirt, down to the open vee of his zipper. My. He popped up faster than a kid for candy. She couldn't make that memory disappear for him. Now, and maybe forever, she'd never make that mental picture disappear for herself, either. But she could slip her hands inside his jeans and slide that fabric down, down, down. He yelped when his bare, bony fanny connected with the cold boards of the deck.

"Is this any way to treat an invalid?" he demanded in a whisper.

"Don't try to get out of this."

"Are you out of your tree? I wouldn't want to get out of this if my life depended on it. I'd just as soon we weren't arrested for public exposure, though. At least until after."

"We might be. But my neighbors aren't kids. Don't have kids."

"Good," he murmured, and then took his turn at sweeping her under. Most of her clothes had undergone major rearranging by then. Her sweater was completely gone. One bra strap seemed to be hanging off her shoulder. Her black slacks seemed to be hanging around her hips—but only for another second or so, because once Fox got motivated, he could have given courses in inspired action.

Yet there was suddenly a moment when he slowed everything down. He threaded his hands through her hair, just looking at her in the moonlight, and then tortured them both by tuning their channel to slow, lazy motion. He scraped his bearded cheek between her breasts, polished her nipples with his tongue, took in each breast. Tenderly. Ardently. He offered a caress of tongue and teeth that pulled at every need she'd never known and made a girl-growl hiss from her throat.

"Oh, yeah, you," he murmured. "Now. Now, Phoebe…"

She was doing the seducing, darn it, but somehow…somehow he was the one strapping her legs around him, probing and then diving in, then fitting the two of them tighter than satin Velcro. Moonbeams danced in front of her closed eyes. Sunshine seemed to shine from the inside of him to the inside of her. He started the ride…a wild, wild ride on the cold porch on their dark, dark night…and something loosened in her that had never been loosened before.

It was the rage, she thought. She'd never been angry like this. That had to be it.

They both seemed to tip off the cliff at the same time. He let out a joyful yell that made her want to laugh…yet she felt the same exuberant burst of joy. Nothing was going to erase that terrible experience for him, she knew that. But for this moment—these moments—that sadness had been bearable. Love had a way of lifting and healing, she believed from the heart…which was why she simply had to offer him hers.

Eyes still closed, still breathing like a freight train, she kissed him and kissed him and kissed him. He kissed her and kissed her and kissed her. They started regaining their breath—and a cold whisk of midnight air made them both shiver…and smile at each other. A private smile that belonged to the two of them and no one else.

No one had ever smiled at her the way Fox did.

No one had ever made her feel the way Fox did.

He stroked her hair back. "You take my breath, red," he whispered.

"And you take mine."

"We're going to catch our death."

"I know. We need to go in—"

"And we will. But I just have to tell you…" He shook his head, still smiling, still looking at her with midnight-dark, loving eyes. "You're the sexiest woman I've ever known. You're my dream."

Her smile died. She froze completely—inside and out.

Nine

Fox turned the corner. Just ahead was Lockwood's restaurant, lit up brighter than the Taj Mahal. His brother Moose had never done anything halfway. You couldn't get in the restaurant door without a tie. A kid in tux parked the cars. Even on a cool spring night like this, the outside garden was decked out with teensy lights and a golden fountain. Hell, the cheapest thing on the menu was $50 a plate.

Fox parked behind the building, next to his brother's BMW. Thankfully there were back stairs, so he could sneak up to Moose's place without being seen. He was wearing old, battered jeans and a USC sweatshirt from his college years—which was held together by threads.

He hadn't played poker in over a year, and wouldn't be now if Phoebe hadn't put the idea of a night out in his brother's head. Fox had to unearth his "lucky" clothes from the depths of his closet.

And he needed some luck, he thought as he clomped up the private back stairs. Not for poker. But with Phoebe.

He thought they'd turned a milestone the other night. Making love—my God, who could deny how powerfully they came together, who they became together? Even for a man who'd never wanted love, who didn't believe he was in a position to offer love—or a life—Phoebe was forcing him to rethink everything.

If he couldn't live without her, he obviously had to find a way to kick himself in the butt, completely heal and start a real life again.

It would seem he couldn't live without her.

It would also seem that he couldn't possibly live without making love to her—preferably every night, possibly more often, for the rest of their natural lives.

Only, she'd freaked after. He mentally replayed those moments after they'd made love. Yeah, he'd told her she was the sexiest woman alive. That didn't seem like an insult, did it? I mean, for damn sure, he should have said she was the most beautiful, the most brilliant, the most wonderful woman in the world before he got to the sexy adjective. But God knew, he meant the compliment with love. He meant it with honesty. And he could have sworn Phoebe didn't need flowery packaging to tell her something straight from his heart.

Besides, he'd known she had a little thing about thinking of herself as unsexy. But that was the point. Why he'd said it. Why he'd wanted to compliment her that way. Guys prayed to find a lover who was honestly, uninhibitedly hot for them, someone who fired up for the same things he fired up for. Yet no male with a brain really thought he'd ever find that. You worked at sex just like you worked on everything else.

Except with Phoebe. She was more than his dream. Every time they touched, she felt like his missing half. He'd reached heights with her he hadn't known existed…and as far as he could tell, she had, too. Yet he'd made that comment, and suddenly she'd run inside on the excuse of their needing to warm up. Then she'd insisted his session time was up. He'd said, what the hell did that matter. She'd said, "Fergus, I thought you were only going to be here for two hours. I've got a baby scheduled to come over tonight. It's not as if I knew we were going to make love."

And that was the crux of the crisis. Not what she'd said. But that she'd called him Fergus instead of Fox.

She might as well have punched him in the stomach.

When he reached the top of the stairs at Moose's place, he knocked once, then freely opened the door. "It's just me," he called out.

But he still couldn't get his mind off Phoebe. He loved his brother, even loved to play poker, once upon a time. Just not tonight. He needed time alone. It wasn't just that he was all riled up about Phoebe, but that he needed concentrated time to think about life. A job. The serious decisions looming imminently in his future.

Still, again his mind sneaked back to Phoebe with another itchy problem. He never had gotten an answer about what happened with her ex-fiancé. That had to be a major key, he figured, because hell, if it wasn't a major key, he was in major trouble. She'd only committed to helping him for a month, and that month was up in a matter of days.

He knew, as sure as he knew he was allergic to clams, that

once that month was over, she was out of there unless he found some way to stop her in her tracks.

"Moose? Where the hell are you?" he called out.

He assumed the poker table would be set up in the den. It always had been. But the den was as quiet as the kitchen, where Fox automatically opened the fridge and pulled out a beer.

The whole upstairs apartment was bigger than it looked, and Moose wasn't one to deprive himself of creature comforts. The kitchen looked like an audition for appliance heaven, and the living room was fancied-up with a home theater, set-in bar, recessed lighting and a lit-up aquarium with exotic fish.

"Moose? Am I really the first one here?"

Past the leather and sleek technology center were a pair of bedrooms and baths, one on either side of the hall, and then came a long narrow sun room that Moose had always used for an office. Now, though, Fox saw the gaming table as he crossed the threshold. He opened his mouth to offer a greeting and instead closed it faster than a gulping fish.

Moose jerked to his feet. "Hey, Fox, didn't hear you come in. You're a little early—"

"I know, I—"

"Fox, you know Marjorie, don't you? Marjorie White?"

"No. I don't believe I've had the pleasure." Fox stepped forward with his hand outstretched because his mom hadn't raised any sons who didn't know their manners. But in a single glance, he could see the gaming table had no cards on it, no drinks, no junk food. No one else was in the room but Moose and this woman.

And where he was dressed like a rag man and holding a

long-necked bottle of beer, she was wearing what his mom called country club clothes. Stockings. Clunks of gold here and there. Blond hair sharply styled. Subtle makeup, little black dress, expensive perfume.

"Fergus, I've heard so much about you for years."

"Well…I'm glad to meet you." He said politely, and then shot a shocked and confused look at Moose.

"I thought you two hadn't met each other before," Moose said heartily. "Marjorie doesn't teach, Fox. But she used to be married to Wild Curly Forster. Remember him? Line-backer, my class, not yours, but turned into the sharpest lawyer this side of Gold River."

"Sure," Fox said, who had never heard of the guy before.

"He died a few years ago. Car accident."

"I'm sorry," Fox said automatically.

"So you both know something about loss," Moose said firmly.

"Say what?"

Marjorie intervened with a quiet little laugh. "Your big brother is springing this surprise on you, I realize. But we don't have to make a big deal out of it, Fergus. He just thought you'd like some feminine company for a change. Let's just have a drink and talk a bit, all right?"

"Sure," Fox said, and again spared a glance at his brother. Murder was too good for him. Hell. Torture was too good for him. "I could have dressed differently, but I assumed I was coming for a poker game."

Moose slapped him on the shoulder. "Marjorie could care less how you're dressed. You two just put your feet up. Get to know each other. I put a couple DVDs in the machine, got some wine cooling. I've got to go check downstairs. We're having a hell of a gig downstairs tonight, company party for Wolcott's."

"Moose, hold up—"

"I had the boys make up a tray of finger foods, so just pull it out when either of you are hungry—"

Marjorie hadn't stopped looking at him, and now a miserable flush climbed her neck. "Fergus, I realize you weren't told about this. I never liked the idea of blind dates, either. But I'd thought, from what your brother said...I mean, it's not like I'm so hard up that I need to be set up."

"Of course you don't." Hell. Hell. Hell. Her feelings were hurt. Fox could plainly see the flush, the trembling mouth, and thought he was going to strangle his brother, and enjoy doing it. He couldn't fulfill that daydream quite that fast, though. "Marjorie, just sit down, all right? We'll talk. I really didn't mean to come across as..."

God knew how he filled out that thought. Cruel? Mean hearted? He really didn't mean to give her the impression that she was too ugly to warrant his time. She was pretty. Very pretty. Actually, she was damn near gorgeous.

She just wasn't Phoebe.

Before he could turn around, his brother had disappeared. There was nothing he could do about it—not for a few minutes. She was obviously mortified and miserable. He couldn't insult her, just because he wanted to kill his brother. Come to think of it, he'd really wanted to kill both brothers, because for damn sure, Bear had been consulted on anything Moose did.

Both of them were dirt. Turncoats. Pond scum.

He served Marjorie a glass of wine and then unearthed the platter of hors d'oeuvres, after which he listened to the entire, unabridged story of her marriage to Wild Curly Foster. Their courtship. His death. Their two children. The money he'd left her. Her evil in-laws. The trip she'd taken to Paris last year to recover from all the stress. How much she missed a man.

When the telephone rang, though, he finally had an excuse to run downstairs. The call was from the local police, asking his brother for a donation. Fox offered them a four-figure gift, but after he hung up he told Marjorie the call had been from Moose—that there was some kind of emergency downstairs; he'd check it out and promised to be right back.

Faster than lightning he charged downstairs, taking the restaurant's back door into the kitchen. He stormed past the clanging pots and steaming smells and cooks yelling at each other, past the computer service area and the maître d's. Finally he located the fink—opening wine for a crowded party in one of the restaurant's private rooms.

Moose spotted him in the doorway. Fox figured his brother must have noticed the steam coming out of his ears, because he promptly aimed his thumb toward the outside.

In the fresh, cold air of the parking lot, Fox darn near took a swing at him. "What the *hell* were you doing?"

Moose lifted his hands in a helpless gesture. "The idea was for you to rejoin life again. To get out of the bachelor house. To budge you off 'go.' To remind you of the good things in life."

"So you thought I needed fixing up with a woman!"

"I didn't say that."

"What the *hell* would you call it, then?"

"What I'd call it," Moose said calmly, "was Phoebe's idea."

"What?"

Moose slugged his hands in his pockets. "She called me two mornings ago. She knew it was my night to have you over. She assumed I'd be setting up a poker game, but she wanted to suggest a different idea. I *do* happen to know a few women, you know."

"Phoebe told you to set me up with a woman?" He still couldn't grasp it.

"Not set *up,* Fergus, for God's sake. She just said part of healing—part of motivating you to rejoin life again—was remembering the good things in life you used to enjoy."

"Like women?"

"Hey. I figured you'd be pissed as hell. But I guess Phoebe figured I'd be the brother who really knew women, you know? So I'd pick someone okay. And Marjorie's heard about you for a blue moon. Kind of had a crush on you from afar, or so they say—"

"I got it, I got it." There was nothing more to say, and he couldn't keep Marjorie just waiting upstairs by herself. He had to get back up there and get himself out of this. But his mind kept reeling in the information that this had been Phoebe's idea. An idea that surfaced two mornings ago…which meant it was the morning after they'd made wild, tumultuous love on her back porch.

The only conclusion he could draw was that their making love must have scared her—really scared her. Badly scared her.

But why…? He didn't have a clue.

Friday morning Phoebe was in the middle of her Baby Love wellness class when she heard a knock on the back door. She scooped up two of the babies and carried the thumb-suckers with her to answer it. Fergus grinned when he saw them.

"Got your hands full, I see." He dropped a kiss on her nose, then moved on past, carrying a toolbox—and shoes that tracked in sand, she noticed. "I just had an extra hour to spend on the waterfall, so thought I'd take advantage if you didn't have any clients in there."

"I don't. I've got a class going in the living room, but that's not a problem. How're you doing?"

"Whistling good. Couldn't be better," he assured her.

Not that Fox had ever complained, but his perky tone was distinctly unlike him. "No aches or pains at all?"

"Nothing worth mentioning. Went to the doc yesterday. He hadn't seen me in a while, claimed I looked alive for the first time in months. Believe me, that was a mighty compliment, coming from hi—"

"So," she said in her laziest tone, "did you have a good time with your brother the other night?"

He peeled off his jacket and started laying out gear, barely glancing up. "You mean Moose's night-out thing? I'll tell you the truth, red. The night did just what I think you wanted it to—jolted me good. And I can hear the babies from here—so you can go back to your class, don't worry about me."

He hunkered down on his knees with his back to her. Her mouth was still open to ask him another casual, lazy question, but somehow that was impossible now. Between the perkiness and the snappy kiss on the nose and the mysterious dark glint in his eyes, he was really acting…indecipherably different.

Had Moose set him up with that Marjorie? Had anything

happened? Was she going to chew off any more fingernails fretting about it?

Damn it. Had he kissed TOW? That Other Woman?

"Phoebe?"

When she heard one of the moms' voices, she quickly spun around and rejoined the circle in her living room. Her therapy room was huge, but still not big enough to accommodate six moms and their babies—at least when the group needed to be spread out all over the carpet. Everybody brought mats for the Baby Love class. The babies were all naked. None was older than four months.

The babies were all happier than clams. The moms were all exhausted and frazzled. Which was why she'd started the program.

"Okay, now. A relaxed baby makes for a relaxed mom…and I'm making you a promise. The more you touch your baby, the happier he'll be. We're going to do four types of massage exercises today. Playful. Enervating. Comforting. And calming. One at a time…"

She usually went around the circle, working with each baby and mom individually. And she intended to this morning, too, but after starting the group with the technique for the second exercise, she popped to her feet and strayed down the hall.

"Hey," she said cheerfully.

"Hey back," Fox said, but he didn't turn around. He'd pulled off his shirt, stripped down to old jeans and boots and gloves for the stone and mortar work. The plumbing was all done for her waterfall. So was the tile part of the pool. Really, the project was nearly done—it just happened to be at the messiest and dustiest part of the construction.

Temporarily, though, she didn't give a rat's tail about her waterfall. Even a few weeks ago, Fox would never have stripped off his shirt—no matter how hot it was—because he'd never have wanted anyone to see his scars.

They were riveting, she thought. Not pretty. But all the wounds were closed now, the swelling and discoloration completely gone. His natural complexion was more olive than pale, so even in early spring his skin had a healthy ruddiness. The breadth of his shoulders, the ripple of muscle in his forearms, spoke of how hard he'd worked to regain strength. She noticed that he hadn't shaved. The fuzz of whiskers on his chin seemed to be coming in blonder than his head hair. Mostly she noticed the strong profile, the good-looking nose and wickedly sexy eyes and…

"Is your class over?"

She jumped when Fox suddenly spoke. "No, no, I just wanted to see how you were doing. You're really moving along!"

"Yeah, the worst was the plumbing. I should be able to finish up the mortar and all this messy, smelly stuff by Saturday. So that'll also give it Sunday to dry before you've got people in here again. That sound okay to you?"

"Sounds good. So you had a really good time on your Moose's night out, huh?"

"Yeah, I'll say. Hmm. Phoebe, I think you need a different shower head than the one you picked out. One with a softer spray."

"Okay."

"You want me to pick it out, get it?"

"Yeah, whatever you think is best. Just tell me and I'll reimburse you. So…we're on for Monday, late afternoon, right?"

"Right. In fact, there's something I'd like to do with you on Monday, if you don't mind."

"Sure. What?"

"Nothing weird. But you've been pushing me to get outside, get more in the fresh air and all…and there's something I'd like to do that afternoon. Unless you object—"

"No, no, that's fine. I can do the exercises with you almost anywhere. So." She cleared her throat. "Whatever you did with Moose, you think you'll do it again?"

He lifted his head. "I hear one of those babies crying. Your class is probably wondering where you are."

She heard the baby cry, too, but still hesitated. It was one of her absolutely favorite projects, the healthy Baby Love massage group, yet still, she couldn't seem to move.

And Fergus suddenly sighed. He pushed up, from his hands on his knees and slowly walked toward her, his hands and torso covered with a thin layer of mortar dust, his jeans crusted with it. He came close enough to touch her but didn't—which was probably a good thing, because eventually she *did* have to go back to the class, and she was dressed for them in a white terry tunic and terry pants.

He came so close, though, that she could see the dark glints in his eyes. His gaze magnetized hers. She couldn't look away. That close, she could no more have looked away than stop breathing.

He said softly, "I think it's cute, Red. Your trying to set me up with other women. God knows, no one ever had the nerve to try that on me before."

She'd have answered him—except that he closed the few inches between them. His hands didn't touch her—his dusty, sweaty torso didn't touch her—but he bent down and brushed his mouth on hers. It wasn't a kiss. More…the threat of one. More…the promise of one.

"You want to know if I kissed her?" he murmured.

"No."

"You want to know if I considered—"

"No."

"Because I'll tell if you ask me. I'll be honest with you. No matter what. You'd be honest with me the same way, wouldn't you, red?"

"Yes. Of course I would," she breathed. But something about the way he'd kissed her, the way he was whispering, the way he was looking at her, had her so rattled she couldn't think straight. She was a pinch away from hiccupping from nerves. Her. The woman who could probably get a Ph.D. in laidback. "I need to go back to my class."

"I know you do."

"We'll talk later."

"Oh, yeah," he murmured. "I know you've got work today. But we're definitely going to talk again. And soon."

She stumbled back toward her class, thinking, all right, now she knew that Fergus had an ugly, evil side to him. A manipulative, wicked side. A side that turned her mind to jam and her sanity to jelly.

He talked to her as if they were lovers. Which, she guessed, they were. But she'd emotionally shut the door on believing they could make it long-term. She'd hoped—she admitted that she'd fiercely hoped—things might have turned out differently. But when he'd praised her for being "so sexy," she'd felt her heart thud like the clunk of a coin down a long, dark well.

He wanted her, she didn't doubt that. But sex, even great sex, was just no measure that he seriously valued or respected her.

Nothing had changed. She had fiercely wanted to heal Fergus—to be the one to make a difference for him—and every day, every week, she'd literally seen her efforts working. He was so, so much better, mentally, physically and emotionally. She wasn't the only one responsible for that, but Phoebe gave herself credit for playing a key role.

That was what mattered. Getting him healed. Not what she wanted. Not what she dreamed.

She stomped back into the class and blurted, "Damn it. We are going to *relax,* class!"

The moms all looked at her as if she were crazy—until someone laughed. And then she tried to laugh, too.

Ten

When Fox pulled into her driveway, Phoebe had to put up with two solid minutes of whining and begging from Mop and Duster. "I know it's Fox, you guys, but you can't go. It's not our truck. And it's raining. And you know I won't leave you alone for long. Come on, you two. Be reasonable."

The dogs had heard all that. They also knew they had the dog door open to the whole backyard, and that their dishes in the kitchen were heaped with food and fresh water. They just didn't want Phoebe to leave, and they loved being with Fergus, besides.

So did she—which was the problem. She pulled her rain jacket hood over her head to run outside. Grumbling clouds swirled, leaking more drizzle than rain for now, but warning that worse was coming. Even at four in the afternoon it was darker than winter, with moments of sudden stillness and then moments when the fresh green leaves suddenly trembled and tossed in fretful anticipation.

Lightning crackled just as she reached the door of his SUV and slammed inside.

"I was coming in to get you—"

"Well, that would have been silly. Then both of us would have gotten wet." She tossed her jacket in the backseat. The wipers and defroster had to be on because of the foggy steam, but underneath all that threat of storm, the temperature was muggy and close. She should have worn her hair up, she thought, and her long-sleeved green tee was probably going to be too warm, as well. "You still haven't told me where we're going."

For the first time, she glance at Fox, then quickly away. That was the trick, she mused. If she just didn't look at those mesmerizing eyes, that sexy narrow mouth, that *look* of him, too hard, too long, she'd be able to keep some emotional distance.

"I'm not trying to be mysterious. I just wanted to show you a place. If I told you about it first, I was afraid it'd color your reaction, so I just wanted you to see it. And I promise, it's not a long drive."

"I couldn't believe how much work you'd gotten done on the waterfall over the weekend."

"Yeah…even working around the hours you need the room, I should have it done by the end of the week."

She'd guessed that. She'd also guessed that Fergus was likely to call off their relationship completely when the project was done—partly because he was at the end of her recovery program for him as well. She had one more intensive exercise she wanted to work with him on, but Phoebe could see for herself that he was totally on the right track. Maybe he wasn't ox strong quite yet, but his shoulders and arms had regained all their muscle tone. He moved with virile, vital purpose again, energy, stamina.

He didn't need her anymore.

"You haven't mentioned having a bad headache in over a week," she said. "You're sleeping better?"

He shot her a look. "How about if we talk about how you're sleeping instead?"

Not well without him, but she could hardly say that when both of them avoided mentioning ever making love, as if saying it aloud would bite them in the butt. She said, "Okay, I get it. I won't hound you about your health for a whole two hours, okay?"

"Good. I'll hold you to it." He peered out the windshield. "Damn. I really want you to see this place. Maybe the rain'll quit."

That seemed as likely as cows flying, judging from the hissing wind and angry sky, but it wasn't as if driving were dangerous. The blacktop glistened as they took the twisting, curling road out of Gold River. Slopes turned into hills, then climbed into more mountainous terrain.

He was right. It wasn't a far drive. He turned down a gravel road that led eventually to…nothing. Where he stopped and braked, she saw a long expanse of meadow, carpeted in wildflowers, leading to a creek that splashed silver in the rain. Boulders on the other side led up to a hillside of rich, emerald-green trees.

"What do you think?"

She cocked her head curiously, unsure what he wanted her to say. Her first thought was that the wondrous place resembled the safe haven he'd described in the first exercise they'd done together...but she couldn't imagine that had any relevance to why he'd brought her here—or what he wanted her to say. "It's gorgeous."

He didn't exactly look disappointed, but something in his expression changed. Suddenly his gaze looked...careful, and his shoulders stiffened with tension. "Yeah, it's pretty. But what can you picture here? I mean, try to imagine it if it weren't raining and gloomy. If the sun were shining down on the water and the mountainside..."

"I think it's gorgeous in the rain and would be even more beautiful in the sunshine." She spoke truthfully but couldn't seem to think. He obviously wanted her to react in some way, yet she had no clue what he wanted from her.

He turned off the engine and just leaned back, staring out the window instead of at her. "I've been thinking about moving. I haven't minded being by my mom, but...I just want my own place. I rented before. That seemed the simplest choice when I didn't have the time or interest in maintaining a place of my own. But now...the idea of a home is a lot more appealing."

She could see his profile, the strong nose, the sharp eyes, but nothing in his expression gave away what he was feeling. "You feel up to making a major move?"

"I know I'm not moving at racehorse speed yet, but yeah. I'm getting there." He hesitated, as if hoping she'd comment more, but again she felt an attack of nerves.

She'd never been short of opinions, and she'd easily offered them to Fox before, but it was different now. The times they'd made love stood between them like a velvet wall. He didn't refer to them. Neither did she.

She knew how to communicate using touch. But she didn't know the words he wanted to hear.

And when she still said nothing, he filled in. "Phoebe, I wasn't trying to lead you into saying something I wanted to hear. But I was specifically thinking about building a house. Right here. I own this property, have for a while. What do you think about it for a home site?"

"I think it'd be gorgeous," she said, and then realized that seemed to be the only word that kept coming out of her mouth.

He motioned. "Probably put the kitchen there—facing east—with big glass doors leading to a deck, so a body could sit outside, eating their grapefruit, sipping their morning coffee." He waited, then went on. "Then I could see an octagonal room, glass walls—the great room facing the mountains and creek. The sun would come in there too strong, but we could fix that by using solar windows. Put the master bedroom upstairs. Make it a solid north wall, but put windows east and west, so the room would get the sunrise in the morning, the sunset in the evening."

When he paused again, she said, "It couldn't sound better, Fergus. It's a beautiful plan."

"Can you picture the house ideas?"

"You bet."

"Could you picture living in a house like that?"

She frowned. "Sure. Who couldn't? It sounds like a dream house. But…I'm not sure it'd be a good idea for you to be out this far in the woods alone, do you?"

"You've got that right. I don't want to live alone anymore." He fell completely silent then, scraping a hand through his hair and then, for a few seconds, squeezing his eyes closed.

"Damn," she murmured. "I knew something was wrong. You're getting a headache, aren't you."

"Not a headache. I just…" He opened his eyes. He suddenly looked so despairing, so frustrated. "Phoebe, I…"

"No," she said swiftly. "I can see you're hurting. Bad hurting. Don't talk. Just turn around for me, Fox. Face the side window."

"You don't understand. I wanted to—"

"No talking! I mean it!" Energy surged through her. She knew what to do when he was hurting. Anything was better than those strange moments when he kept waiting and waiting, clearly counting on her to say something and her failing to come through. Whatever that had been about mattered, but if Fox was hurting, *that* took precedence over any and everything else.

"Lean forward," she said quietly, firmly. "I told you before, I had another exercise I wanted to give you. It's like the first one we did. An exercise you can use whenever you're in pain or stressed. Not just for now but whenever you feel stressed.…"

He turned toward the driver's window—not at a perfect angle, but good enough. She knelt behind him—again not easy to do from her seat, but she could manage. Thankfully he was wearing an old, loose sweatshirt that she could push out of the way. She closed her eyes when she felt his warm, supple skin under her fingertips again. Maybe she had no oils to work with today, no soothing warm water, no props. But she had her hands, to knead into his hair, into his nape, around his temples and forehead. And she had her heart, her love, to convey through the sense of touch.

"Okay now, Fox," she whispered, "this is called the rainbow exercise. I want you to picture yourself standing at the beginning of a giant tunnel that's entirely made of color—"

"You've got to be kidding me."

She considered taking a small nip out of his shoulder, but that would be too loverlike. A headache was serious business. Healing him was no joke. "Just go along with me, okay?"

"Okay." He used that patronizing tone men used on women when they were pretending to be patient, but she didn't care. She'd won what she needed. His attention.

"Okay, now close your eyes and imagine this rainbow tunnel. Just like with a real rainbow, the first part is red. You're going to take an imaginary step inside where it's all red, Fox. I want you to feel that red, smell it, taste it, touch it. There's huge energy in that color, isn't there? Passion. Anger. High emotion…

"And then we're going to keep walking, slowly, into our rainbow. We're going to walk past the red into orange. Feel how bright and colorful and splashy the orange is? And now we're walking into yellow. All warm and healing and sunny. A happy color, yes? And you're feeling washed in that yellow. Drenched in that yellow. It's bathing you from head to toe.…"

She rubbed and stroked, his head, his temples, playing out the rainbow exercise, talking softly, soothingly. Lovingly. She could feel the knots in his neck start to ease. Feel those big strong shoulders give up some of their tension.

He was such a sucker for a head rub. Again she felt her heart surge. It was such a simple joy—knowing that she was the one who could reach him. Knowing she was the one person who could relax him, whom he could trust enough to be himself with, to let down his heart with.

"The green is so beautiful, isn't it? You can almost smell all the green things—the grass and leaves. The emerald is so alive, so full of life. But then, at last we come to blue, Fox. A deep, rich royal blue...but not dark. This is a clear blue. This is the blue color that makes you think of peace. There's no stress in this blue. No worries. No fears. Feel the blue, Fox?"

"Yup, I feel your damn blue, red."

She grinned and dropped her hands. "Okay...that's it. Just kind of wake up from this slowly. How's the headache?"

Slowly he lifted his head. Slowly he turned around. She was still crouched on her knees, waiting to see his face, to study how he was doing. The storm clouds had thundered on, but it was still raining outside—a clean, soaking downpour that hissed in the leaves and washed down the meadow. She could see his face much clearer now, and the intensity in his expression startled her.

"What did he do to you, Phoebe?"

"What?"

"The guy. The jerk you were engaged to. What did he do to you? And no ducking out this time. You promised that you'd try to be as honest with me as I was with you. You promised you'd *try*. And I told you what happened to me."

She sucked in a breath, feeling suddenly at a loss. "I didn't heal your headache? The exercise didn't work?"

"Red, you've been healing me from the day I met you. How about giving me a shot?"

"At what?"

"At helping you heal this time," he said softly, and then repeated insistently, "What did the son of a gun do to you?"

She clicked up the lock and pushed out the door. She could

have grabbed her jacket, but at the moment she just didn't care. Rain sloshed down, not hard, but too relentlessly to escape it. It slithered in her hair, matted her eyelashes.

Still she took off, hiking fast, and only moments later realized that Fox had caught up and was keeping pace beside her. He said nothing, just walked with her, getting as soaked as she was.

"Darn it, Fox! It's not something I can explain. Not to a man."

"Then forget I'm a man and just think of me as a friend."

"For Pete's sake. I *do* think of you as a friend. But I'll never forget you're a man in this life. No woman would."

"Um, I'm not sure if that's a compliment or an insult."

"It's just a statement of fact."

He said quietly, "Find a way to tell me."

Like it was that easy. And damnation, but the warm rain was squishing in her shoes now, and making her long hair feel heavier than a rope.

Besides, she didn't know where to start. "In high school…I went out with a lot of boys. Always had a good time. But also always pulled back before it went too far. I just really wanted to save it for the right guy. Girls still believe there'll be one perfect guy for them when they're in high school. Or some of us still did—"

"Okay."

"So anyway. That was the point. That I'd waited. That I thought Alan was The One. So when we got engaged…"

Fox wasn't going to waste time on euphemisms. "You did the deed. And he hurt you?"

"No."

"He scared you somehow?"

"No. Nothing like that. It went great."

"So…"

She turned on him in a fury. "If you catch cold from this walk because of me, I'm going to shoot you myself."

"Threat accepted. So go on."

She lifted her hands in a helpless gesture. "So that was the problem. That it went great. I didn't understand at first. We were engaged. Why would he be unhappy if things were going well when the lights went out? Yet from that first night, he started pulling back."

Ahead, a rabbit hopped into their path, stared at them and then hopped back under cover like any sane animal would have done.

"I guess you could say I got more adventurous. I was…blind. This whole part of life seemed…great to me. Natural. Wonderful. And I believed I loved him, so there was nothing I wasn't willing to think about or talk about or try."

"And?"

"And he was repulsed."

"Say what?"

"You heard me."

"I couldn't have," Fox said bluntly.

She sighed. There was a time she thought nothing would mortify her, but trying to talk about this did. "I could claim that we both wanted to break the engagement, but the truth is…he wanted out. It's not like he didn't want to keep sleeping with me, but he shut me off any time I brought up marriage plans after that. The better it got between the sheets, the less he trusted me. Anything I said or tried to say, somehow I ended up feeling dirty. Amoral."

"Phoebe, we may have to run through this again, because

something's wrong with my hearing. Something *has* to be wrong, because I couldn't possibly be hearing what you're telling me."

"I know you're trying to be funny. And it is, in a way. There's nothing new about the old double standard. It's been around since the beginning of time. I'm not blaming him. I'm saying there was something ingrained in him. And maybe it's ingrained in a lot of men and women. That women who are…sexy…must be of low moral character."

"That's ridiculous."

She persisted quietly, firmly. "There's a fear that a woman 'like that' won't be faithful. That if she's a great lover, she won't make a steady wife. I know, I know, we all *say* differently out loud. Alan *said* differently, too. But that's how he felt deep down. The more times we slept together, the more he pulled away, the less he trusted me, less he shared with me. Oh, for God's sake. Let's head back to the car and get out of this ridiculous rain before we both catch our death."

"Wait a minute—" He hooked her arm, not roughly, but determined to spin her around to face him.

She faced him, but she also shook her head. "I really don't want to talk anymore about this. I know what you'll say. That it's all wrong. That he was a creep. That of course a guy wants a hot woman. I mean, come on, we're not kids."

"Maybe I wasn't going to say any of that."

"Oh, yeah, you were." She lifted her face, ardently wanting to kiss him—wanting to be kissed. Actually wanting anything but to still be talking about this. "But I don't need logic or that kind of reassurance, Fox. I was just trying to tell you what happened. How it made me feel. How it affected me."

"You moved away. Gave up regular physical therapy completely. Concentrated on work with babies." He added, "I understand it took you a while to get over him. But it's been a while. You *have* to know it isn't that way with me. I can't believe you'd paint me with the same brush as that jerk."

"It's not about painting you with the same brush." She knew it'd be impossible to explain. Even to Fox. Especially to Fox. "It's about…feeling different about myself. I grew up thinking that sensuality was a good quality in myself. He…crippled that."

"You let him cripple that."

She felt stung. "Come on, that's not fair. When you knife someone where they're the most vulnerable, it's pretty hard to just…go on…as if your life hadn't been seriously changed."

Fergus touched her cheek, whispered, "You think I don't know that?"

His voice—his words—struck her with the surprise of a slap. He *did* know that. As totally unalike as their problems were, it wasn't being physically injured that had crippled Fox. It was being hit in the heart, because it was a child who'd injured him, and it was children where his whole self-image—as a man, as a leader and teacher and a role model—was founded. She'd always understood. When a child betrayed him, he felt as if he'd betrayed the child, as well.

And now she saw the parallel. When her innermost nature betrayed her, she'd felt as if she had become her own worst enemy. How do you recover when something you had believed was totally good in yourself turned out to hurt you?

Fox looked at her. Rain had soaked through his sweatshirt. It dripped from his brows, had turned his hair dark. "Is that where you want to leave it, red? You can do what I did. I gave up teaching, my life."

"I didn't give up sex. I made love with you, didn't I?"

"Yeah, you did. Which is really fascinating, when you think about it. You took on a man who was running straight to loserdom. No job. No future. Wallowing in self-pity, hiding in dark shadows. So what the hell were you doing, sleeping with me?"

"That's completely different, because you were never a loser. You were never at fault for what happened to you, even if you thought you were. None of that was who you were. You were just...hurt. You just needed time to heal."

"Maybe that's true—but you couldn't have known that. You took a chance on me. You took a huge risk with me. But now...you just want to walk away?"

She frowned, fiercely confused, sick to her stomach. Darn it, he was deliberately rattling her. "Fox, I never said that."

"Well, I want you to think about it. Because I'm not disappearing, red...unless you send me away. I'm not positive where I'm going, but I won't be hiding in the shadows anymore. I am sure of that. And I want to be sure of what you want from me."

She heard an implicit ultimatum in his voice. Not a threat. Just a fish-or-cut-bait warning—the same one she'd been waiting for weeks now. "I can't be, Fox! You don't understand!"

"Oh, yeah," he murmured. "I understand." And he turned away from her and stalked back to his car.

Eleven

Fox, standing at the stove in his mother's kitchen, pointed the royal finger at his mom. "No. Sit. You are not to help. You are supposed to sit there and drink wine and let me do the work."

"You're treating me like a dog," Georgia complained. "Sit. Stay. What kind of language is that to use with your mother?"

"Down, girl," Fox repeated when she tried to stand up again. "This is my night to cook for you, remember? You said you wanted to do this exercise of Phoebe's. That means you're supposed to put your feet up and I'm supposed to do the dinner. That's the deal."

"Something is very scary about you lately," Georgia said darkly. "At least when you were sick, I could order you around. You still didn't obey much, but you didn't give me all this lip."

"I think we always gave you a ton of lip, Mom." Before he could stop her, she'd sprinted out of the chair—carrying her wine—and was trying to see over his shoulder at the progress of the sizzling food on the stove.

"That isn't remotely related to beef Stroganoff," she announced.

"You've got that right."

"I bought all the ingredients for your favorites. Beef Stroganoff. Double blueberry pie. Waldorf sa—"

"Sit."

Muttering ominous threats, Georgia retreated as far as the counter stool, but she still looked at him with nosy, suspicious eyes. Mother eyes. "What's going on," she said finally, flatly. She didn't make it a question.

Fox deserted the stove long enough to set the table—at least, his version of setting the table. He scooped up some forks and knives from the silverware drawer, added a couple of plates, then tossed some napkins on the middle of the table. He wasn't sure everything was going to be ready at the same time, but whatever. He could cook well enough not to starve. Putting together a complete dinner—especially the dinner he was trying to create tonight—was impossibly tricky.

"Fergus Lockwood, answer me," his mother said firmly.

"What's 'going on' is that this is the last dinner you have to put up with, as far as risking life and limb on something I cooked. I'm at the end of Phoebe's crazy program."

"The whole family loved the program, Fox. It made all of us feel we were doing something for you, instead of just sitting back and watching you hurt. That was awful."

"Well, I'm not admitting it out loud—at least to Phoebe—

but I've liked it, too. What can I say? I've got a helluva great family. But there's just no need for it now. I'm better. Really better." Since he was stuck talking about sticky stuff, he eased into another little matter. "It's time I moved out of the bachelor house."

"Why?" she demanded instantly. "I've loved having you so close! And the house is just sitting there. There's no reason on earth—"

"I know. You'd like all of us close. And we *are* close, but I need to get my own life back together. You know the property up on Spruce Mountain? I want to build a house up there."

"Oh. That's not too far." Georgia took a sip of wine, looking relieved. "Fergus. You put the knife on the right of the plate, not the left. That's a beautiful site up there. Still in the school district…in case a body ever wanted kids…but peaceful and quiet and all."

He motioned her to the table and started serving dishes. "So, here's the plan. You're hearing it before anyone else. I'm going to spend the year building a house up there. And next fall I'll be teaching again."

"Not this year?"

"Not this year. I'm going to coach the basketball team. Keep my hand in with the kids. Work with some of the liners." The "liners" was the term he and the principal created for kids who were on the line between failing and making it— those who could fall the wrong way if something didn't happen to pull them out of a slump. "I talked with Morgan about it two days ago. It's a done deal."

"You really are putting it back together," his mom said quietly, and then looked at the dishes in front of her. "Fox, since when did these become your favorite foods? What's this?"

"Chicken with cilantro."

"And this…well, I can see this is the holiday potato dish—"

"Yup. And dessert is a marshmallow sundae with chocolate ice cream." He added kindly, "You can have the sundae with dinner, if you want. This isn't like growing up. I won't tell if you have dessert first."

His mother lifted a fork, then put it down and just stared at him.

"What?" he asked.

"It's Phoebe, isn't it."

She didn't phrase it like a question, just like she almost never phrased things like questions when she already had a mom sense about the answers. So Fox didn't try to balk or duck.

"Yeah, it's Phoebe," he said quietly. "But don't start counting on grandchildren, Mom, because the truth is…I think I lost her."

"Oh, Fox, you—"

"No." This time his voice turned firm. Not disrespectful. Just firm. "You want the secret side of stuff, I'll give it to you. I love her. Completely. Totally. Enough so that she's the only thing in my head, the only woman I can even imagine spending my life with. But she's not seeing me the same way. I can't open a door she wants locked. And that's all I'm willing to say. Besides, this dinner is supposed to be about you. I want to hear how the bridge club's going, what's new with the neighborhood crowd, how your arthritis is."

"But, Fox, I—"

"This is the deal. No dessert if you keep asking questions." He added, "This is between her and me. There's no one else in the universe but her and me. Not as far as our private lives go."

And he couldn't talk any more about it. Not without panic climbing a sharp ladder up his spine. She hadn't even blinked when he'd talked about building the house for the two of them, much less given him even a tiny sign that she might be willing to build that home with him. And as far as the whole rotten thing her ex-fiancé had pulled on her...hell.

Fox just couldn't see how to make any move without making the situation worse. If he tried to make love to her, she'd think he wanted her for sex. If he didn't try, she'd think he'd stopped wanting her. That jerk had done a number on her from the inside, and Fox couldn't remember feeling more frustrated. That someone could twist Phoebe's sensual, loving, nurturing and, you bet sexy nature against her made him see red. Bull red. But short of finding the guy and beating him up, there was little Fox could do—and besides, that would only make him happy.

He wasn't used to feeling impotent.

In fact, he'd never felt the sensation before.

But if Phoebe needed to know how much he respected her, he'd already shown her how much he did...by reaching out to her. By revealing his most vulnerable side. By sharing his weaknesses with her the way he'd been unable and unwilling to share with anyone else.

Fox didn't just respect her in theory; he respected her with his heart. The more critical problem was Phoebe herself. The jerk had dented her self-respect. And that was something he had no way of fixing for her.

He looked down at Phoebe's cilantro chicken and the infamous holiday potatoes—the potato dish no man had been able to resist since the beginning of time. And suddenly he couldn't eat.

He had one more occasion to see her, but he doubted it would help. He'd lost her.

And he knew it.

Exhausted and frazzled, Phoebe opened the van door and let Mop and Duster leap up on the seat. They faced the window and determinedly ignored her.

"Look, guys. Everybody has to have shots. The vet loves you. The nurse loves you. You hurt their feelings when you treat them like they were torturers, did you ever think of that?"

Neither pup bothered to turn around. She'd pay all day for taking them to the vet. Probably have to feed them steak. Take them for extra walks. Suck up for hours. She knew what to expect. They'd been through this before.

Phoebe drove straight home, relieved it was Saturday, because she'd lost all her usual energy. She didn't want to work, didn't want to see people, didn't want to do anything. As soon as she got home, she was inclined to lock all the doors and mope in peace with the dogs.

At the base of her driveway, she stopped at the mailbox, picked up three bills, five catalogs and a reminder that she needed to renew her physical therapist's license this coming fall. She was still shuffling through envelopes when she glanced up and realized that there was already a vehicle in her driveway. A white RX 330.

Fox's car.

The pups noticed it at the same time she did and, turncoats that they were, promptly commenced a barking frenzy until she braked and let them out. They zoomed for the door, Mop quivering with excitement, Duster's tail swishing the ground in equally ardent fervor. "What is it about him," Phoebe muttered, but it was a silly question, when she already knew what it was about Fox that inspired the female of the species to fall totally and irrevocably in love.

She shouldn't have been that surprised he was here, because she'd given him a house key weeks before. It just made sense. He tried to work on the waterfall when she didn't have clients and he wasn't in her way. Usually, though, he didn't show up early on Saturday mornings, because she often had neighbors over...and, besides, this Saturday she'd just thought he wouldn't come.

He hadn't called or been around since their walk in the rain.

She knew she was to blame, which ached all the more—because she'd only told him the truth. She couldn't seem to get past what Alan had done to her—how to get past the whole feeling that she wasn't...good. That the sensual and sexual part of her nature was a flaw instead of something good and natural. The thing was, when a girl got down and naked with a man and then he crushed her for it, it did something to her spirit. Her heart. Her self-respect.

And Phoebe believed she'd had no choice but to be frank with Fox...until she'd gotten home that day, walked into her bedroom, peeled down for a shower and started crying her eyes out.

Maybe she'd told him the truth...but she suddenly realized there were other truths. She kept remembering what he'd said at the house site—how he wanted to build a deck off the kitchen, a place to sit outside, eat grapefruit in the morning....

Grapefruit. Her vice, not his. Her goofy favorite food, not his. He'd been talking about living in that house with *her.* Building that house for *them.*

And until that grapefruit word poked in her mind and stabbed her sharply, she just hadn't realized that Fox was thinking about her seriously. Not as a lover. But as a wife. Not as a red-hot mama when he needed healing.

But as the kind of woman he might be willing to share a grapefruit with when they first got up in the morning.

Now she took a gulping huge breath. From the sound of the pups barking, they'd already located Fergus in the back room. She peeled off her fleece jacket, stashed her bag and mail on the kitchen counter, pushed off her shoes and tried to think how to handle seeing him, greeting him.

No magical or brilliant ideas occurred. She shook her hair loose, took a big breath and then walked to the doorway of her therapy room—then stopped, still.

The waterfall was done. Or it sure looked that way.

Fox was crouched down with the dogs, making a fuss, rubbing tummies and baby talking to them. There was still a mountain of trash and debris that he'd obviously just started to clean up, but the waterfall itself took her breath away.

It was her dream. The backdrop wall and sides were mortared in river stone. There were steps, as if you were in nature and really walking from shallow water into a deeper pool before you stepped under the waterfall. The tall windows above had the effect of skylights. You could lie in the pool, look up and see sunlight or stars, be secluded from the rest of the massage room environment. Lighting had been built into the lower pool. The outside steps had places to set ferns and plants.

"Oh, Fox," she whispered hopelessly. "It's so, so perfect."

He spun around at the sound of her voice and immediately stood up. If the light hadn't been straight behind him, she might have perceived his expression, but as it was, she caught his dusty knees, his rough-brushed hair, but his eyes were in shadow. "You're here just in time."

"In time for what?" she asked, and then shook her head for asking such a silly question. "Obviously in time to help clean up—"

"No. That'll wait. I need a victim, an experimentee. Translate that to mean 'sucker.' Your waterfall's done, ready to test. I know it *works,* but I don't want to put everything away until I'm positive we've got it all the way you want—height of the hidden shower head, water pressure, water temperature and all that stuff. I don't think we'll have to make any major plumbing adjustments—please God—but I still want to test the details."

"Sure. What do you want me to do?"

"Just use it the way you'd use it. Close the drain. Turn it on. Fill up the pool the way you would if you were using it with a client. Just make sure everything's the way you expected, then we'll drain it and call it quits. I'll keep cleaning up in the meantime."

Something inside her froze for the oddest second. It was as if her heart understood she had a choice. One choice. Right then. A choice, a chance, that would disappear if she didn't take it.

Fox turned away again. Flanked by the dogs, who seemed to think he desperately wanted their company constantly, he started stacking spare parts, gathering trash, putting away tools. The whole time he kept up a conversation. "Now, you're used to using oils in your work, right? You can't in this. You'll need your clients to take a 'clean' shower to get the oils off before they soak in the waterfall tub, or it'll be too slippery."

"I hear you," she said, as she pulled off her shirt. Fox didn't glance back, just kept working.

"And then, I've been thinking about a way you could rig up a sling for babies. I assume that's part of what you want to do, right? Use it for the little ones?"

"I had in mind using it for all ages. But when I'm working with babies, part of my idea was having their moms in there with them. So both of them could relax at the same time," she said, as she peeled off her jeans and socks.

"Yeah, I figured that. So this sling idea…it'd be like a little hammock. Soft. But water flowing in and around it. Obviously you wouldn't leave a baby alone in it, but it would be a way for a small child to feel the flow of water without it overwhelming him." A couple of hammers and crowbars made a heck of a racket when he piled them in one long metal container.

Slowly, her stomach starting to curl, she unsnapped her navy lace bra and let it fall. Then walked barefoot into the new waterfall tub and turned on the faucets. "That sounds ideal for the babies," she said. She stood there, not getting wet yet, just lifted her hand to the spray until she had the water temperature nice and warm.

She wasn't completely naked yet. She was still wearing her favorite thong—the navy satin one, with the red, white and blue flag in the triangle. They weren't the underpants of a shy, retiring girl. They weren't underwear for a woman who wasn't inherently in-your-face sexy. Which, of course, was why Phoebe had always worn the kind of clothing where no one could see them.

"Okay…well, while you're letting the pool fill up, I'm going to start making a bunch of trips out to the truck. It's going to take me quite a—" He turned around. Saw her.

Dropped a crowbar. Then a hammer.

While he was speechless, which she suspected wouldn't last long, she stepped under the waterfall spray. "You got the water pressure perfect," she called out.

He dropped the whole damn toolbox.

She lifted her face to the pelting spray, feeling the water gush and rush and slink down her face, her throat, her body. Her hair went from a tidily brushed mass into a heavy, thick, water-soaked rope in seconds. She closed her eyes, trying not to feel how hard her pulse was thudding, her badly her tummy was twisting, how scared she was.

When it came down to it…this was how she used to feel when she was younger. About herself. About life. It would never have occurred to her that it wasn't a joyful thing to enjoy the feel and the smell of fresh warm water on her bare skin, to love the explosion of her senses. To want to be this free—for a lover. With a lover. Open. Open in her heart, open in her mind, open to wherever the senses could take them both.

It had been gone—that freedom, that feeling—for a while now. And it wasn't totally back. Phoebe wasn't positive she'd ever totally get it back…but she knew, positively, that's how she wanted to be for Fox. With Fox. With the man she loved.

"And you've got the temperature perfect," she called out, and in that second, when she was blinking water out of her eyes, she almost jumped to the ceiling…because there was Fox.

Right there. His eyes inches from her eyes. His mouth inches from her mouth. He was still wearing all his clothes, except for his boots. His work socks already looked heavier than cement, and the rest of his work clothes were molding to his body faster than glue.

"Most of us," she said tactfully, "remove our clothes before taking a shower."

"Don't you mess with me, red."

She sobered, softened. "I'm not messing with you."

"This is a pretty brazen, bawdy thing for you to do. Stripping in front of me. Getting naked in front of me."

"Yeah, I know," she said regretfully.

"You could give a guy ideas. Bad ideas. Ideas like…that you know how delectably beautiful that body of yours is. Like…that you want me to notice how delectably beautiful that body of yours is—"

"Fox?"

"What?"

"This is what you're going to be stuck with. A brazen, bawdy woman. Who likes to get naked. For her lover. Only for her lover. No one else."

"Oh, I hope so," he whispered, and then leaned down and took her mouth. It was a kiss that started out hard and firm and just got more tenacious. The pelting warm water couldn't compete with this steam.

Her Fox, her crazy wonderful Fox, seemed to forget that he was standing there in all his clothes. He framed her face in his hands and kissed her and kept on kissing her, closed-eye kisses, tongue kisses, silver kisses, come-on kisses, claiming kisses.

She was still feeling nervous and worried. But maybe not

quite as worried and nervous as she started out, because a competitive streak seemed to kick in.

She could do kisses.

In fact, she could do downright fabulous kisses. For the right man. And Fox was so totally the right man.

She made him suffer through an intensive repertoire. She tried whisper-soft kisses and ardent, take-me kisses. Wooing kisses and shy, silky kisses. Kisses involving tongues and teeth, and kisses that barely touched, only hinted at what the future might hold. Could hold. If he was a very, very good boy.

"Phoebe?" he gasped in a breath.

She took the chance to gasp in some air, too. "What?"

"We're drowning."

"That's not the serious problem, Fox. You want to know the serious problem?"

"Yeah, I do."

"You have all your clothes on. And that really is a problem that needs fixing immediately."

"I'll help," he assured her, and there was a grin. A dark, intimate, wicked, pure, guy grin. The memory burst in her mind of how she'd first seen Fergus…so low, so sad, so unreachably angry and lost. It wasn't her fault that that grin inspired her to huge, vast heights of risk. Getting wet clothes off a guy was no easy task…but she was up for it.

He was also definitely up for it, in every sense—particularly as she followed each loosened button with a kiss everywhere and anywhere she discovered bare skin. By the time she'd battled four shirt buttons, he was ripping off his belt, trying to tear off his jeans.

By then, the water in the pool had filled to knee height.

Unfortunately, everything suddenly went kaflooey. His jeans were too soggy, too stuck to him, to pull off the rest of the way. He tried. She tried. They bumped heads and staggered back, and both ended up sitting in the water with the water-fall exuberantly splashing water on both of them, and Fox, laughing, roared out, "Damnation. I need *help!*"

"You think I'm not trying?" She'd started helplessly laughing, too, and between his sitting and bracing and her pulling, they managed to win the war with his pants.

"You're not supposed to have *fun* when you're this desperate," he grumped.

But his laughing and grumping was what sealed his fate, she thought. And hers. Because the more they battled his pants, the more they laughed, the more they loved…the more she knew it was going to be all right with Fox. To be herself. Always. That this was the one man she could be with.

Fear melted away, not all at once, but in flashes of searing sensation…like when his teeth scraped the hollow of her shoulder. Like when his hands slid down her ribs, around her spine, onto her fanny, where he clenched his hands and drew her tight and hard against him. When she reached back to turn off the water—before the pool overflowed all over kingdom come—he could barely seem to give her that spare second before he reached for her again, too impatient and hungry to wait.

"I love you, red. Not just want you. I *love* you. Now. Tomorrow."

"And I love you back," she said fiercely.

"I mean *love*. And you can take it to the bank, we're going to love the sex. It's going to be hot and wild and inventive for a long time."

"You think?"

"I think. Because I trust you." He lifted his head for just that moment, so she could see his eyes. So he could see hers.

And then he sank inside her, wrapping her legs tightly around his waist. Sunlight blazed through the skylight, shining gold on his shoulders, on his forehead. The water glistened on his skin like magic crystals. Night would have offered more concealment, more privacy, but this, Phoebe thought—she *knew*—was how she wanted to be with him. Naked, physically and emotionally. Her soul as bared as his.

Her risks as great as his.

"Take me," she whispered. "Higher. Hotter. Every which way, my love."

"No," he whispered. "You take me. All the way."

Needs spiraled the more she clung to him. Tension built the more he teased and stroked. She twisted in the water, claiming him. He swirled her beneath him, claiming her. The doorbell rang. The dogs barked. Her cell phone beeped. He sank under the water once, stealing a kiss that way…but by then their playfulness had turned serious. Heart serious. Future serious.

For so long, Phoebe had felt unsure of herself. Not as a person. Not as a worker. But as a woman.

Fox didn't give her that confidence back. But for him, she found that steel-strong well inside of the woman she wanted to be. The woman she could be. With a man who challenged her to reach for it all.

When it was over, he sank back against the tile, gasping, pulling her with him, both semi-floating in the warm water until they caught their breath. His cheek nuzzled her cheek. "Are you going to kill me if I tell you you're the most beautiful woman alive?"

"No."

"What if I told you you're the brightest, the most creative, the most generous and wonderful woman in the universe?"

"I guess I'll survive if you told me that, too." She sighed, knowing where his teasing was leading up to, because she knew him so well. "Go ahead. It's okay. You can say it."

"I don't want to tick you off. Especially right before I discuss something serious with you."

"You won't tick me off."

And out it came. "You're the sexiest woman in the galaxy, red. You're my dream of a mate. You make me proud to be a man, because of how you respond to me. With me."

"All right," she said warningly. "Now you've done it—"

When she reached for him, determined to mete out the punishment he deserved—and earned—he stopped her. "*Wait,* wait. I really do need to ask you something serious first. And before that, there's something I have to see."

"What?"

He insisted they get out of the water, and then he chased her upstairs. His excuse was that they were both more wrinkled than prunes and needed to get out of the water, but she figured out pretty quickly that he'd built up a humorous curiosity about her bedroom.

In the upstairs bathroom, they toweled off and then sprinted for her bed, diving under her down comforter until they warmed up again. Then he leaned back against the pillows, pulling her onto his chest, while he looked around.

"That's what I couldn't wait to find out. What color your bedroom would be, because of all the colors you used downstairs." He shook his head in surprise.

"I didn't have a lot of money to decorate when I moved

here. And what money I did have, I needed to use on the downstairs where clients could see—"

"And that's why you chose white up here?"

She looked around at the familiar furnishings—the down comforter and rug, the painted dresser and giant wicker rocker and antique bench. "I didn't want virgin white," she said honestly. "Or bridal white. But when I came here, I kind of wanted blank-slate white. Because that's what I was trying to do when I moved here. Start over. Figure out who I was all over again. Start with a blank slate, if I could."

He scooched down, so they were face-to-face on the same pillow. "Would you consider putting a marriage date down on that slate, red?"

Her heart stopped, then came damn close to bursting.

"Don't say no," he insisted. "Hear me out. I want to build that home for us. For us—and for any kids we might want to add along the way. I know I'm unemployed and don't look like such a great bet right now. But I've got a good slug of savings put away. And I'll start some real-work teaching next fall."

Damn the man, but if he didn't force her to kiss him again. Softly. On the temple and cheek and chin. She had to kiss him. Softly. On the temple and cheek. "I'm glad," she whispered.

"You knew I'd go back to teaching."

"I know you adore kids. But I didn't know if you'd realized you were healing."

"I wasn't. Until I met you. You healed me, Phoebe. But it scared the hell out of me when I realized you were hurting, too. And I had no idea how to be the healer for you."

"Fox."

"What?"

"Love's what heals." Since she'd kissed his one cheek, she had to kiss the other. Beneath the covers, he was starting to perk up again. Oh, this man was going to be trouble for a long, long time. "Love's what's always going to heal," she whispered.

"Does that mean—"

"It means, yes, I love you. From my heart. With my heart."

"And does it mean—"

"Yes. Yes. Yes."

He stopped asking questions. That seemed to cover it all.

* * * * *

SILHOUETTE® Desire™ 2 in 1

THE DYNASTIES: THE ASHTONS
BETRAYED BIRTHRIGHT by Sheri WhiteFeather

CEO Walker Ashton had always put business before pleasure but when, on the search for his mother, he met Tamra Winter Hawk, his thoughts definitely turned to pleasure. Walker didn't know why, but she made him yearn for a forbidden liaison…

MISTAKEN FOR A MISTRESS by Kristi Gold

To discover who had killed his grandfather, Ford Ashton was prepared to deceive and seduce the late billionaire's mistress. But Kerry Roarke was not all *she* appeared to be either. Could love develop with so much deception between them?

HEART OF THE RAVEN by Susan Crosby
Behind Closed Doors

Dark, mysterious Heath Raven hired private investigator Cassie Miranda to find his baby. She was a smart, sultry woman who fuelled all his long-denied desires. Yet after she found his son, would they lose the deep connection they had forged?

THE SULTAN'S BED by Laura Wright

Divorce lawyer Mariah Kennedy trusted no man—especially tall, dark, gorgeous and ruthless ones—but Zayad Al-Nayhal was irresistible and suddenly she was sleeping with the Sultan.

BOUGHT BY A MILLIONAIRE by Heidi Betts

When millionaire Burke Bishop hired Shannon Moriarty to have his baby, Shannon agreed to keep things strictly business—but soon she realised Burke would make the perfect husband. Would Burke agree to Shannon's change of terms?

JARED'S COUNTERFEIT FIANCÉE
by Brenda Jackson

Jared Westmoreland needed a date and immediately thought of beautiful Dana Rollins, but they ended up having to pretend they were engaged! With the passion quickly rising between them, would Jared's faux fiancée turn into the real deal?

On sale from 16th June 2006

Visit our website at www.silhouette.co.uk

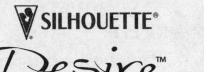

FROM *SUNDAY TIMES* BESTSELLING AUTHOR PENNY JORDAN

They had shattered her past.
Now she would destroy their futures.

Pepper Minesse exuded sexuality and power. She presented a challenge men wished they could master. But Pepper had paid dearly for her success. For ten years, her thirst for revenge had fuelled her ambition and made her rich.

Now it was time for the four men who had taken something infinitely precious from her to pay too – their futures for her shattered past.

On sale 7th July 2006

FREE!

2 Books
and a surprise gift!

We would like to take this opportunity to thank you for reading this Silhouette® book by offering you the chance to take TWO more specially selected titles from the Desire™ series absolutely FREE! We're also making this offer to introduce you to the benefits of the Reader Service™—

- ★ **FREE home delivery**
- ★ **FREE gifts and competitions**
- ★ **FREE monthly Newsletter**
- ★ **Exclusive Reader Service offers**
- ★ **Books available before they're in the shops**

Accepting these FREE books and gift places you under no obligation to buy, you may cancel at any time, even after receiving your free shipment. Simply complete your details below and return the entire page to the address below. You don't even need a stamp!

YES! Please send me 2 free Desire books and a surprise gift. I understand that unless you hear from me, I will receive 3 superb new titles every month for just £4.99 each, postage and packing free. I am under no obligation to purchase any books and may cancel my subscription at any time. The free books and gift will be mine to keep in any case.

D6ZEF

Ms/Mrs/Miss/Mr ....Initials................................
Surname .... **BLOCK CAPITALS PLEASE**
Address...
....
....Postcode ....

Send this whole page to:
UK: FREEPOST CN81, Croydon, CR9 3WZ